# HIGHER EDUCATION

# HIGHER EDUCATION

## INDIRA TAGORE

EAST HOLLYWOOD PRESS
HOLLYWOOD, CALIFORNIA

Published in the United States
by East Hollywood Press

First Paperback Edition 2021

Library of Congress
Control Number: 2020909313

ISBN: 978-1-7350863-09
Ebook ISBN: 978-1-7350863-16

Designed by Euan Monaghan

Email: inquiries@easthollywoodpress.com

For BD

# CALIFORNIA, 2002

Given our national anxiety, perhaps my father's trepidation shouldn't have been such a surprise. And yet it was. What I'd long imagined as a drive south through California's grapevine proudly celebrating my arrival at college—and therefore my devotion to all filial expectations—inexplicably became an anxious journey intensified by my father's emotional distance and the intentional absence of my mother and sister. I feared their absence was designed to finally facilitate a father-to-son discussion of sex, but thankfully it wasn't to be. Instead, our conversations took place well above the surface. We talked tersely about the 49ers and their quarterback struggles since the forced retirement of Steve Young by concussion two years earlier. We discussed—or, rather, I did, as if trying to resurrect the father I knew and loved through the sound of my voice—the incomparable dominance of Barry Bonds and how, only one year removed from his record-breaking, 73-home run season, he was now leading the Giants through the playoffs and into a likely World Series clash against the Anaheim Angels. I talked and talked and talked, but nothing I said could free him from his apprehension.

By the time we'd reached the Los Angeles Mountains and stopped at Taco Bell for lunch, my father's response to my tireless monologue had become little more than a grim smile and an occasional nod of the head. It was only when we were leaving the rest stop at Tejon Ranch and about to ascend the Los Angeles Mountains that he momentarily lost the sobriety that had enveloped him for those last four hours. There, at the freeway entrance, an American flag so large it could've draped five cars fluttered at half-mast against the clear blue sky. The sight of it was a somber reminder that we'd been attacked, that we were now at war, and that we should never forget, and overcome, my father teared up as he sat perched over the wheel. I wanted to say something, but for the first time all morning I had finally run out of words.

At Irvine, after loading up my tiny dorm room, my father stood like so many other parents under the golden afternoon sun, staring in silent amazement at the swarm of exuberant freshmen and the world we were about to inhabit. For the second time that morning he teared up, but cry he wouldn't, no matter how much I sensed he wanted to weep like my mother had earlier that morning. Dressed in her best *sari*, a crimson *tico* centered just above her eyes, my mother had placed her thumb into a small container of vermillion powder and blessed my forehead, her heavy sobbing a mixture of pride, loss, and fear. My little sister eventually succumbed too, but only after repeatedly asking if she could join us on the ride down to Irvine, and only after her arms locked around my waist and she begged me not to go. I could tell my father also wanted to hug me, much like most of the Indian fathers dropping off their children. But that was something we rarely did, especially in public. Instead, much like my high school graduation and my *janoi*, my father shook my hand in awkward congratulations as the sea of people around us ebbed and flowed. The surrounding crowd was a mix of races very different from our home in Fremont, and so perhaps that was what finally compelled him to offer some kind of parting advice, to protect me from whatever it was that had darkened his mood. I don't know. My main thought then was typical of most young men and women about to begin college far, far away from home: that for the first time in my life I was going to be free—an illusion, I soon learned, whose beauty would eventually be shattered.

My father, meanwhile, seemed momentarily lost in the college's staggering diversity. It was a campus, Irvine College proudly advertised in its marketing, without one truly dominant racial or ethnic group, a place where minorities comprised the majority and Indian and Asian students combined to form almost fifty percent of the population. But there weren't just Asians and Indians before us. There were also Hispanic students, some of whom proudly bore crosses around their necks, their sobbing, visibly emotional parents calling out to them in mellifluous, melodic Spanish. There were also many Arab or Persian families, with mothers easily identified by their varied coverings—multicolored burkas or hijabs—and fathers, dubious like my own, standing before cars adorned with stickers of whichever colorful flag represented the nation they'd once called home. As for the African American and white students, their parents seemed lost and speechless in the cacophony of different dialects and voices, their sense of place disrupted and suddenly smaller than it perhaps had ever been. And there were Indians, of course, young men and women who, like me, stood awkwardly and in awe beside fathers stoically unconvinced that their children were actually leaving home, so many of our foreheads stained with crimson and blessed by rice.

We were all so many. We were all so different.

As I walked my father back to the parking lot, I couldn't subdue the surprising upswing of emotion bringing me to tears. Quite suddenly, I missed him, even though I'd been eagerly awaiting this moment my entire life. It was then my father said what would come to shape so much of my freshman year at Irvine. After opening the driver's side door of the SUV he took in the chaos flowering around us one last time, and then he was looking at me there before him, my brown cheeks wet and glistening under the afternoon sun. And perhaps because of my tears or perhaps because this was what he'd been wrestling with all day, he confided, as if sharing a secret, "You're going to be all right. Just do one thing for me, okay? Stay with our own kind. Do that, and you'll be just fine. I promise."

Had I not followed his advice, would it have made any difference? There are times I like to believe that everything that transpired could have been avoided if I had followed my heart and ignored his words. There are also times I like to believe that I had no choice and that my father's advice was not really advice at all, but rather some irrefutable truth of my being. For my father is a proud man—proud of his American success, proud of his Indian culture, and proud that the children he raised would always, at least in his estimation, consider themselves Indian first and foremost. What I didn't realize then— and what I would eventually learn the hard way—was that it was not only my tears or his pride that provoked his advice, but fear as well. For he understood far better than I the fear and anxiety pervading our current time and so, like any reasonable, loving father, he only wanted to protect me from everything he believed was far outside my control—our times not least among them.

What I was to learn throughout my freshman year at Irvine, however, was that our times are what we make of them, and that while our fathers can love us, they can never protect us from the pain required to face our fears. Or the pain required to be yourself.

# 46

My dormmate Sudeep arrived the following morning. I was out getting coffee in the cafeteria when he arrived, so when I returned I found him and his parents straining to squeeze as much of the furniture they'd brought into our small room. That he was an Indian shouldn't have been as a big a shock as it was, given that the Freshman Housing Department at Irvine was known for housing students based on race. Nonetheless, the sight of him and his parents there brought on a strange sense of disappointment. I don't know who I expected my roommate to be (a white guy with a surfboard?), but the fact that he was an Indian seemed unexciting, boring, as though, because I had an Indian as my roommate, I was still in my privileged Silicon Valley cocoon. I felt strangely let down at the sight of him, even though I knew my father would have felt quite the opposite.

Much like Sudeep's father, whose eyes, upon noticing me

standing quietly sipping coffee in the doorway, softened immediately. A warm, paternal smile relaxed his face. He offered me his hand and said his name, "Harshad," excited at what I assumed was the prospect of his son spending the next year with someone he believed he could trust. "*Kem cho*," he added, a Gujarati greeting I'd been hearing all my life and that essentially made up most of my fluency in my parent's native dialect. "That's Sudeep, our son."

I repeated the phrase and then introduced myself: "Rohan." And then, looking at Sudeep trying to wedge a very nice— but way too large—teakwood bookshelf into a corner, added, "How's it going?"

"We really lucked out with the size of our room," he said, huffing, his back to me.

"They put us in the penthouse," I replied, smiling at Sudeep's mother. I now noticed she was wearing a *tico*, like my mother had yesterday. Her long black hair was tied in a ponytail straight down her back, and she wore several gold bangles around her wrist that sparkled in the bright morning light cutting through our one and only window. I repeated the greeting.

Her smile was like her husband's, warm and relieved but also enthusiastic, and when she shimmied through the morass of cardboard boxes and bags of clothes on the floor between us, she too extended a hand.

"Neema," she said. "It's nice to meet you."

"You too."

"So," Harshad began, standing beside me now, "where are you from?" He took care to enunciate each word, to make sure, much like my father occasionally did, that his listener understood that he'd been speaking English for quite some time.

If the room was bigger than twenty by twenty, then I was the Mahatma. Even in the pictures on the college website the rooms looked tiny, but given the outlandish cost of living any-where else, and given the proximity of Tarnopol Hall—the name of our part of Irvine College's freshman housing com-munity—to the engineering buildings, it seemed like a wise choice. I wondered, standing there with three other people and all of our stuff littering the floor, how any studying—let alone anything else a young man might desire—could get accomplished in such a small space. The beds were bunked (I'd already commandeered the bottom) and there were two desks side by side opposite the bed (where Sudeep now attempted to wedge a bookshelf). Opposite them, on the wall by the door, were two small knee-high dressers that looked wide enough to store about two pairs of socks.

"Fremont," I said, checking his eyes to see what might register. Everything did.

"Sudeep," he said delightedly. "Did you hear? He's from Fre-mont. We're from Pleasanton."

"Pleasanton," I repeated, once more overcome by disappoint-ment at hearing he'd grown up a mere fifteen miles from me.

Sudeep momentarily gave up on the bookshelf and rose to look at me. For the first time that morning, my disappointment and assumptions were challenged, for while Sudeep's parents seemed all too familiar, Sudeep clearly wasn't. It was his hair that caught my attention, hair decidedly unlike mine or anyone else I knew in Fremont. Long and shaggy, his curly black locks fell in no particular order down his head, covering his ears and resting unkempt upon his shoulders. It wasn't quite an afro, but it certainly wasn't the serious, businesslike haircut of someone trying to please his parents—let alone any future employer. No, there was something hippyish about his thick, curly hair, as if he were brazenly announcing to the world—and those of us who chose to try to fit in through our square, side-trimmed corporate cuts—"This is the hair I was born with, take it or leave it."

"This isn't going to work," he said, frustrated, his shaggy black hair bouncing atop his shoulders. "You're going to have to take this thing home. Fuck!"

"Sudeep!" Neema cried theatrically. "*Beta*, please watch your mouth."

"Dude," Sudeep said, and now I could tell his annoyance was about more than just the bookshelf. "He doesn't care."

At this point Sudeep's father launched into a Gujarati diatribe that, though I couldn't quite make it out completely, was fueled with enough bluster and profanity (which I, for the most part, understood) to make me wish I wasn't there. Sudeep's eyes glazed over in the way of all children who've been lectured by their parents their entire life, and for a moment I felt embarrassed for him, even though I could sense that this was more of a charade, a play being put on by Sudeep's parents to appear something they actually weren't—but probably wished they were.

"Now leave that thing alone," Harshad concluded. "Deal with it later. I want to eat. Are you hungry?" he asked me.

"No," I lied, my stomach growling at that precise moment.

"Come on," Neema said. "We're going to the Cheesecake Factory. Do you like the Cheesecake Factory?"

"I'm okay," I said, then sipped my coffee in the hopes of silencing my audible hunger.

"Come on," Harshad said. "Eat with us."

"I don't want to impose," I replied, because I didn't, even as I knew that, were I to truly resist, Sudeep's parents would feel insulted and our year would begin on the wrong foot.

"You're not imposing," Sudeep said, hurdling clumsily over an unpacked box. "Come on." He ran his hands through his long black locks. "I'm fucking starving."

**45**

I was right about the charade. Sudeep was everything to them: their only child; indeed, the literal embodiment of whatever it was they perceived as the American dream. He got away with more profanity during our one hour lunch than I'd gotten away with during my seventeen years at home, and each and every time the word "fuck" fell from his lips I felt both terribly embarrassed and, paradoxically, tempted to use the very same language as him. For I'd never heard a person my age converse with their parents in such a confident, adult way; he was so passionate I almost felt seduced into using some profanity myself just to try and legitimate my positions—as unclear as they were—within the discussion.

We—or rather, they, for I found myself, as the guest, more observer than ardent participant—discussed a plethora of issues during our lunch, and I could tell that his parents, F-bombs or not, relished every second of their fleeting time together, proud of the fact that they'd raised a young man so hypercritical of everything and everyone. Whatever faults he might've possessed, their eyes gleamed with the satisfaction of knowing they'd raised someone who undeniably thought for himself, someone who would meet all of the challenges of college head-on—indeed, with a raised fist.

"Let's get one thing clear," Sudeep passionately posited at one point, "the only thing that Cheney and that fucking snake Wolfowitz care about is profiteering from war. That's it. Look it up. They own more shares of Halliburton than anyone—and rumor is they didn't even have to sell their fucking shares when they came to office. They'll make *millions*."

As Sudeep paused to bite his crab cake sandwich, I tried to remember what Halliburton or who Wolfowitz was, but nothing substantive came to mind. Lost, I only smiled at Sudeep's mother, who encouraged me to continue my pasta Alfredo by her raised fork.

"And believe me," Sudeep resumed, his mouth frothing with tartar sauce, "they don't give a fuck about the people in Afghanistan, they certainly don't give a fuck about the suffering taking place in Kabul—or that had been taking place under the Taliban for damn near fifteen years—and they certainly don't have a plan about what this tiny, barren, heroin producing shithole will look like ten years down the line. I bet they can't even catch bin Laden. I mean, those assholes couldn't find saffron in India!"

To such a litany of charges, Sudeep's father could only shrug off the profanity at best and offer up an alternative hypothesis somewhat more hopeful, something stemming from what I could easily deduce—easily because my parents often seemed to suffer from the same naïve optimism—was an immigrant's idealism regarding their new home's political intentions. To this, and to any such impossible charge, Sudeep would recoil in animated disgust, doubling down on his positions, positions whose ardor and militancy he seemed incapable of relinquishing. Listening to his tireless ranting, I couldn't believe that this was the kid (man) with whom I would be living for the next year. I didn't know whether to order dessert or a subscription to *Foreign Affairs.* I felt at a loss to offer anything credible amidst his bombastic rhetoric and because of that I felt nearly invisible and strangely out of place in an environment in which I knew I belonged. Occasionally he would pause and turn to me, as if offering me a window to interject, but humbled by his intensity and uncertain in my positions regarding the war, I only deferred (or, worse, sheepishly agreed), hoping, by my silence, to save some face.

For the fact was, prior to Irvine and the War on Terror, my personal politics were truly nonexistent. I'd yet to vote in a presidential election—or any election other than one at school—and though my father, a Democrat like virtually every other Indian in our community, would always urge me towards that party, the truth was I'd yet to fully think out or formulate my own positions about the world around me. Like most normal freshmen (except Sudeep, apparently) mine was a truncated, undeveloped politics shaped primarily by the tragedy of that awful September day last year, when our lives and our collective memories were forever scarred by those two crumbling buildings and a psychopath with a very long beard in some cave in Afghanistan. I knew, in a sense, what I was for and against—President Bush made sure every American understood that—but any ideological understanding—or nuance—was as of yet undeveloped in me.

Like your average college-bound seventeen-year-old, I had been more concerned with AP exams, SAT scores, and application essays, with simply trying to accomplish the infuriating—if mundane—requirements needed to apply for college than anything remotely political. In our household—and practically every other Indian household in Silicon Valley—there could be no mistaking how important and necessary and, indeed, out of the question *not* going to college was. In fact, in our household and most others in the Indian community, college was merely the starting point. Ours was a world where advanced degrees were actually expected; amongst my father's friends, unless you held at least *one* master's degree, you were looked down upon as someone not only living up to your potential, but you were failing to take advantage of the economic opportunities America had to offer, the most obvious being high-paying jobs in medicine, law, or any of the hard sciences. As such, and arguably to my detriment, the Taliban, the War in Afghanistan, al-Qaeda, the political maneuvering in Washington, the looming 2004 election, the potential consequences of war on our nation or our collective psyche—or my generation in particular—these were things I'd barely given a moment's thought, so preoccupied was I with my immediate familial expectations. Embarrassingly, but quite normally I thought, these political actions and debates existed somewhere beyond the scope of my life, not simply Washington or on the nightly cable news shows, but in an area that seemed far removed from my everyday existence. Until now.

"For real," Sudeep said at one point, "you think I'm kidding you, but if you really think about it, what political benefit does

Bush have to actually catching bin Laden. So long as he's out there, releasing those fucking video tapes, they can continue to wage their war on terror unabated, independent of any congressional oversight, hidden beneath the fucking Patriot Act which essentially lets them stick a bug up anyone with brown fucking skin. And that means you," he said, pointing a finger at me from across the table. "Wait till you fly home for Thanksgiving. One sight of you at LAX and you know what they'll see? A fucking terrorist."

"I'm not a terrorist," I said, trying to smile at his parents, who only shook their heads at their son's escalating absurdity.

"No? No? Tell me, Rohan, what *is* a terrorist? *Define* terrorist. It has no fucking meaning. It's one of those fuzzy fucking political terms that you can't nail down. Tell me, you're a history major—"

"I'm majoring in engineering," I interrupted, cutting him off. This elicited a broad smile from Harshad and Neema, as if further confirming my esteem.

"An Indian majoring in engineering. What a surprise? Well tell me, Mr. Engineer, what does the term terrorist mean?"

He didn't really give me a chance to answer—though if he did I'm not quite sure how I would've responded.

"*Exactly.* Like I said, it's one of those fuzzy fucking terms that have no real meaning. Well let me ask you this, Mr. Engineer, what political action *hasn't* used terror—or fear—to achieve a political aim? If you break it down, terror—either verbal *or* violent—*is* politics. Fuck, even our idiot President George fucking Bush is using it right now on all of us and we don't even realize. The Terror Alert's high! The Terror Alert's low. What the fuck is a Terror Alert anyway? I'll tell you what it is—it's fucking *terror.*"

On and on he went, moving from one political topic to another with an ease and fluency unlike any I'd ever witnessed in anyone my age. It was a strange experience, listening to my new roommate vigorously discuss what I had always considered adult topics. Listening to Sudeep and the way his family ardently discussed issues of national importance, I was quickly learning that politics was no longer merely for adults. Perhaps it was now for me.

# 44

What I also learned, after we'd returned to our dorm room and Sudeep had carried his bookshelf (lamenting, along the way, his tragic loss) to the parking lot and said *aawjo* to his parents, was that Sudeep was much more complicated—or contradictory, or cool, or just plain old normal—than I could've ever imagined. As soon as he returned, with his parents, presumably, back on the 5 and heading north to Pleasanton, he immediately locked our door and began rummaging through one of his duffle bags.

"I thought they'd never fucking leave," he said, buried elbow deep inside the bag.

"That was a fun lunch. Thanks again for having me."

"My parents can be fucking lame sometimes," he confessed. "So don't hold it against me."

"They were fine," I said. "They were great."

"I promise," he said, revealing an emerald green prescription bottle from his bag, "I'll make it up to you."

"Are you sick?"

Whatever was in there stank. Bad.

When he popped the lid, our room flooded with a ridiculously strong blend of flowers, mint, pine, and some other unknown, unnamable magic ingredient.

"Oh I'm sick," Sudeep said, his head, and hair, bouncing rhythmically atop his shoulders. He revealed a tiny, palm-sized glass pipe from his bag. "Crazy like a motherfucker." His laughter was sardonic and mad, full of life but also bursting with something else, something dark and unclear that made me feel both terribly frightened and excitedly alive.

"This is the best shit you'll ever smoke," he said, picking out a tiny green morsel and letting it rest on his fingertip. It stuck there as if it were glued. He wagged his finger at me, attempting to flick it like a booger but to no avail. He eventually squeezed it into the glass pipe. "My buddy goes to Stanford and gets this shit from Palo Alto. Says all the guys at Cisco smoke it when they're writing code. Sounds dumb, I know, which is why I don't really believe him, but when you think about it all those fucking tech guys have to be stoned on something to come up with all that crazy shit, right?"

I didn't know. All the tech guys I knew from high school were, well, exactly like me, especially when it came to drugs. Up until that moment, and as incredible as it may sound (or not), I don't think I'd ever physically seen marijuana, let alone smoked it (or is it toked it?). I'd seen movies like *Friday* or *Animal House* or *Dazed and Confused*, so I was attuned to the general humor surrounding marijuana, but all throughout my high school education I'd never encountered anyone either smoking it or, for that matter, wanting to. And it wasn't as if I'd spent my entire high school career locked in the library doing advanced calculus (even if that's how I suddenly felt); I, like many of my close Indian friends, would occasionally party and drink alcohol, but to be perfectly honest these were rarities that oftentimes followed some sort of special occasion like a particularly stressful test or graduation. In fact, our concerns were so far removed from drug experimentation I can't recall a close friend of mine even offering it up for suggestion. We were all too concerned with what was coming next: college and then graduate school and then either medical, law, or post-graduate school, too focused on what our parents wanted—or expected— of us. And even though I knew that deep in my core I'd done all the right things in high school, the truth was, sitting there watching Sudeep expertly handle the glass pipe, I suddenly felt as if I'd failed in some strange way.

"Open that window," Sudeep instructed me.

"You're going to do that here?" I asked, painfully aware of how cowardly—or stupid—I sounded.

"Dude, it's not heroin. It's weed. It's from the earth, man."

Pathetically (and deeply embarrassed), I added the following as a means of justification: "But this is a non-smoking room."

"*Dude*," he said calmly, as if anticipating my response, "everything's taken care of. Look," and here he withdrew from his bag the brown cardboard tube that accompanies a roll of paper towels. It was filled with fabric softener. "All you got to do is blow into this, all right?"

What I wanted to do was leave, but I knew that doing so would put me in some kind of precarious position with my newfound roommate. Not to mention make me look like something—or someone—I didn't want to look like. Though what that was, exactly, I wasn't quite sure. All I knew was that were I to defer, for whatever reason, I would seem exactly like the caricature he'd jokingly painted of me over lunch, a caricature that too often fills the minds of people when they think of Indians. I could hear him referring to me as Mr. Engineer, and though, when you really thought about it, it was hard to make wanting to be an engineer condescending, Sudeep had done it in a way that made me feel as if, for everything special I aspired to be, my aspirations were actually the very same as everyone I—and he—knew—and were therefore not very special at all. Whether right or wrong, it was humiliating to be thought of in such a mechanical way, even if Sudeep had no real malicious intent and was simply trying to be amusing and toy with his own engineer of a father (whose expectations for him, I'm sure, were exactly the same as mine). Nonetheless, he'd touched on a strange source of shame for me, something that troubled me even while I worked assiduously to excel at every scholastic endeavor I faced in high school. For I was acutely aware that, for all of my academic successes, I was missing out on something distinctly American, some strange version of sex, drugs, and rock n'roll that was typical and normal and, for many my age, expected. Especially here.

It didn't take long for Sudeep to read my consternation. "You've smoked before, right?"

I blushed.

"Oh man! You're a virgin—fuck!"

At that word, I blushed even deeper, accosted now by a

shameful terror. I peered at our tiny window, wondering if I could fit.

"All right, it's all right," he said, missing it, or perhaps showing mercy. "No problem. Look, I don't want to peer pressure you into anything, especially this. That's not my style. We should all come to the magical herb on our own terms. And besides, if we're going to be living together I want us to, you know, be cool—I don't want there to be any shit between us, especially on the first day. The quarter's too long and I'm going to be smoking a fuckload of weed, know what I mean?"

"I just don't want us to get into, you know, umm, any, umm, trouble, that's all."

"Have you ever wanted to smoke?"

"To be honest," I lied, "I'd never really given it much thought."

"Well," he sang, rising from the floor, "no time like the present."

He opened the tiny window separating our bunkbeds from our desks. The window was probably no bigger than two by two and it opened to only half that. I felt the ocean breeze, cool and salty and rich with potential, as if calling on me to act, or act out. Sudeep took a seat on the desk near the window and peered outside, up and down, left and right.

"How does it look?"

"Not as good as it's going to," he said, offering me the pipe and the paper towel holder. He fished out a tiny lighter from his jeans pocket. "What do you think roommate? Should we christen it together?"

I looked at the lighter, the pipe. I looked at Sudeep. He looked at me. His smile, wicked and playful, rested atop a nose and eyes whose familiarity reassured me of some antiquated ideal. He was, after all, one of our own, right?

"Maybe just one," I said, taking the pipe from his palm.

"Trust me," he winked conspiratorially, "that's all it'll take. Here," he held up the paper towel holder packed with fabric softener, "I'll handle this." He drew it close to the windowscreen, positioning it for me. "I'll light it and you inhale—you've at least smoked a cigarette before, right?"

"Of course," I lied again, though now with a touch more irritation, decision.

"Do you have any?"

"What?"

"Cigarettes."

"No."

"Damn. Anyway, hit it like a cigarette but hold it in a little longer. When you're ready make sure you blow it out through this fucking tube or our room's going to smell like Jamaica, know what I mean? And then we're *really* going to be in trouble."

"Dude," I said, "you're freaking me out."

"Sorry, but this shit stinks. I'm not kidding."

"I got it."

"You got it?"

"I *got* it."

"All right," Sudeep said, bringing the lighter to the pipe. "Batter up."

He flicked the lighter once and then twice and I felt light-headed even before the dancing turquoise flame ignited the emerald herb before me and I inhaled quickly and deeply as if in strange competition with some unknown prototype and then Sudeep took the pipe away and studied me with comical caution and my lungs burned and ached with gentle relief and

I wanted to keep everything inside but I couldn't so I exhaled coughing, grasping for the paper towel holder, fumbling haphazardly in the descending, darkening haze, and though some of it passed safely out the paper towel holder and out the window most of it, well, didn't.

"Fuck!" Sudeep sat wafting the remaining smoke like he was trying to put out a fire. "Dude, what the fuck was that?"

Coughing, I crumbled to the ground, my lungs afire and my lips contorted into some strange semblance of a smile.

"Are you all right?" he asked.

"Do you smell that?"

"*Banchod.*" Quickly, expertly, Sudeep drew the pipe to his lips and took a long hit, holding it in for what felt like ten, twenty minutes, and from the floor where I was splayed I watched him, and the sun outside, high amidst the perfectly blue sky, and it looked like the sea, the sky, the sea looked like the sky, and then he let it out through the tube and I smelled flowers, or clean linen, or perhaps it was flowers, yes, flowers, and we were in a field surrounded by daisies, and Sudeep took another hit, and then another, and he was smiling at me and shaking his head and by the time he'd finished I was floating on a bed of orange daises and golden dandelions and drifting into the most blissful dream, a dream that this was what college was supposed to look and sound and smell like, a dream within a dream within a dream.

When I awoke Sudeep was gone. Apparently, I had passed straight out on the floor, for when I surveyed the room what little sunlight remained sat boxed by my feet and ready to escape out the window. Judging by the clock two hours had passed. My mouth was painfully dry and my head heavy with fog. I awoke startled from a dream with the guilty feeling that it had actually happened. In it, a beautiful girl, someone with very fair skin and emerald green eyes, leads me through the woods, summoning me to her with an extended hand. I know I should not follow her even though I am powerless against her beauty. She is not of my kind, I think as I trail behind her, she is not for me. Yet still her beauty beckons, and I follow, a fool under some magical spell. She wears sheer white silk, and through it I can see the fullness of her breasts as she turns to me, an arm extended and waving me closer, closer, closer. Her black hair shines in the glorious sunlight. Her neck is so pure and white it takes my breath away; I feel terribly guilty for desiring this thing, so unknown and alien, so forbidden. Eventually, I arrive at a small clearing with an azure pond. Lotus flowers rest atop the water; I stop and stare at them, and the water, and the sky, so high and blue. She calls out to me to follow her, asking if I want her, offering me the strangest freedom. She moves slowly into the water, and I watch as she retreats, as the sheer silk becomes wet and the azure water rises to her knees, her waist, her breasts. She holds her breasts in her hands like some bountiful offering, enticing me to join her.

The instant I step foot in the water the sky darkens, the surrounding trees crouching closer until they've nearly built a canopy above us. Whispers abound. Eyes, hidden and disappointed, watch from the darkness. By the time I'm up to my knees, the whispers turn to screams; I can feel their weight, their animosity, their vicious sadness. I stare at the beautiful girl, who now swims in the center of the pond. Even in the darkness descending upon us, her emerald eyes sparkle, dazzling me with their beauty. By the time I'm up to my waist, the voices become recognizable, and in their filial outrage and disgust I feel a brutal sense of loss, as if I've committed the most terrible crime.

It was the guilt that startled me awake.

I rose from the floor and peered into the tiny mirror beside our dorm room door. My eyes were bloodshot and my face looked different, strange. Something was off—I didn't look quite like myself, even though I knew it was my self staring back at me. I left the room and headed out of our building, passing a surprising amount of students still anxiously moving in, many of them Indians like Sudeep and me, or perhaps Indians not like us at all. Nothing looked as it once did, and though I saw some real familiarity in the Indian mothers with their *ticos* and occasional *sari*, I felt an odd kind of guilt making eye contact, feeling, as I moved quickly through the crowd, as if I held some embarrassing secret.

I left Tarnopol Hall and the throng of weeping parents and began to wander around campus. I tried recalling the route my parents and I had taken when we first visited over a year ago, but because it had been so long, or perhaps because my head was still foggy from that strange dream—and the weed—I couldn't quite remember the way. Nothing looked familiar. As I wandered forward from Tarnopol Hall I eventually appeared at the science buildings, recalling, as I passed them, that most of my classes would take place—at least as a freshman—in the Engineering Hall and the Engineering Lecture Hall. In fact, I had two classes there tomorrow. I stood outside of the closed buildings, surveying them, so majestic and full of promise, and I felt a thrill very much like I'd felt when my parents and I had come before. Before, having as of yet made my decision, I looked upon these buildings with the scrutiny of deliberation; now, I admired them like some excited competitor, eager to step foot inside so as to begin my conquest.

Engineering Hall, with its glass-exposed stairways, seemed stoic in its simplicity, its dark brick and three stories embodying a place where only hard work and shrewd deliberation could lead to breathtaking discoveries. I stared up at it partially in awe of its architectural beauty—it looked like the prototypical college building, therefore rendering *me* the prototypical college student—and also aware that something significant awaited me inside, an opportunity, perhaps, to show the world who I was and what I was made of. I felt a delightful thrill contemplating the challenges awaiting me inside, so much so that I impulsively thought of my father. I wanted to call him and tell him how excited I was to finally be here, at college; recalling my earlier escapade, I thought against it, realizing, guiltfully, the shameful irony I would be enacting.

I moved on through campus, stopping occasionally whenever I found myself possessed or overcome by the beauty of a particular building, aware of the fact that starting tomorrow my life would forever change—or finally begin. Truly alone now for the first time in my life, I felt in total control of my being, completely free to conduct myself in any way *I* saw fit. Never before that moment had I felt so empowered; I felt a strange, terrifying responsibility, both to myself *and* my parents. I feared I might let them down; I feared I already had. Nonetheless, mixed within this trepidation grew an exhilarating, beautiful anxiety, a sense that I was on the right path in my life and that everything, eventually, would work out for the best. All I had to do was follow what was in my heart.

I soon found myself moving away from the buildings and out towards the very center of campus: Zuckerman Park. The sun had not totally set and the sky was fuchsia with a few high clouds moving inland. It was getting cold. When we had walked through the park on our visit, school had been in session and students could be seen milling around or meandering through, some throwing a football or kicking a soccer ball or simply idling the day away. Now, only a handful of people were around: an Asian couple hanging out under a massive oak tree, a blanket spread beneath them; two white guys wearing fraternity letters throwing a baseball, the smack of the hard leather into worn mitts a rhythmic heartbeat of some essential pastime. Eventually I found an empty space I could privately call my own. I moved up the grass towards the trees, the sound of the baseball popping off in the cool distance. I sat beneath one of the massive oak trees and sprawled at its base.

I sat there until I saw stars.

However prepared or confident I might've felt the night before staring at Engineering Hall and Engineering Lecture Hall, all of it seemed to vanish immediately the first morning of classes, as I found myself anxiously immersed in what felt like the entire freshman class of Irvine chaotically vying to make it to class on time. Campus abounded with students scrambling around the quad everywhere, haphazardly running around as if lost—and some were. More than once I saw students—their faces glazed with distress, some fighting back tears—walking around with maps clutched tightly in their hands, glancing uncertainly up at the buildings and then back at their map and then back at the row of stoic redbrick buildings towering over them. They raced around as if shot from a cannon, bumping into you and anyone else in their myopia, furtively checking their watches as they tried to deduce the location of their class and if they could make it on time. It was one giant wave of energy and emotion, of intellect and curiosity, of fear and anxiety that left me generally wishing for a traffic cop to emerge and safely shepherd these lost souls to their futures. And even though I knew exactly where *I* was going, I too felt swept up in the storm and equally confused. So much seemed at stake—and it was only the first day!

Whereas the freshmen seemed visibly lost, the upperclassmen, however, were easy to identify. Already back with old friends, most of them walked in packs, their peace made with the general madness of Day 1. They embodied calm, moving languorously through the quad with their colleagues, without care or caution as to whether they'd make it to class on time. Too often that first morning I found myself spying the grassy quad in strange admiration at a group of upperclassmen as they joked with each other, once or twice pointing out a freshman for ridicule or, noticing someone they hadn't seen since last year, stopping to catch up. You could hear the familiarity in their voices; you could see the comfort in their demeanor; you could feel the confidence in their beings—in their being at Irvine. It was magical.

Of equal magic was the amount of beautiful women parading around campus, their long legs—cinnamon, white, dark brown, black—and bare shoulders casually exposed to the rising sun and offering everyone a glimpse of their tantalizing allure. I had never seen anything like it. They were everywhere. And every time I felt under the spell of one that simply couldn't be any more beautiful another one even more stunning came sauntering around some hidden corner, transfixing me with her sensuous gait and compelling me to trail admiringly behind. They wore everything; they wore nothing. Jeans shorts were undoubtedly in vogue, for I noticed that at least half of the young women strutting to class that morning wore shorts that enticingly framed the generous swell of their tanned thighs. These shorts were so blessedly short there were times you could see just a hint of cheek peeking out from the faux-torn denim, and too often I caught myself staring from beneath my Way-farers at a particular goddess, dumbfounded by the voluptuous-ness of her proportions and the sheer casualness with which she carried herself.

Not before long I found myself drowning in a sea of sumptuous brown legs and straight black hair, as one of the dark
beauties in tightfitting jean shorts I so powerlessly followed
inexplicably led me to my intended destination—Engineering
Lecture Hall and Chem 101. Once we all squeezed inside and
I had taken my seat, I noticed something that, in many ways,
symbolized much of what I had seen on my adventure across
campus that morning, even if I wasn't totally aware of it at the
time. There was a social organization to campus that, now that
I was planted squarely in the home of my major, you couldn't
ignore. And even the most naïve believer of our nation's diversity could not deny what was so obviously apparent: most of the
students walking to class that morning and all of the students
sitting in this massive lecture hall were separated by ethnicity.

The lecture hall, with its five hundred seats, crystalized this
phenomena for me. If you had drawn a line down the middle
of the auditorium you would have had the Indian students on
one side and the Asians on the other. And that was it. There
might've been a white face salted in here or there, but mostly the
lecture hall was divided along these lines, and as I sat near the
middle I realized that there were even a handful of seats to my
right that were empty, as if to further demarcate our differences.
And that wasn't all. For within our broad ethnic separation,
there existed further separation, especially among the Indians.
On our side of the lecture hall, we were separated, consciously
it felt, by the kind of Indian we were—or envisioned ourselves
to be. The Indians like me, for example, first-generation Indians
born here who wanted to consider ourselves mostly American
(even if our parents had other ideas), we sat in the middle of the
hall, along the aisles and towards the back, speaking English

or playing on our laptops, dressed in jeans, shorts and T-shirts. The other Indians, though, the Indians who we traditionally (though only somewhat derisively) called FoBs (Fresh off the Boats), they were located mostly in the far left-hand section of the hall, sitting at or near the front of the room. You could easily identify them by their clothes: many of the women—and they outnumbered the men—wore *kurti* tops with jeans, while the men, many of them in white, wore some kind of *kurta* with slacks. They could also, perhaps more importantly, be identified by their language, for rarely did you hear English issuing from their side of the room. A symphony of different Hindi dialects emanated from where they sat, as did, I quickly noticed, a whole mélange of Mandarin or Cantonese rise from the immigrants seated to my far right. It seemed, for the moment at least, that the first-generation Indians and Asians populated the center of the room, while our brethren, the young men and women assiduously following the very path of our own mothers and fathers, sat on the edges, marginalized, cast out of the very group they so vigorously strove to enter.

These distinctions became even sharper once class began. Professor Xian, Chinese, mid-fifties with a head full of dark, shiny hair, strode up to the lectern, dressed professorially in a bow tie and tweed jacket. The class fell quickly to attention. I don't know why but I began sweating. Dr. Xian stood there for a moment, surveying all of us, his receptive, empty vessels. I knew he was a leader in his field: according to his profile on the college website, he had once been a high-ranking executive at GE and now sat on at least two executive boards of major Chinese state-owned chemical companies. I chose him over Professor James, who taught the only other section of Chemistry 101, for those very reasons. I wanted only the best, and Dr. Xian, based on his resume and professional success, fit the part. Feed me, I thought. Teach me everything I need to know to be just like you. To be *better* than you.

When he opened his mouth, however, I immediately realized I'd made a tragic mistake. And I wasn't the only one. You could almost feel a collective groan emanate from the Indian side of the room, even though no one dared physically utter a sound. His English bordered on indecipherable, and not because he spoke low or the microphone at the lectern was malfunctioning. His was a recent immigrant's English: choppy, mispronounced words with sentences lacking proper verb conjugation. Was this some kind of joke? I peered around the room, hoping it was, waiting for the real Dr. Xian to please stand up.

For certainly I wasn't paying the tuition I was paying to learn something as difficult as college-level chemistry from someone whose English wasn't fit to give driving directions. The other Indian students looked around the room as well, sharing conspiratorial glances, frantically seeking some kind of advice, escape, or interpreter. And perhaps I shouldn't have been surprised to see some of the Asian students—though not all, for many of them, American born like me, bore looks of severe frustration—listening intently, jotting down whatever Dr. Xian said they felt was relevant or important, but I was.

Watching them, I was dumbfounded at the way they nodded their heads agreeably and copiously took notes. I was stunned at the laughter that occasionally sprung forth throughout the lecture (What was so funny? Did he tell a joke? What was it? *Why are you laughing!*), amazed that they could crack his puzzling English into something, well, *meaningful*. Then again, perhaps

I shouldn't have been *that* surprised. As the child of Indian immigrants, I too had familiarity trying to decipher non-native English. Too much, in fact. Whether a recently immigrated cousin or my mother's own tongue when I was in elementary school and embarrassedly forced to translate her English questions into something my overwhelmingly white teachers could answer, I understood the bravery—and, too often, humiliation—of someone trying to speak a second language in America. What I couldn't understand, I guess, was why I had to understand this while trying to learn, well, *chemistry.*

At the end of class, a small group of Asian students surrounded Dr. Xian and began eagerly questioning him—in Mandarin. As the lecture hall emptied out amidst whispers of dropping the class, I sat there defeated, watching those students converse with Dr. Xian, their shared laughter rising throughout the cavernous auditorium like some immutable future.

I watched and I listened and I thought, perhaps with *too* much bitterness: that should be *me.*

# 41

You could smell the smoke the second you entered the hallway. Our room was three floors up, and the instant I'd traversed the stairs I could smell the minty, florid scent suffocating our entire floor. I peered up and down the hallways, hoping, foolishly, that it *wasn't* coming from my room. Mercifully, the hallway was empty. I walked down to one end of the hallway and threw open a window and then to the other end and opened that window and at my room I stood at the door. I could hear a wellspring of voices, of laughter, rising from beyond.

Reluctantly, I entered.

"Rohan!" Sudeep bellowed, cracking up, his crimson eyes obscured by his curly black locks and the dense, smoky haze. "Where the fuck you been? Everyone," he said, gesturing to the crowd packed into our tiny room, "this is my roommate: Rohan! Where you been, man?"

"Class."

"Class? Dude, it's the first day."

"You didn't go to class?" I asked, genuinely perplexed, because when I left this morning he was awake, and dressed, and holding books.

"No one goes the first day," he said. "Come on man!"

"How do you know?"

"Oh," he said, loading the glass pipe with a tiny green morsel, "I know."

"Won't they drop you?"

"They'll only drop you if you miss the *second* day," said the guy seated beside Sudeep on the floor. In total there were three others: two girls and him, all with the same, stoned, glassy-eyed look as Sudeep. "And even then it depends on who your professor is." He offered me his hand. "Naresh."

"Rohan." I shook it. "Hi," I said, turning my attention to the two very pretty girls seated on my bed.

"Dipika," said the darker of the two. She wore a white ruffled skirt complimented by a tightfitting shamrock green polo with all three buttons undone and when she offered me her hand I couldn't help notice the gold bangle around her wrist, shimmering through the haze. "I hear you're from Fremont."

"Yeah," I responded, though it sounded more like a question. I glanced over at Sudeep, wondering, embarrassed, just how much these girls knew. "What about you?"

"Artesia," she replied.

"Where's that?" I asked, aware now that the girl seated beside her was blatantly eyeing me. She was much, much lighter than Dipika, her skin so fair and even I thought for a moment that perhaps she wasn't Indian. But I could tell. I could see it in her eyes, almond and wide yet so light brown they appeared almost hazel, eyes that, when they finally met mine, sparkled with something akin to danger. She smiled when she noticed me notice her.

"We call it Little India," Dipika said, embarrassed.

"Is that good or bad?"

"I know right?" Sudeep said, then hit the pipe and exhaled a thick plume.

"Dude," I said. "What the fuck?"

"What the fuck what?" Sudeep coughed. And laughed. He coughed-laughed.

"What about that gizmo you had."

"Gizmo?" His confusion sounded real, but his eyes, so red and narrow, told another story.

"You know, that thing you said you blow into, to clean the air?"

"Dude," Sudeep said, passing the pipe to Naresh, "don't worry about it."

"Don't worry about it? What about our R.A.?"

"*I'm* you're R.A.," Naresh said, igniting the bowl.

The girls laughed, giggling at each other.

"Is he serious?" I asked them.

"You're in my Chem class," the fair-skinned one said. "Dr. Xian."

"Dr. Xian!" Naresh shook his head disappointedly. "No, no, no! That guy can't speak no English."

"Don't talk about my dad like that," Sudeep said.

I looked at Sudeep and tried not to laugh and then Naresh seated on the floor beside him and then the fair-skinned girl on my bed. Was this the girl I followed into Chemistry class earlier this morning? Could be. Her legs certainly fit the description. Her tightfitting jean shorts showed more than enough of her enticing flesh and smiling at me (as if reading my mind) she uncrossed and slowly recrossed her legs.

Inexplicably, I suddenly thought of my father, our drive to campus, and my fear of him finally broaching the subject of sex with me. In high school the entirety of my sexual experience consisted of a brief, clumsy foray into dating an Indian girl named Sheetal (now at Stanford) during my senior year, an arrangement that seemed purposely designed to ensure we had prom dates rather than anything resembling true romance. And while it did ultimately result in an hour-long make-out session immediately following the dance, our swift, mutual dissolution upon graduation only served to reinforce what we both intuitively knew: that we would never allow anything to get in the way of our real goals of college and making our parents proud. Nonetheless, before and throughout that time, my parents were careful to say very little about sex or dating (or even Sheetal, for that matter, whose Stanford admission I knew had to impress them), a silence whose bewildering logic left me strangely ashamed whenever desire stirred within me. Because I love them, I excused their silence due to their arranged marriage and the difficulties I sensed they faced when contemplating how best to tackle what must have felt like an alien issue. Of course, what I truly wanted was to have my father grant me permission, and to grant it in the grandest terms—to have him tell me that sex was natural, that it was healthy, and that there was absolutely nothing wrong with having as much of it as possible so long as some kind of protection was used. The child that has ever heard that from a parent is the luckiest child in the world.

"Dr. Xian," Naresh said. "Brilliant fucking guy. Broken fucking English."

"I *hate* that phrase," Dipika said. "*Broken English*. I can't tell you how many times I've heard people say that shit about my mom."

"So what? We've all heard people say shit about our moms. About our moms, about our dads, about our cousins. Doesn't mean it ain't true."

"How long you been here?" I asked Naresh.

"I'm in my third year but I'm still technically a sophomore."

"You like it?" I asked.

"I never want to leave," he said, hitting the pipe again before passing it to me. "Let me say this though," he advised as smoke escaped his lungs. "Whenever you have a chance, take an Indian. There aren't that many of them—they're mostly in computer science or whatever—but the handful around knows the deal, know what I mean?"

"What deal?" I asked.

"Dude!" Sudeep laughed. "Come on man! What the fuck do you think?"

"We take care of our own," the fair-skinned girl said. "I'm Padma, by the way."

She offered me her hand. I took it. It was soft and warm with nails the color of saffron.

"Are you a Chem major?" she asked.

"Engineering," I said.

"What kind?"

"Civil? You?"

"Biochemical," she said proudly, and then, perhaps reading the reluctance with which I held the pipe: "You going to be able to handle that?"

I looked at her.

"Don't be scared," she said. "I'm here for you."

"Yo, check this out," Sudeep said, his voice filling the room. "Check this out. I just got a great fucking idea. Yo, this is like the best fucking idea I've ever had. Ready," Sudeep waited, so as to draw our undivided attention. "We should start an intramural cricket league." After a dramatic pause, he clapped his hands and said, "Bang!"

"Yes," Naresh said, high fiving him, the two of them breaking up into delirious, ecstatic laughter. "Yes! That would be *so* tight!"

"What do you think Rohan?" Sudeep asked.

"I've been known to play a little cricket from time to time," I said, an understatement if ever there was one. From seventh to eleventh grade, I played in a highly competitive summer cricket league in Fremont, leading my team, as head bowler, to two championships. Those teams were awarded the misfortune of going to India to compete in winter tournaments around Gujarat, exercises in futility that reiterated and reinvigorated our—and our parents'—academic hopes and dreams.

"I love it," Naresh said. "Whenever I go to India I always go to the Mumbai cricket yards to watch the people, the crowds, the games. And you know what? This could get us all to organize around something, something that's—I don't know—truly *ours*."

"I hate to burst your bubble, but isn't cricket an *English* game?" I asked.

"You know," Dipika began, "it could be fun. You could use the practice soccer fields. I think people would be into it."

"Yo!" Sudeep exclaimed, shaking Naresh by the shoulder. "There you go!"

"We should do it," Naresh said. "We should definitely do it."

"Are you a virgin?" Padma asked me.

"What?"

"You know," she said, pointing to the pipe.

"Oh." I blushed. "No. Not at all."

"Rohan's an old pro at this," Sudeep interjected. "Aren't you?"

"That's one way of putting it."

"I want you to impress me," Padma said.

"Do you?"

"Yes," she said, leaning on my bed, an elbow propped on her knee, her face resting in her palm and alight with intrigue. "Don't you *want* to impress me?"

"Yes," I replied. "Though I can think of a better way than this."

"Like what?"

"I don't know if you can handle it," I said.

She let this linger like the smoke between us.

"But if you're good..." I began, and somehow burying my anxiety (or was it shame?), I somehow managed to steadily bring the pipe to my lips. I hit it so quickly I wasn't even sure I drew smoke. But I did. How I exhaled without coughing was a miracle. "Then perhaps I'll show you one day."

"Promise?" Padma took the pipe from my hand.

"Promise."

I could tell by the way she hit it that she was experienced in ways I could only imagine.

She looked at me, at all of us, and asked, "You know what we should do?"

Stoned silence; something vaguely akin to anticipation.

"We should go to the park."

# 40

We found a place near the center of the park, squarely in the sun, a large piece of green the five of us could comfortably call our own. Naresh had retrieved a large blanket from his dorm room—the room, coincidentally, directly across from ours—and Dipika, Padma, and myself sprawled upon it while Naresh and Sudeep threw a football across the wide expanse of grass. Sudeep would loft the ball high in the air and Naresh, laughing at nothing, everything, would wave his hand in the air as if calling for a fair catch and then reach up for it and either bungle it off his fingertips or lead it straight into his chest. The girls and I watched and laughed and occasionally Padma would glance at me and through her Wayfarers I could feel her hazel eyes, curious, provocative, and playfully shy, and I would smile at her and then she would smile at me and then we would turn our attention back to Sudeep, now almost twenty yards away, as he cocked his arm and hurled the tiny football through the clear blue sky.

And then Dipika was telling us about her older sister, Hetal, Harvard Medical School, thirty-three and single and terribly alone. Dipika was talking to all of us but it sounded as if she was addressing no one in particular, perhaps just the beauty of the day fading before us, the blue sky and the setting crimson sun. Occasionally she would stop her story and zone out on one of the many small groups of students walking through the park, their Mandarin or Spanish or Korean interspersed with high-pitched laughter, and then Dipika would look at Padma and me and, stoned, ask, "Where was I?" and we would all crack up so hard I usually wound up crying.

"Your sister," I said, wiping away tears.

"Right," Dipika responded, "right. Anyway, she calls me and she tells me how lonely she is, how much she really wants to get married. I mean, she says these things to *me*, her eighteen-year-old sister. As if I can relate? But I'm her sister and I love her and she's all the way in Boston, alone for the most part, and so I let her vent, you know? And you know what she always comes back to: I want to have an arranged marriage. Can you believe it? I'm like, 'What? You want to marry a total stranger? What the fuck's wrong with you?' And you know what she says: 'I just want to find a nice Indian guy to marry.' And I'm like, hello, you're at fucking *Har*vard. They're, like, everywhere. And you know what she says? 'All the Indians here want white girls. They want trophy wives to show they've made it in America. They're not interested in a girl like me.' I mean, can you believe that shit?"

"That's bullshit." Padma shook her head. "She's just not looking hard enough."

"This is what she tells me! I mean, what do you think, Rohan? Why do so many Indian guys want white girls?"

"I don't know if I'm the right guy to ask for this," I replied.

"Why's that?" Padma asked.

I could feel her through her Wayfarers, intrigued and delightfully flirtatious.

"Because if I ever came home with a white girl my father would kill me," I confessed, and even though such direction had never been explicitly given, it felt utterly true, like some unspoken bond holding my family—and my father's hopes and dreams—together.

"Good boy," Padma said, and here she reached out and patted my leg, touching me for the first time beyond our cursory handshake. I studied her hand there on my thigh and smiled at her and, much to my delight, she smiled back.

"That's not the question you should be asking, anyway," Sudeep said, ten yards away. He cocked his arm and flung the football through the air, leading Naresh across the grass beyond the paved path and near the trees. "The question you should be asking is: why do so many Indians not want *Indian* girls?"

"I don't know. You tell me Joe Montana?" Dipika asked.

"Well, since you asked," he said, drifting backwards several feet. We all gazed high into the dimming sky and watched the ball arcing gracefully towards him. "I think your sister might be on to something, when she mentions this idea of trophy wives.

I mean, that's part of it. They want to feel like they've made it, like they are finally *American*—like they belong or something. And it might sound foolish or whatever, but you'd be surprised how many Indians, particularly from outside California—you know, Indians who haven't grown up around a lot of other Indians—feel as if the only way they can be 'themselves'—what the fuck ever that means—is by fully assimilating into what they believe is the mainstream American culture. Which, in their eyes, means white. Or at least anything that generally means a middle-class or upper-class lifestyle. But there's something else at play too, something perhaps even more dangerous. And that's where your sister probably feels *really* up against it. And that's the idea that for some Indian guys, marrying an Indian girl means keeping faith with the traditions of their parents, of India. It means continuing something that, because they think of themselves as fully American—or because they *want* to—represents—I don't know, what's the best way to put it?—a step backwards, as if they're not advancing if they don't marry *outside* their race."

"So," Dipika said, "in your eyes, it's all about economics."

"First of all, everything is about economics," Sudeep said dryly, throwing the ball back to Naresh. "Don't get it twisted. Everything arises from an economic base. But what I'm alluding to is perhaps something more dangerous. And that's the sense that, for some Indian guys, their culture lacks something for them—or, worse, is backward or deficient in some way. And what they see in too many Indian girls today is their parents' culture, their parents' ideology mirrored right back at them. And it scares them to see themselves like that. To see themselves as Indian in the *cultural* sense of the word."

"So they marry white women?" Dipika asked.

"So they marry *other* women."

"You need to lay off that crack pipe," she said, igniting all of us, Sudeep included, to laughter.

It was then we heard the chanting, an organized, powerful upswing of emotion and protest rising up throughout the park. I sat fully up from my languid, sprawled position, and under an almost crimson sky the marchers came raging through the park, striding across the paved path like some strange corporeal manifestation of dissent, perhaps twenty or thirty students at most, each of whom shouted in vibrant, impassioned unison, "Iraq is not al-Qaeda! Iraq is not al-Qaeda!" over and over again. Some of them held signs of Osama bin Laden marked with a red X, others signs picturing Iraq with the phrase "No WMD" written across it. Others clutched large placards of President Bush, his face bedeviled with crimson horns and the words "Warmonger" stamped across his mouth while still others touted signs saying "We Are Not Terrorists." Their chanting boomed rhythmically across the serenity of the park, halting everyone in their otherwise mundane activities to take heed of their strange, visceral plea—or charge.

"Speaking of backward cultures," Naresh said. "Our campus version of the Arab League."

It was only then that I realized the girls (there were only a handful) wore colorful headscarves covering their hair while the guys wore white tunics, those most commonly seen in various Arab countries and, unfortunately, most recently seen in the endless footage of Osama bin Laden, al-Qaeda, and the Taliban that had been repeated constantly on every news channel since 9/11.

"I can't believe those girls are wearing headscarves," Dipika

said, the protestors passing directly before us now, their placards rising and falling in unified vehemence.

"I know, right?" Padma replied. "I mean, especially after everything they've done."

# 39

English 101. 8:30 am Tuesday morning. This time I was
pleasantly surprised to find myself in an actual classroom—as
opposed to some gigantic lecture hall—and that, among the
handful of students already seated and waiting patiently for
our professor to arrive there wasn't one particular demographic
dominating the room. I took a seat near the back, in the middle
but not quite, at a position where I felt I could participate but
also, if need be, fade into the background depending on what
was taking place. English was unequivocally my least favorite
subject, something that too often left me feeling, particularly
when it came to writing or thinking about literature—let alone
poetry—as if I was faced not with something containing a
plot, characters, or dialogue, but rather some inscrutable riddle
wherein my academic—and therefore professional—future tee-
tered on edge.

Too often in high school I found myself wondering what
all the hubbub was about regarding literary analysis; characters did what their writer intended them to do—beyond iden-
tifying that, what was all the fuss? Themes, motifs, subplots,

historical context, all of these things puzzled me to the point of frustration—trying to correctly identify them, let alone write about them in an intelligible way, caused me more headache and anxiety than I could bear. My preference for—and excellence in—science and math over the liberal arts perhaps resulted from this disconnect between a place where there was undoubtedly only one correct answer and a place where there were many, a place where rules, laws, and theories governed and predicted outcomes and a place where those things were neither predictors nor guides but rather carcasses trampled over and subverted. Needless to say, I wanted to get through my English requirements with as little friction as possible.

I was about fifteen minutes early and so, to pass the time, I flipped through what I knew to be one of the required texts for the class. It was titled *America Today*, a five hundred page anthology containing writers ranging from Thomas Jefferson to Martin Luther King Jr. to the provocative filmmaker Michael Moore. Rumor had it (and this coming from a stoned Naresh) that most English 101 professors assigned a novel as well, though, mercifully, when I'd gone to the bookstore yesterday I didn't see anything listed, much to my relief. The last thing I wanted on my plate besides Chem and Calc was fiction.

Students slowly trickled in. Two Indians, two African Americans, pairs of Asians, a kaleidoscope of faces so varied that—with class about to begin in less than five minutes—our classroom resembled an ethnic hodgepodge, the antithesis of what I'd seen in my Chemistry and Calculus classes yesterday. This soothed me for some reason, made me feel as if I was finally on some front line of progress, even if my father's words still rang loudly in my ears. I wondered what he would think of Sudeep and Naresh. Certainly those were not the kind of Indians he wanted me to stick to in the hopes of saving myself trouble. If anything, those guys *were* trouble. Or at least more trouble than anyone I'd ever known back in Fremont. Nonetheless, I wondered if my father would perhaps prefer their kind of trouble to whatever he feared lurked in the faces of those so unlike mine.

A pair of girls entered and surveyed the room. Among the empty seats, there was only one pair remaining and it was directly behind me, against the wall. Every other seat was a single, including one directly in front of me and one directly to my left. The girls smiled as they squeezed past and after sitting behind me began chatting loud enough for me to hear.

"Oh no," one of them said. "The whole thing is a scam. You know that shit. Don't get it twisted. The whole thing is a scam so the book publishers can gouge us broke-ass college kids. And for what? So they can reprint some edition with one new essay in it? I mean, why does this book cost eighty-five dollars?"

"Someone needs to come up with an electronic book reader, you know?" said the other. "Something where all these books can just be free and you can carry them around like a disk or something. I mean, my Algebra book cost a hundred bucks!"

Like everyone else in the classroom, I felt their pain. And I was about to relate it when *she* walked in. It felt as if the world had stopped and the only thing moving was her. I stared. I couldn't help but stare. She moved with such innate sensuality it was as if she was a melody embodied, a perfect song made soft and fair and oh so young. Her long black hair shone brilliantly in the morning sunlight slanting into our classroom; her lips, supple and full and playfully agleam with a naturalistic hue of pink, ignited fantasies so shameful I blushed, right then and there. Did she feel me staring? It seemed as if she was looking right at me, that her sharp, lime-green eyes were reading everything I suddenly felt, dreamed, and desired, but that, perhaps having encountered such stares her entire life, having grown accustomed to the magical power of her beauty, she was blessedly able to ignore the spellbound admiration of lesser beings.

For that's what I felt like seated in my chair: a lesser being, a mere mortal in the presence of a goddess. And a fair-skinned goddess mind you. Hers wasn't the lightness of Padma, something akin to brown but distinctly Indian and that, in our culture, marked you as especially beautiful. Hers was the real thing, pure and untainted, American and yet something distinctly other, as if, beyond her bewitching beauty, there was some mystery locked in the strange harmony of her shiny black hair, green eyes, and pure white skin. Had I been forced to stand I wouldn't have been able to, so overcome was I by her beauty.

Before I knew what was happening she was in front of me, her hand atop the back of the empty seat before me.

"Is this seat taken?" she asked.

I looked at her, the seat, and her again. When I opened my mouth nothing came out.

"Is anyone sitting here?"

Powerless to speak, I nodded, no. She took the seat and pulled a notebook and pencil out from her backpack. And even though I knew I was risking humiliation, even though I knew it was totally rude—and not to mention, you know, probably creepy—I watched her do this. I couldn't help myself. She wore tightfitting black jeans with a white sleeveless blouse that swooped modestly around her neck and that invited you to admire her arms, which, upon closer inspection—*stop staring!*—were a tad pink from the sun. There were freckles—*freckles!*—upon her shoulders, and just the sight of those magical imperfections were enough to make me crazy—and *ashamed!* For I knew she wasn't for me! I knew she could never *be* for me! I also knew, conversely, that I could probably never be for her—*whoever* she was! Nonetheless, I also knew that I had never before been shaken by someone—by *beauty*—in the way that I now was and so what did any of that other shit matter?

I don't know if she felt my eyes, but she turned around to me. Like a fool I smiled back and then glanced over at the door, wondering where our professor was. It was past time and I was sweating. Profusely. I glanced back at her and there she was, still facing me, her gentle face alight with the most graceful curiosity.

Instead of asking me "Why are you staring at me you weirdo?" she asked, "Did you get the book for this class already?"

"Yes."

"I looked in the bookstore and I couldn't find it. Where did you get it?"

"Amazon."

"Amazon?"

"Online," I clarified.

"New or used?"

"Used."

"How much?"

I thought of the girls behind me and said, softly, "45."

"That's not bad."

"I got lucky."

"Where are you from?"

To that question I lacked the proper compass. "What do you mean?"

"Are you from California?"

"Fremont. The Bay Area."

"L.A.," she said. "You like it here?"

"It's been," I paused and, inexplicably comfortable, comfort*ed*, I stared into her eyes searching for the right word. "Interesting."

At that moment our professor stumbled in, a staggering blur of dishevelment and confusion. She carried coffee and a bagel clumsily in one hand and a thick stack of what I assumed were our syllabi in the other. She looked at us and then at the desk and lectern at the front of the room and then back to us and then dropped the stack of papers onto the desk. They held tenuously in a stack before toppling and spilling to the floor. We looked at her and then the papers and then her.

"English 101?" asked in a breathless, confused tone.

A handful of people said yes; others, groaning, shook their heads.

"I'm Dr. Green," she said, glaring at the toppled syllabi. "And I've had a hell of a morning. Give me a minute."

The girl before me rolled her eyes in disbelief and said, "I'm Azada."

"Rohan."

"Nice to meet you Rohan."

"Thank you," I said, an idiot, a robot, both.

It was then I noticed the necklace and charm resting upon her chest. Where I found the courage—or stupidity—to say what I did I do not know.

"Interesting necklace," I whispered, feeling, as the words became real, as if I'd just done something terribly wrong.

She looked at me curiously before turning to her necklace and charm. The charm was a small gold disk inscribed in a style of lettering Americans had seen all too frequently in the news this past year.

"Do you like it?"

"What does it mean?"

"All glory to Allah."

# 38

"Here," Sudeep said, a cigarette fuming from his lips. He handed me a red plastic cup filled with foamy beer. "I want to get into that beer pong game. You down?"

Apparently, weekends started on Thursdays at Irvine. The jury was out as to whether this was good or bad. Part of me wondered if this was a recipe for disaster, as if by offering virtually no classes on Friday the college was perhaps sanctioning what it had to know was inevitably reckless behavior in an age group more prone to play than work. Another part of me, however, felt that perhaps this absence offered a clandestine lesson, an opportunity for us aspiring young men and women to try and successfully manage our time, to use that freedom for whatever study or research our fields required. Like an exercise in proper time management. Or blistering self-denial. Either way, when Sudeep informed me we were going to a rush party at one of the two Indian fraternities on campus, I felt myself caught between two opposing desires: to please my parents by being good and studying—and to please myself by trying to get laid. Luckily, I had Sudeep's trademark eloquence to push me over the edge. "Dude," he'd said, pipe in hand, "it's the *first* weekend. Who the fuck does homework?" Who indeed?

The DJ stood behind an Apple laptop playing *bhangra* music infused with early nineties hip-hop in the crimson darkness of the basement as a strobe light flickered occasionally, igniting the crowd to surge and pump their fists in the air as weedsmoke hung like some caliginous ceiling and Sudeep polished off his beer and then looked at the Indian working the keg of Bombay Ultra and he was so dark I could only make out the gleaming white of his teeth and Sudeep handed him his cup as Snoop Dogg was rapping over the pounding drums and when Sudeep took his beer we headed upstairs and outside into the backyard where on a sand volleyball court brightly lit under the clear black sky a game of four on four was going on and sipping our beers we watched them beside four guys smoking a blunt and beyond the court was perhaps thirty yards of grass and beyond that another fraternity house where a party was also underway, the house, at least three times larger than the Indian fraternity's, illuminated and throbbing with music and laughter.

"Who lives over there?" I asked.

The guy smoking the blunt exhaled, studying me with nearly closed eyes. "The Reds," he said.

He handed me the blunt. I looked at Sudeep. Sudeep smiled approvingly. I hit it and passed it to him.

"Who are the Reds?" I asked.

"You know, the Chinese? The Communists. They're Commies over there," he said.

"Stop fucking with me," I said.

"Why would I fuck with you?"

"To fuck with me."

"I like this guy," he said, retrieving the blunt from Sudeep. "Where're you from?"

"Fremont," I replied. I sipped my beer. It tasted flat and stale and appropriate.

The guy looked at Sudeep.

"Pleasanton," he answered. "You?"

"San Diego," he said.

"Never been down there," Sudeep said.

By now the other three guys smoking the blunt had circled around us. Two of them wore shirts with the fraternity's letters on them, Greek letters I knew to read Delta Sigma Eta, or DESHI as they were commonly—and accurately—called on campus, as deshi (or desi) is a common shorthand among Indian immigrants and their children throughout the diaspora for anyone from the subcontinent. One of the guys, perhaps the oldest and undoubtedly the heaviest, took the blunt between two fingers and held it to his lips and hit it and hit it again and then stared out at the volleyball court and exhaled. He wore a gold chain with an Om medallion around his thick neck that glimmered under the lights.

"San Diego's cool. Cool but white. Whiter than you could imagine. It was a culture shock coming here. I'd never seen so many Indians in my entire life. So many Indians and so many Asians. It felt like I was in the Taipei airport on my way to Mumbai there were so many fucking Indians and Asians."

"Are you a brother here?" I asked.

"Damn right," he said, smiling, the blunt having magically

appeared between his lips. "Darpan," he said, hand extended. I shook it and then Sudeep shook it and after we introduced ourselves Darpan hit the blunt and passed it to me.

I stared at it for a moment pinched fuming between my fingers.

"Do you like it here?" Sudeep asked.

"Let me tell you something, guys, and I'm not trying to bull-shit you here because part of my job as a brother is to rush smart, good-looking guys like yourselves. But we're the shit. And it's not just because of the parties we throw or the hook-ups we have with the Indian sorority or the chronic we get, it's much more than that. It's the cultural shit we do, shit, to be totally honest, I didn't even realize I needed or wanted when I was in white bread San Diego. Are you okay?"

Apparently, this was addressed to me, staring at the blunt as if I were holding a gun. "What's in this thing?" I felt like I was a thousand feet tall—and growing.

"Meth," Darpan said.

"Meth?"

"Meth," Darpan repeated seriously. This ignited the other three guys—*brothers*—to laughter.

"Stop fucking with me."

"Why would I fuck with you?"

"To fuck with me."

"I *really* like this guy," Darpan said. "It's weed, man. Is it too strong for you?"

"I don't know. Maybe it's the beer," I said.

"It's definitely not the beer," one of the guys said. "The beer's not strong enough for *anyone*."

"Here, *banchod*, let me take that off your hands," Sudeep said, taking the blunt from me. "He's new to the game."

"You speak Hindi?" Darpan asked Sudeep.

"Not as much as my parents would like," Sudeep replied.

"Well, that's another thing we do here. We've set up a Hindi club where we meet once a week and learn Hindi. We've been lobbying the college to offer real classes but they won't for some reason. As if French is more fucking relevant in today's world than learning the language of a billion people."

"That's the problem with Western institutions," the older, heavyset guy wearing the Om medallion said, "they're too Eurocentric." He had the kind of accent I'd heard all my life from cousins and *kakas* who'd come over to America on H-1B or student visas, a carefully enunciated English inflected with the exotic illusion of worldly intelligence. "Perhaps the Socratic Method is essential to a liberal arts education, perhaps it isn't. I don't know nor do I profess to know and nor do I really care to know—I'm a computer science major and I'm looking to get paid. But what I know for sure is that these liberal universities insidiously promote the idea that European culture is the best and all other cultures, Indian or otherwise, are somehow less worthy of attention or critical study."

"Orientalism," Sudeep said.

"It's more than that," he replied, though there was an undeniable twinkle in his stoned eyes at Sudeep's reply. "Part of what we teach here, part of what we advocate—and perhaps I shouldn't say teach because that sounds too much like, I don't know, we're proselytizing some dogma when what we're really doing, or trying to think about, is how *our* culture—that of our parents, what *we've* been brought up and raised in—how that culture has value, an inherent value, something certainly as good as anything Europe—or even America—has ever produced. Part of what I like to think we do here, together, as brothers, is understand how that value should be treasured and, well, continued."

"I'm too stoned for this," I said, because, well, I was.

"I know, right?" Darpan said. He took one last hit of the blunt and dropped it to the ground. "Enough of this shit! You're scaring the kids. Come," he said, arms wrapped around Sudeep and me. "Let's go play some beer pong and see if we can get you two laid."

# 37

At a certain point throughout the night Padma and Dipika appeared and it might've been when we were playing beer pong outside on the gravel driveway with two fraternity brothers from Houston who talked with a Texas twang and who made Sudeep crack up every time they said "Git in there" to the ping-pong ball ricocheting off the table and into the clear night sky or it might've been when we were inside playing a card game called Asshole with several flirtatious members of an Indian sorority who made me drink simply because I was a freshman or it might've been afterwards when we wound up in Darpan's bedroom listening to The Doors and smoking a six-foot glass bong but honestly I can't be totally sure. Darpan had a blacklight poster of Shiva's blue face superimposed onto a gigantic Om symbol and in the crimson darkness Shiva looked ominous and foreboding and even though I didn't want to stare the truth was as the bong circulated and smoke clouded the room I felt as if Shiva was trying to communicate some eternal message through his menacing, omnipotent presence and so all I could do was stare spellbound into his eyes, his bloodblue visage hauntingly illuminated by the blacklight as if powered by some strange, essential knowledge.

And then we were downstairs in the basement and the DJ was playing some Bollywood song I knew from a childhood visit to India mixed with deep house music and apparently Padma knew it too for soon our laughter morphed into lyrics and the words were coming back to me, words I'd long forgotten but that now, as Padma, her arms draped around my neck and her breath hot in my ear, sung forth, reminded me of a very long car ride from Bhagada to Rajasthan and of my mother, seated beside me and my younger sister in our rented sedan, singing those very words every time the song had managed to come onto the radio. Hearing the song—*Ek Do Teen*, or, simply, *absurdly, One Two Three* in English—so mellifluously sung by Padma made me yearn, with perhaps too much nostalgia, for my mother, my parents, for home in all of its insularity and protection, and perhaps because I was drunk or perhaps because I was not drunk enough I held Padma tightly in my arms and felt immensely proud to belong to something so large and real, to have somewhere to return and now, perhaps, somewhere to go.

Padma looked alluring in a cherry red dress that stopped high above her knees and plunged enticingly down her chest and her lips matched her dress perfectly and her long black hair hung curled down her back and her exposed shoulders and I don't know how many times I told her she looked amazing but at a certain point she placed a finger on my lips and held it there. Her touch upon me, I was blissfully aware that I was succumbing to a force whose intentions seemed irrationally rational, that I was, here in the basement of this fraternity house on campus, immersed in a tradition where desire was expected to act upon desire.

What happened next happened so fast I'm not quite sure who made the first move. Soon my arms were below her waist and hers were around my neck and we were looking into each other's eyes and a strobe light flickered and soon we were kissing, her cherry red lips wet upon mine, softly at first, very, very softly, as if merely resting there, touching, but soon hungrily, as if emboldened by the darkness and music and being so far from home, and I remember at one point laughing and she was too and then we were kissing again and like a fool I tried clumsily to kiss her neck and ears and she let me for a moment but probably because I had no idea what I was doing she pulled me to her and kissed me hard and then we were on the street staggering to her dorm room and in our heavy silence we smiled elated with drunken anticipation of what we knew awaited and twice we stopped in the middle of the empty street and made out under the sharp white glow of the half-moon and when Padma stared into my eyes I could see the moon and stars reflected there and when she said "This is crazy. *We're* crazy," I could only smile and bring her lips to mine.

In her dorm room Padma tried to light some incense but I told her not to because it would remind me too much of my mother and she laughed and told me her mother would light incense every Saturday morning before a picture of Ganpati and from her bedroom Padma could hear her mother ringing a bell and gently chanting and something about the memory made Padma kiss me hard and in the shadowy darkness we collapsed atop her single bed and even though I knew I wanted this I also felt strangely terrified in my excitement, as if what was about to take place—this magical thing that had brought me such trepidation and, oddly, shame—was not the way I'd always envisioned it.

And how *had* I envisioned it? Like most young men, no particular dream dominated my clandestine, masturbatory fantasies, but something about being in this darkened dorm room drunk made me realize that, no matter how I'd dreamed it would happen, this wasn't quite it. There was something cliché about it, something decidedly unspecial, something trite compared to the unique image we all hold about ourselves, particularly at that age. Nonetheless, I knew that that didn't make it any *less* desirable. In fact, because there was something cliché about it, it made a strange kind of sense, as if, by getting it done now, I could finally move on with my life and relieve myself of this ludicrous albatross once and for all. And under the circumstances, wasn't this a story I could be proud of later, perhaps when I was in graduate school and recounting to my then fiancée my first time?

Padma had taken my shirt off and was kissing my chest, moving about me with a sophistication and confidence that made me wonder if she too was like me. The way she moved, the skillful way she danced her tongue down my chest, made me consider her, yet again, as someone decidedly experienced. First drugs and now sex—this girl was unlike any Indian girl I'd ever met. How far would she go? How far had she gone *before*? I resisted the temptation to inquire, even as my mind raced with curiosity. Tensely, I waited in silence, my abdomen quivering as she proceeded down my stomach. Soon, she sat up on my thighs and through the darkness I felt her look at me. I looked back. Should I say something? Like what? Keep going? Don't stop? I *love* you? A million things came to mind, each more absurd than the other.

Instead, as she sat up on my thighs, I reached for her, taking hold of her bare legs, and slowly, tenderly, I began stroking them, watching Padma through the shadowy black as she watched me, her breathing, as I touched her, rising, rising. Padma eventually took my right hand and led me under her dress. I felt past the billowy cotton and then, beneath it, I felt her thighs, taut and warm and blessedly smooth, and soon there was lace, and she ended there, ended or rather began, began truly and completely and as only she could, and guiding me she let me go where there was no longer anything between us.

Out of the darkness erupted a volcanic sigh, so deep and powerful I had to ask if I was hurting her.

"What?" she whimpered. "Are you kidding?"

"Does this hurt?"

"No," and then, crumbling onto me, she kissed my lips, and, with my finger still inside her, pressed herself hard against me and rasped, *"Don't you fucking stop."*

And so I didn't. First one, and then, as her gentle whimpers became moans, two, I went where I'd never gone before. In my utter powerlessness I felt a strange, burgeoning sense of control, as if I was learning yet another lesson, this one of the flesh and desire and, dare I say, self, and Padma, her eyes occasionally open, would peer at me through the darkness with such blistering elation I felt pangs of shame as I peered into her soul. Would she remember this? Would I? Did it matter? I couldn't help feeling like it did, even if, at that very moment, the only thing that seemed to matter was the sheer pleasure coursing through Padma's blistering fair skin. It was as if she had been plugged into an electric socket, so hot did she burn, so beautiful was her rapturous candescence.

The man in me wants to rewrite the scene so as to make it sound as if I knew what I was doing and I was the one who brought her to this luminous point. But to say I did most of the work would be disingenuous (not to mention, well, implausible). With my fingers inside her, Padma moved her body against mine with an efficiency and skill that made me occasionally feel as if I wasn't even there. Like an expert basketball player who knows exactly where she needs to be on the floor to get her shot, Padma positioned herself atop me and grinded her hips until she scored—over and over and over again. In fact, she scored so many times I was beginning to wonder if I would ever get to score, let alone shoot.

At a certain point she rose before me and unhooked her dress and let it fall in a heap to her knees. I watched mesmerized through the darkness as her body took shape before me, her breasts, the first pair I'd ever truly seen, there in the darkness like some divine gift. She crawled to me in only her underwear and, as I sat slightly up on the bed, told me to kiss her there. I did. Against the thin cloth and lace frill I kissed her and I could taste her salty wetness and I could feel her there, the hair coarse and sparse and the skin buried there delicate and strange like some clandestine treasure conjured from the depths of my innate desire.

She held my head in her hands and pushed me against her, into her, and I kissed and kissed until I was no longer kissing but rather sucking her there, playing her like some voluptuous instrument that filled the darkness with her enraptured tune. Like a fool, I'd expected shyness, reticence, a willingness to play but a sense of decorum befitting a good Indian girl from an immigrant family much like mine. Why I thought that—and why I didn't think she would—or *could*—be like a stereotypical girl whose high school experience had, in many ways, sexually prepared her—I can only say resulted from my own lack of sexual experience and the effects of having parents who neither discussed sex nor admitted its existence in any outward way. For not the first time in my brief stay at Irvine I felt guilty in the safety of my assumptions—the stereotyping stereotype—and with Padma in my mouth I felt a crazy rush to break free of that absurd prison, to recalibrate—indeed, *destroy*—my thinking through the experience now awaiting me.

If I had once been drunk, Padma there before me seemed to wash all of that away, and in her flesh I discovered a wellspring of clarity, feeling, and sensation. I clutched her behind, bringing her closer to me, my fingers working beneath the thin piece of fabric in frantic, delirious search. Overcome, I ripped her underwear off, shredding them like paper, embarrassed by what I'd done but also deeply, strangely emboldened by what now stood before me. There it was. There *she* was. I inhaled the moist, fecund aroma as if I would never again get to breathe such rarified air (and given my past sexual history it seemed like quite the possibility). There it was. *There it was!* There were so many things I wanted to do I felt ashamed just thinking about them. I could feel Padma's eyes and hear her panting, and so I peered up at her through the darkness, fearing, in my delirium, that I'd done something terribly wrong or crossed some obvious line.

Padma, in all her splendid mercy, only began laughing.

"What's so funny?" I asked.

"I can't believe you just did that."

"Was that bad?"

"They were my favorite underwear," she said, her laughter illuminating the darkness.

"I'm sorry."

"Did you enjoy that?"

I had to think about it for a moment. "Yes."

"Then it was *totally* worth it."

And then she was on top of me, naked, and soon I too was naked and I could feel her, could feel her there open and waiting for me, could feel myself slipping in ever so slightly, just, just a touch, and even that millimeter felt unlike anything I'd ever dared dream, and I wanted to ask about some sort of protection but I also didn't want to ruin the moment but I deeply wanted to ask about some kind of protection but I also wanted this to happen more than I'd ever wanted anything to happen but I was also terribly afraid of what might happen without protection and even more intrigued by what might happen without. Briefly, there in the darkness, I could see the horrified disappointment on my father's face when I broke the news that I was going to be a father at only eighteen and he a grandfather at not yet fifty. Conversely, I could also hear my conscience—not to mention Sudeep—ridiculing me tomorrow and every day for the rest of my life for failing to seal that most elusive of deals and remove that most embarrassing of stigmas. I would have to kill myself—*and who could blame me?* No one but the only man I ever wanted to make proud.

I reached for her ample, soft breasts and cupped them, drawing them to me, and Padma, my willing accomplice, rose ever so slightly to assist me. One after another I kissed them, caressing them and occasionally holding her dark nipples between my lips, suckling them playfully and then seriously as if some starved newborn driven insane by some unspeakable desire. Padma's sighs climbed slowly throughout the darkness, escalating until finally she kissed me hard on the lips and then sucked my neck, her body now slithering atop me like a boa constrictor preparing its prey. Once more I could feel her there, could feel the singeing stickiness urging me forward. I felt myself sliding inside, deeper this time, deeper than ever before, so deep that Padma elicited a sound so voluptuously carnal it was unlike anything I'd ever heard, and I felt both completely lost and utterly at home, powerless to my desire and powerful in my enormity, and even though I knew that what I was doing couldn't be any more natural I could also hear a voice rising from deep inside my brain, admonishing me for risking what can only be described as, well, everything.

I thrusted twice before pulling out.

"What—what's wrong?" Padma rasped, frantic, confused.

"We—I—I mean, don't you think we should, I mean, I don't have any, you know, I don't have any protection or anything."

"It's okay," she panted, breathless. "I'm on the pill."

"You are?"

"You sound surprised."

"I am."

"Rohan, are you *kidding*? I couldn't *wait* for this," she said, gesturing to the darkness. "I plan on having a lot of sex in college. Don't you want to have a lot of sex?"

This I didn't have to think about. "Yes."

"Then fuck the shit out of me."

# 36

At one point during that first weekend my mother called. We were lounging idly at Zuckerman Park, Sudeep, Naresh, Padma, Dipika and a few others we'd met throughout the weekend, and there was a football flying through the air and somewhere beyond us a hacky sack was being kicked around in a circle and Radiohead was playing from a vintage boombox beneath a cloudless blue sky and though I had been stoned earlier in the day by then it had pretty much worn off and left me divinely mellowed. My cell phone—given to me by my parents the week before college, a gift that, at the time, was on the cutting edge of technology—buzzed in my pocket and even before I looked I knew who it was.

I slid it out of my pocket and saw the only name I'd ever called her my entire life and I thought about the last time we'd spoken and felt guilty for it and then I glanced at Sudeep drifting backwards through the grass, tracking the football, his curly locks bouncing upon his shoulders, and then I heard Padma laughing beside Dipika and momentarily entranced I caught sight of her black hair fluttering in the gentle wind and feeling me she turned and winked slyly before returning to Dipika to burst in concordant laughter.

"Mom," I said, turning away from the girls so as to shield the phone from their escalating, stoned laughter.

"Hello?" she said, the excitement in her voice unbound. "Do you remember me? Do you know who this is?"

"Mom, yes, of course," I said, feeling, suddenly, like an elementary kid whose mother stops by recess to check on him but, by simply doing so, embarrasses him instead.

"I thought you forgot about me," she said, and though clearly joking I could still detect her hurt, her worry, her pain.

"Come on, mom."

"I miss you."

I looked at Sudeep as he hurled the football and then Padma and Dipika, flat on their backs, their hands clutching their stomachs in exhausted laughter.

"What's the noise over there? Where are you?" she asked.

"I'm outside—at the park. Remember that park we walked through when we came to visit?"

"Yes," she said, and I knew she could hear the girls' laughter, that she was slowly trying to make sense of what it could mean—or meant already.

"I'm out here with my roommate," I said, spying Padma flat on her back. She turned to me and blushed.

"How is he? Is he nice?"

"We seem to be getting along."

"Is he smart?"

"I didn't give him an IQ test."

"You know what I mean," she said. "What's his major?"

"English I think. Or maybe history. I think he's a double-ma-jor."

"Is he Indian?"

"Mom, yes! He's from Pleasanton, believe it or not."

"And he's not in computers or science?"

"Why does he have to be in computers or science? Not every Indian wants to be in computers or science."

"His parents must not have done a very good job raising him."

"I met his parents. They're very nice people."

"Are they Gujarati?"

"I don't know. I didn't ask for their passport. What kind of questions are these?"

"I just want to make sure you're all right?"

"Mom," I said, unable now to free my eyes from Padma's legs, exposed by her ruffled red skirt. "I'm fine."

"I'm worried about you."

"Why?"

"I miss you. Your sister misses you."

I was still admiring Padma's legs when I said: "I miss you too."

"Do you want to talk to your sister?"

"Mom, look, I'm sorry but we're actually going somewhere and..."

"Oh," she said, and I could feel her shock, among other things. "Well, I didn't realize you were so busy."

"I'll call you later," I said, ashamed of how I sounded. "How about tomorrow?"

"I don't want to put you out."

"You're not putting me out. Please stop saying that."

"Rohan?"

"Yes."

"Don't forget about us."

"*Mom*," I said, though it was more of a whisper.

"Okay?"

"Yes, of course. Now please, *stop* worrying. You don't have to okay? I'm fine. I'll call you tomorrow."

"Promise?"

"Yes," I said guiltfully, knowing, as I watched Padma light a cigarette, that it had already been broken.

# 35

After about three weeks, life seemed to take on an order of its own, and though I knew that this wasn't quite the dutifully scholastic order and singular purpose I'd eagerly envisioned with my parents when we'd first visited Irvine, I nonetheless felt that the shape my college life had taken was something productive and exciting, educative and playful, a life that successfully managed to shuffle between my academic interests and ambitions while giving sufficient respite for the rambunctious idleness that some say lies at the heart of American higher education. During the day there were classes to attend, classes that I, dutifully, had yet to miss at that point; I always remembered, each morning as I awoke to shower and shave in our communal bathroom, a horror story my mother passed along about a distant cousin, a child of engineers who, when he went away to his Ivy League college, turned into someone he hadn't been while living at home; foremost of his crimes against his parents—let alone himself and his clan—was missing classes, which had the snowball effect of eventually landing him on academic probation; in and of itself this was an embarrassment and a slight which still damaged his parents. That this sequence of events eventually caused him to drop out of his Ivy League school as a senior and then move to Hollywood to try and become an actor—and thereby shaming his parents—well, my focus every morning was to try and consciously prevent that snowball from even taking shape. The last thing I wanted was to become an actor.

So: during the day there were classes, and then, on the way back, there was always time spent on the quad, at either Zuckerman Park or in front of Tarnopol Hall, seated on the low brick wall there or amongst the picnic tables sprawled on the green grass, and more often than not you'd see someone you knew (either Naresh or Sudeep or one of the fraternity brothers we'd befriended, guys who, as rush neared, were quickly trying to play larger roles in our lives) and they'd call you over and under the cloudless blue sky you'd sit and stare at the parade of long, bare legs passing by and there was always someone offering you a cigarette and so you'd sit there and smoke and even though smoking wasn't something I particularly enjoyed I did find myself enjoying these moments, moments outside of the classroom yet surrounded by peers, freshmen like myself all undergoing the same strange transformation: learning how to live with the newfound freedom of being away from home. To say it was exhilarating would be to trivialize the relevance of these seemingly mundane interludes, for in our collectively

disembodied discourse we vigorously discussed subjects ranging from our classes to girls to sports to girls to classes to our
parents to India to—with Sudeep—politics and back again, a
rambling discourse that awakened me—as our conversations
inevitably moved from the sunniness of the quad to the smoky,
crimson darkness of someone's dorm room or the boisterous
frothiness of a house party somewhere on campus—to the vast,
complex richness of life outside of my immediate academic
concerns. In our agreements, in our discord, in our tenuously
blossoming friendships, in our jocular hijinks and shenanigans,
in our idly passing time doing nothing but staring at beautiful
girls, the clear blue sky, or the stars and crescent moon, we
were collectively engaged in the kind of learning that can never
take place in the constructedness of a classroom, a place where,
because power is typically delineated, freedom is intrinsically
repressed—no, ours was a diffuse discourse, passionately cham-
pioned and refined and reconstructed through skepticism, intellect, and intoxicants, a blistering, mutating discourse whose
vibrancy seemed to ensnare us all and bind us as something
beyond merely freshmen or Indians. Something new was being
created: us.

And there was also Padma, of course. Were we dating? Were
we boyfriend and girlfriend? Were we—dare I say—lovers?
These questions too often occupied my brain, and not merely
when, after Chem class or spotting me meandering across the
quad, she would eye me flirtatiously and after taking my hand,
lead me to her dorm room and, silently, drop to her knees
before me. And incredibly, some days, that was seemingly all
she wanted—*from me!* To drop down before me—*and nothing
else!* A blowjob in the middle of the day—*the middle of the*

*morning!* What had I done to deserve such awesome treatment, to be blessed so by the gods above!

Like a lucky fool, I struggled with the meaning of these interludes—as if a sexual relationship between two consenting adults needed meaning! *Yet still I struggled!* For didn't we have to have some kind of defined relationship, didn't there have to exist some kind of propriety, in order for whatever it was we were so (seemingly) openly sharing to make sense? Didn't there have to be something *underlying* our sexual conduct, or was the entire campus indulging in the very sexual freedom we were? Was this how it was at college—and American adulthood in general—sex minus the need for any real kind of meaningful relationship? Didn't I owe her something—shouldn't I want to? And didn't she want something from me? Beyond the sexual, wasn't there something Padma *needed* from me?

These were just some of the questions I struggled with during those early weeks at Irvine, questions that seemed urgently important but, because I was so deeply mired in the haze of the first real sex of my life, I couldn't quite formulate the strength or intellect to verbalize. For, to be truthful, they seemed quite ludicrous given the pleasure at stake. Even if I knew they were relevant. Even if I knew that by asking them, perhaps we might save ourselves a whole lot of pain later on, when and if this thing ever fell apart. It was too easy, and because of that I couldn't help feeling terribly guilty on my solitary—yet deeply satisfied—walks back to Tarnopol Hall. The man inside me whose passions and desires demanded the very satisfaction and attention Padma readily provided was pleased beyond imagination; paradoxically, the son of my parents was ludicrously stuck pondering how my behavior would, in any sense of the word, make them proud. What if they were aware of my actions—what kind of judgment would they level? I shuddered to think. And what about Padma and *her* parents? Such a good, intelligent, beautiful Indian girl—but was she really good? Was I? What did good even mean in this context?

Also during this time the drumbeat of war seemed to take on an increasingly strident and divisive tone, as the War in Afghanistan was entering its first full year and, alongside it, the urgency of our President to invade Iraq seemed to grow louder and more vociferous by the day. Osama bin Laden had yet to be caught (and wouldn't be for nearly a decade), and though many of us on campus and back home were curious of the connection between Osama and Saddam, the truth was that most of us found ourselves too mired in our own lives to pay the kind of diligent scrutiny required by young men and women our age, voting men and women who should, perhaps, always have their civic duties foremost in mind. We were all still scarred by 9/11, and we all still wondered aloud if and when we—the American we, the big We, a We that, whenever discussing the horrors of that day and the subsequent fallout, seemed to ring of some strange, uniting patriotism, a kind of solidarity that seemed earnest and real but felt, paradoxically, hollow in too many ways—would ever capture Osama bin Laden, but the truth was as the months had passed and our President had urged us to just shop and continue on with our lives, I'm sad and ashamed to say that's what too many of the young men and women of my generation did, especially until the launch of the Iraq War. I would be lying if I said I knew many Indians from Fremont who volunteered to fight al-Qaeda—they were in or on their way to college with dreams to become doctors and engineers, and no matter how noble the fight against terrorism seemed, ours were parents whose sole concern was ensuring the economic and physical survival of their only children, and so enlisting to fight enemies a continent away was out of the question. And so this perhaps explains why I—and so many of the Indians at Irvine—didn't have quite the emotional connection to or acute interest in what was taking place in Afghanistan. We knew this was a war that needed to be fought; we knew, like our President so seriously summarized, that revenge had to be taken; sadly, like too many Americans, we also knew that no one we knew thought it was worth fighting enough to actually fight themselves, and so perhaps that was why we were able to hold our shameful positions with practically no guilt at all.

I would also be lying if I said that there wasn't already deep-seated anti-Muslim sentiment in the Indian community prior to 9/11—not just Fremont, but the small but burgeoning community of Hindus in and around the Bay Area—and I would also be lying if, back in India, there wasn't a visible and cultural distinction between the interactions and political ideals of Hindus and Muslims. This was something that had been going on for centuries, perhaps ever since the sixteenth century when the Mughals had conquered much of India and subjected the Hindus to Muslim rule for some three hundred years. From my own experience as a visitor to India, I saw how the Muslims in the villages were treated, their neighborhoods segregated from the Hindus, and I heard how my *kakas* and cousins openly derided the Muslims for the way they lived, what they believed, and what they clandestinely felt was the real Islamic political agenda. Since 9/11 I hadn't been back to India, but there were times, listening to my father's friends over the summer or over holidays, where I could easily envision India's "I told you so" mentality, a mentality that had long wished for something akin to the destruction of Pakistan and the reclamation of the vast Himalaya mountains, among other things. And this might've been why most of the Indians in our community, though initially skeptical and generally distrusting of President Bush because of his Republicanism, felt him prudent in invading Afghanistan and somewhat supportive of his idea to preemptively invade Iraq: their forefathers had been subject to Islamic rule in the past and so—rightly or wrongly—they were easily able to subscribe to the threat of terrorism and the fear of a planet under Sharia law.

Of course, like most young men and women my age, I prided myself on being an open, tolerant, and critical individual, someone who never judged a book by its cover because I had, as an Indian American, too often been the victim of stereotyping that always hurt and, whenever it occurred, made me feel not only less than American, but as if there was something severely lacking in me. And so though I heard this anti-Muslim discourse around the community—and even occasionally from my father—I tried to formulate my own thoughts regarding people that, at least from my perspective, had just tried to live their own lives but come under the rule of a brutally repressive regime that had happened to harbor someone with the financial resources and the political zeal to enflame the disenfranchised and underemployed of the Middle East and seduce them into the glory of what by now everyone knew as jihad. To judge an entire global population—let alone those here in America and born here just like me—based on that one historical aberration—or even distant history—seemed distinctly *un*-American, even if there were some Americans who wholeheartedly sub-scribed—whether because of 9/11 or fear of the unknown—to the very same stereotypes and assumptions propagated by some in the Indian-American community.

And so it was too at Irvine, no matter how hidden or obscured by the beautiful weather and blue skies and the generally easygoing nature of campus in general up until then. With the Indians I hung out with you could sense distrust even if it wasn't always vocalized; so too with the non-Indians, whether Asian or Hispanic, white or Black. If a girl walked across campus with a headscarf, or a man with a full-length beard, tunic, and turban, people stared and stopped talking, and in their silent gaze you could feel uncertainty and fear and perhaps even anger—with 9/11 still so fresh in all of our minds, and another war lurking on the horizon, such a sight seemed like some kind of strange affront, even if everyone knew (or hoped) that that person had nothing to do with that terrible day. To feel or think such things was absurd, and by and large we all knew it, yet still it happened, and still, whenever someone clearly marked as Muslim passed by, people talked, wondering not just about the gall of someone openly expressing their identity—and thereby expressing their freedom of religion—but also whether or not it was their patriotic duty to do something to stop it. Nonetheless, the fear was there, the distrust was there, and though I believed it mostly irrational and foolish, as our President urged us to war, our campus still felt swept up in a mania that demanded revenge, blood, and, abstractly, victory, but that, as history would show, tragically lacked reason, compassion, and vigorous discussion.

And so, while there were oftentimes jokes and malicious

insinuations typically made whenever someone walked by with an outwardly Islamic marker, there was blessedly nothing too menacing yet to occur on campus, nothing as of yet to indicate the shameful horror to come.

# 34

One place where reason and vigorous discussion was always taking place, however, was Dr. Green's English 101 class. To my dismay there was a novel on the syllabus, Joseph Conrad's *Heart of Darkness*, a novel I was hazily familiar with from the eleventh grade but whose arcane, impenetrable nature eluded me then and, apparently, still. I thought I had escaped this absurdly abstruse text as a high schooler; when Dr. Green handed out the syllabus and explained that, given our current political climate, we would be spending quite some time explicating it, I seriously considered dropping the class then and there so as to save myself the horror of spending weeks trying to decipher passages as inscrutable as "within the toil of a mournful and senseless delusion."

Which, in many ways, might describe my own toil in English 101, were my explication vaguely correct. Because we had yet to actually write or turn anything in, the delusion that I would pass this class—and not just pass but earn an A, as was mandated by my higher authorities, lest graduate school at MIT or Stanford fail to materialize—was still very much a reality, no matter how senseless or unlikely. The thought of having to write a 5-7 page paper about Marlow or Kurtz was as dizzying as trying to decipher the true meaning of Marlow's tale, something that, to use Conrad's words, or, rather, Conrad's unnamed narrator's words, was "not inside like a kernel but outside, enveloping the tale which brought it out only as a glow brings out a haze …" Exactly. Whatever the fuck that means. And yet by week three I was still there, and with the drop deadline rapidly approaching, still heavily weighing the prospect of escaping the darkness of Conrad and perhaps trying my luck next quarter with something a little less inscrutable—or, in other words, easier.

The one thing working against that line of reasoning was Azada, whose beauty and charm cut through the darkness like a shining beacon of light. Even weeks after that startling—and disorienting—first impression her heavenly looks still managed to hypnotize me every Tuesday and Thursday morning and leave me momentarily dazed. Though we had never spoken outside of class, inside of it we were growing increasingly chatty, an enticing development that further eclipsed any reasoning suggesting I jump ship before Marlow docked and made it to Kurtz. There were a million reasons why I knew we could never truly be anything together, yet still I felt drawn to her presence, captivated by her beauty. It had almost become ritualized, my desire to see Azada in the morning, for after I'd showered and dressed and was on my way across campus, I couldn't deny myself the pleasure of imagining how Azada might look or what she might say, an almost adolescent daydream that felt childish but nonetheless excited me for class. Whether jeans, jean shorts, or a skirt, her legs always looked lovely, and as she sauntered to her seat before me I was always immediately under her spell, my shameful eyes tracing her as she strode towards me bearing the gift of her allure. And as if that wasn't enough, she would always look me square in the eyes (Did she know? Did she feel what I felt? What *did* I feel?) and say good morning, and there, as we waited for class to begin—Dr. Green was never on time—we'd chat about absolutely nothing, making the kind of mundane, innocent small talk that always existed on the surface but that, at least in my eyes, seemed to be slightly tinged with something more, something else, a hint of flirtatiousness perhaps, but a conversation always rich with kindness and sincerity.

And what made our interactions perhaps even more inter-esting—at least to me, I had yet to find the courage to query Azada on the subject—was the fact that she rarely wore that charm I'd seen around her neck three weeks ago. *All glory to Allah*. It was a phrase that had entered American conscious-ness since 9/11, a phrase fraught with many different meanings for many different people, and so while part of me wondered whether the charm she'd worn truly signaled an aspect of her identity, another part of me wondered—indeed hoped—that it was just jewelry and nothing more, something her mother had perhaps given her as a gift and that, depending on her mood or the weather, she decided to trot out simply because it worked to beautifully accentuate her pale, comely neck and draw atten-tion to the fullness of her breasts.

On that morning there was no necklace, only a tightfitting crimson tank top that exposed her shoulders, among other things. Based on how often she offered her shoulders to the public's eye I had by now deduced that this was a part of her body that she was especially proud of—and why not? Hers were fair, statuesque shoulders, shoulders whose silhouette seemed designed to catch the attention of men everywhere and lure them in so they could admire the tiny freckles sprinkling her shoulders and arms, imperfections on any one else but on Azada, symbols of the complexity of true beauty. As the days went by I'd wanted to ask her about them, about who she got them from—her mother?, her grandmother?—but because I was afraid of the answer, or of seeming like a creep, or perhaps because I was just afraid, I never did, choosing instead to zone out on those tiny pink specks whenever Conrad's prose became especially enigmatic.

Dr. Green was focused on a particularly puzzling piece of the novel, a segment of Marlow's yarn regarding, apparently, the rationale behind Kurtz's foray into the darkness of the Congo. In her traditional lecturing style, she stood at the front of the room before the lectern with a black whiteboard marker clutched in her hand. Hers was an easygoing style, calm yet occasionally impassioned, her voice rising when excited to carefully enunciate a point she deigned needed clarification. When she really wanted to goad or provoke us into a response, however, when what we were giving didn't quite meet her standards—which, surprisingly for us overachievers, was every day—she would fill the room with a pregnant, elongated pause, eyeing us all suspiciously, her furrowed brow locked somewhere between disappointment and menace, all as she waited—and waited—in the tense, uncomfortable silence.

Currently, she was waiting for someone to address the question she'd put forth. I looked at the novel before me and reread the passage for what felt like the fifth time, or tenth if you included high school: "An idea at the back of it, not a sentimental pretense but an idea; and an unselfish belief in the idea—something you can set up, and bow down before, and offer a sacrifice to …"

I looked at Dr. Green; she looked at us; I looked at Conrad, reread one more time, and considered sacrificing myself at the altar. Luckily, someone beat me to it.

"It's money," someone said. "The whole thing's about money. That's what they're all about."

"Who?" Dr. Green said. "That's what *who's* all about?"

Someone chuckled somewhere before an uncomfortable silence again filled the room. I looked at Conrad, at Dr. Green, and now finally at Azada's shoulders. She was craned over her desk, studiously peering down at Conrad, writing something into the margins.

"It's not about money," someone finally said, breaking the silence, "though in many ways money is a part of it—it's *always* a part of it. What I think Marlow's trying to say here is that there is something more at work, a sense that, I don't know, when he uses the word 'unselfish'—it rings dangerously close to some kind of crusade to me, as if they're doing God's work."

Dr. Green's eyes ignited with intrigue. "What about this? What about this idea of doing God's work? Is your classmate on to something here?"

"I think you got to take it back to the sentence before this one," an Asian girl said. She seemed uncertain but the words streamed forth nonetheless: "When Conrad writes that it's 'the taking it away from those who have slightly different complexions,' what he specifically means is going into the Congo and stealing ivory, but clearly—or *not*—" and here she laughed, submitting defeat to Conrad's elliptically enigmatic prose, and now so too did many of us, frustratingly aware that what we thought was clear about Conrad was anything but, "he's also referring, I think, to the whole imperial act—the *colonial* act."

"Good," Dr. Green said, scanning us. She pointed to someone beside me. "So what does this mean?"

I watched as his face blanched.

Dr. Green waited.

Repeated her question to him.

He looked down at Conrad, now at Dr. Green until, finally, admitting: "I don't know."

Dr. Green smiled. Bitterly. "Normally I would say that's okay, that not knowing is a sign of learning, but in this instance I'm afraid it's not good enough. You are all here because you're supposed to be some of the brightest of the brightest—I know you know that. I know that's how you like to think of yourselves. And that's good—up to a point. Because some of you are pretenders to the throne—our job here is to weed out those pretenders, to let the cream rise so to speak. Now, we've spent considerable time on this novel already—and I'm sure many of you have spent time on it in high school. We—*you*—need to come prepared to class—either with questions about what you don't know—or with something you can add to our discussion. So, let me ask again, what does this mean?"

"It means," Azada began, looking up to address Dr. Green and all of us with her gentle—yet confident—voice, "that the colonizer needs some kind of idea beyond the mere taking of— what's the word?—resources in order to justify what they're essentially taking by force. And this, I think, is equally important both to the country they represent, but also the place they try colonizing. In other words, there has to be something," and here Azada glanced down at the book before her, a book I could see was riddled with marginalia and highlighted red and blue, "something 'unselfish' that's beyond or helps to hide the real reason a country chooses to invade—*oops!*"

Apparently, Azada blushed, for though I was behind her I could see her neck darkening crimson. It occurred to me to reach out and touch her shoulder in consolation, among other things. Azada looked down at her book as if to shield her face, or hide her embarrassment, until, overcome, she finally began laughing.

Others, myself included, followed, not necessarily because we got the joke but because Azada, in her bravery, had offered something sizable worth dissecting even if she'd perhaps veered a little too off course. Perhaps.

Dr. Green beamed. "Freudian slip?"

Azada, still blushing, shook her head. "I meant to say colonize, I guess. I don't know. I'm sorry."

"Don't be sorry. There's nothing to be sorry about. What about this idea of a colonizing—or imperialistic—country needing, as Azada put it, an idea to sell to their country? Can we think of any historical examples?"

Buoyed by Azada's bravery, challenged by her intelligence, I began speaking, and even though I wasn't entirely convinced that what I was saying was entirely relevant—let alone correct—I wanted Azada to hear my voice and know that I had her back in some way.

"What about the British?" I said. "I'm thinking of their colonization of India. All that was about, historically anyway, was spices and tea and maybe even salt, a kind of 'taking it away' from the native people and profiting from their work and resources. And at first, from what I've been told, it was the Christian missionaries who tried—unsuccessfully—to convert the Hindus because, in many ways, they thought their kind of worship—their idolatry—was something savage or vulgar. I think this might be what Conrad is alluding to here—that by calling them savages—and therefore something that needs some kind of salvation or fixing—the work of these missionaries—ostensibly sent by the Church of England and therefore the King—the work of these missionaries can be seen, to use Conrad's word, in the proper 'light.' Is that what you're talking about?"

I would be lying if I said the look Dr. Green gave me didn't make me proud; she recognized me, she *heard* me, and now, perhaps, she knew me as her student. She was beaming now, and you could feel the class stirring as the sun rose to shed more and more light into our classroom.

"That's precisely what I'm talking about. I think you've hit the nail on the head. What—what's your name?"

"Rohan."

"What Rohan indicates here is the way in which imperialistic or colonial ideas—this concept of going to another country to take or exploit their peoples and or resources—requires some way to sell it to its people in order for it to become politically feasible. And so when Conrad, via Marlow, talks about this elusive 'idea,' he keeps it vague and ambiguous because, historically, different state powers have used different ideas to justify their actions—and sell it to their people. Does anyone else have another example?"

"How about today?" someone from the back corner offered.

"What about today?"

"Well, I can't help thinking about the war we're in now," he said. "I mean, I guess we should've invaded Afghanistan to get al-Qaeda, though even that itself seems a little fuzzy to me. What I'm confused about is Iraq. It seems like it's more of a cover—an 'idea' as it were—to sell to us so we, or someone, can go in there and get all their oil."

"What about this? Does anyone else see it this way?"

Azada immediately raised her hand. "I think the idea isn't necessarily some kind of connection here between Saddam and Osama—which everyone in the Muslim world knows is patently absurd." Her voice was confident yet cautious, her arms and shoulders lightly glossed with a patina of perspiration. I could sense she was exposing herself in ways she might not otherwise have preferred, and because of that I found her courageous. "Saddam's Ba'ath Party is abhorrent to people like Osama, and so for anyone to think they have some kind of connection is ridiculous. But, for me, that's only one part of this enigmatic idea, for there is something else that helps to 'sell' this idea of war, something that in itself is a scary word because typically when you sell something you make money—and what kind of money is made during war? *Who* gets rich? *How* do they get rich? Sorry—what I'm trying to say is that the real 'idea,' at least from the perspective of the Muslim world, is this idea of good versus evil, or the Axis of Evil as Bush puts it. For if they—Saddam, Osama, Iraq—are evil, then by default America must be good. And honestly, I think that's a dangerous position to take."

"How is that a dangerous position to take?" someone else said, a boy seated in front of us to the left. "We were attacked by some maniac in a cave because he hates how we live, he hates our freedom. In this instance how could we not be considered good?"

Azada tightened. People stared at her now, their eyes enflamed by something between outrage, disgust, and embarrassment.

"I think," she cautiously began, "that that's a narrow interpretation."

"Of what?" someone else chimed in. "We were attacked by a maniac!"

"Yeah," someone else cried. "A maniac who wants to impose his religion on our country!"

"I think what she's trying to say," I interjected, "is that merely going to war because you think you're 'good' is an untenable position. And also more importantly, what does good even mean? What is evil? We might be able to call Osama evil for what he did to us—I think everyone could agree with that— but it's unclear to me that we're good by default—or that that is enough reason for us to invade a country—especially if it's for oil. Though that's not really it, is it? For there is something else at play in this idea of good and evil. It's the connection between the idea of evil and certain kinds of people—in this case anyone who looks a certain way or believes something different or comes from a certain place. Now, because we've designated them as evil—or terrorists or savages or whatever—we stereotype them, we think of them as bad or evil, and we can then justify doing whatever we want to them, treat them as less than human..."

On and on I went, unleashed, my discourse springing from somewhere inside I never knew existed, parroted perhaps, though perhaps wholly original, wondering, as I saw Azada's beatific smile turned to face me, what would dad say, what would mom say, what would Sudeep say...

# 33

It was later that afternoon when I saw Azada again. Or, rather, when she saw me. I was on my way home from American History, meandering through Zuckerman Park and, to be quite honest, reflecting on everything that had transpired earlier in English, when I heard someone calling my name. I spotted her seated high upon a hill beneath the cool shade of a maple tree, partially secluded from the path I'd been walking, her long legs crossed before her amidst a pile of books. From where I stood she looked just like any other college student. I wondered if she felt that way. I looked at her seated up there in the shade. I could've looked all day long.

"Doing some reading?" I said, after I'd finally approached her.

She wasn't wearing sunglasses, and because the sun was still very much above us, she had to squint and cover her eyes as she looked up at me. She smiled. "I can't see you. Here, sit down." She picked up her backpack and purse and slid some things around.

I sat beside her and took in the view. "Quite the perch you have up here."

"I like sitting in the shade."

"Well, you picked the right spot."

"I wanted to thank you," she said. "For today."

"You don't have to thank me."

"No," she replied. "I do. What some of those people said—"

"They're assholes," I said, cutting her off. "Don't worry about them. If they'd read the book they would've drawn the same conclusions."

"Well, I'm not too sure of that. In fact," and here she picked up her worn copy of *Heart of Darkness*, "I've been rereading it and I'm not sure *I* agree with my conclusions."

"That's Conrad. What did Dr. Green say? He has a way of destabilizing all interpretations."

Azada laughed. "I know. That's what makes him so fucking awesome."

"That's one way of looking at it."

"You don't like Conrad?"

"Let's just say English isn't my favorite subject."

"No! English is awesome!"

To that I had no reply.

"What's your major?"

"Engineering," I said, feeling guilty for some reason. "How about you?"

"English," she said, beaming.

"What do you want to do?"

"Please don't tell me you're one of *those* guys."

"What guys?" I blushed.

"Guys who think you have to *do* something when you graduate college."

I thought about this for a moment. "Well, what are you here for?"

"To learn."

"Learn what?"

"How to think for myself. To formulate my own opinions, live my own life. You know, all that good stuff."

"That's fine, I guess. But eventually you're going to need a job," I said, thinking, she's wrong. So wrong. If you knew she was wrong before she's even more wrong now and so you should get up and leave immediately. Thinking, she's utterly beautiful and completely unlike any girl you've ever met and you should stay for as long as she lets you.

"And I'll find one. And if I don't like that job I'll find another. Or another. I mean, what? You're an engineering major, right? Do you really think you're going to be an engineer for the rest of your life?"

I looked at her, peering at me inquisitively with her catlike, lime-green eyes. "To be honest, I haven't really thought that far out."

"Well, perhaps it's good that we ran into each other then." She smiled. "I mean, and this is just my opinion, but gone are the days in America where people stay at the same firm, or even in the same *field*, for their entire lives. *Especially* in fields like technology or science."

She was right—up to a point. It was true there were a lot of people in the Bay Area who lost their jobs when the dot-com bubble burst and were now looking for work or had been for quite some time. But it was equally true that those who had been able to hold on were doing better than ever, especially given the occasionally obscene stock options that accompany jobs in Silicon Valley. Nonetheless, our community was hit especially hard, and not simply because the economy had been artificially inflated. Lately, it seemed—and this according to my father, someone generally proud of his Indianness and the success of Indians in general—that technology companies were employing more and more H-1B visas, and though the Indians coming over were happy to have the chance for their own kind of immigrant success in America and, generally, the Indians who had preceded them were ecstatic that a new generation was coming to continue a culture they missed and loved, there was also a general malaise and unspoken truth held by the long-time Indian residents that they were being shed for cheap labor that could easily be manipulated due to its immigrant status. And for the talented and educated Indians cut away by this new influx of cheap labor—not to mention the burst bubble—they were now left to fend for themselves in fields (technology, science, engineering) where being away for barely six months created (or so went the canard) a serious erosion of job skills. Too often I heard my father complain about a friend at Philips or Cisco who'd been laid off and, though handed a generous severance package, had struggled so long to find meaningful work he was considering buying a gas station or 7-Eleven to make ends meet. It was a humiliating end for someone with multiple advanced degrees who had seemingly done everything right in America.

I looked at Azada. "Perhaps you're right. You *are* right. I mean, what you're saying, I guess, is that there are no guaran-tees—"

"Exactly! There *are* no guarantees. Nothing in life is guaran-teed—especially some capitalistic notion of a *job*."

"And that's fine, I guess. But that doesn't mean that science isn't worth studying. Just because everyone will die one day doesn't mean we shouldn't study medicine or try to make a better world. And it certainly doesn't mean engineering isn't worth studying."

"I'm not saying it's not worth studying—of course it is. What I'm saying, I guess, is that we should never put all our eggs in one basket. We should never assume that just because we major in something that that is how our life's going to go. It rarely works out the way we think it will—let alone the way we want it to—and too often, people get heartbroken when they think they're going to *be* something for their whole lives and it doesn't quite work out."

"Are you speaking from experience?"

She looked at me, smiled, and now glanced out at the park and the shadows growing long on this hot October day. She was still staring into the shadows when she asked, "Why do you want to be an engineer?"

I was ashamed to admit the answer. It seemed childish, especially there, with her. But it was true nonetheless and I wondered, momentarily, if she would understand. And to be perfectly honest, this was the first time I'd ever seriously considered the question beyond all that was expected of me. And that too seemed like an embarrassing and even shameful revelation. Spying Azada's long legs, it seemed absurd that I'd come here to this place under such pretenses—absurd too that I couldn't answer the question the way she asked it.

It was then that the protesters' vehemence exploded throughout the park. Azada and I turned simultaneously towards them as they came striding across the grass, picket signs bearing eviscerated visages of Bush and Cheney held aloft in their rising and falling hands. There were fifteen or twenty of them, a contingent slightly larger than the groups I'd seen previously, young men in white tunics sporting various lengths of beard and young women in colorful headscarves and even—strangely on this hot October day—two women in black burkas, full-length body cloaks that enshrouded everything sans their eyes. This I had never seen before in person, either in India or back home and certainly not here at one of California's most liberal and esteemed colleges.

Azada and I watched and listened—the whole park watched and listened—as they stormed past, chanting "Iraq is not al-Qaeda!" with obscene disgust. One of the signs read "Bush is a Terrorist," and something about his face marked with devil horns and his eyes colored crimson unnerved me to the point that I was about to say something. Before I could, though, one of the girls wearing a bloodred headscarf glanced our way and raised her hand. Azada raised her own, tickling the sky above. The girl in the bloodred headscarf smiled and shook her head.

"Friend of yours?"

"She's my roommate. We go way back."

I let this sink in.

"Do you agree with them?"

Azada turned to me and, a beautifully crooked smile upon her pink lips, said, "I haven't decided yet."

Against my better instincts I relented to Sudeep and agreed to rush Delta Sigma Eta. He'd been rushed hard over the last two weeks, spending night after night at their house doing what I could only imagine, and whenever he did finally return sometime after midnight he was either so wasted he could barely talk—and therefore fell clumsily asleep the moment he staggered into our room—or he was humming with all the fraternity had to offer: "It's more than just some dumb version of brotherhood—though I guess there's that too. I mean, the more I think about it, the more I guess it would be nice to have someone to count on and trust. But not just someone—Indians, guys just like you and me who've gone through what we've gone through." As to what that was exactly he didn't specify. "And I mean, there's an appeal there I like. But it's more than that. What I really like is all the cultural stuff."

"You like the *parties*," I'd said at least once over the course of that long week when he'd continuously pleaded with me to do it with him. His initial desire to join was surprising, given that Sudeep had always struck me, beyond his penchant for marijuana, as someone eager to live on his own, unencumbered by the biases and opinions of others (especially a group), someone who took seriously the idea of freedom and individuality. But something, I guess, had changed—in both of us.

"Of course I like the parties. I'm not going to sit here and say I don't like the parties. I mean, I've had my dick sucked twice by two different girls since I've been up there, but that's not the point. There's more to it than just sex. Remember that cricket thing I was talking about? Well, I told the brothers about it and they think it's a great idea! And because we'll be approaching the school as a group, as an organization—as a *minority* organization—they think we can get it done. And *I* came up with it!"

My concerns, of course, were not with creating a cricket league, however audacious and fun that sounded, or even rushing a fraternity, however socially beneficial that sounded, but rather with my studies, with Chem and English, American History and Advanced Calculus, classes that already seemed to take up all of my time. In fact, I had already taken my first major test in Chemistry (one of four), and my grade, a B-, was equivalent to a slap in the face. I thought I'd given it all I had, having pulled an all-nighter with Padma beforehand and so, going in, I'd felt enormously confident. Nonetheless, the day the tests were handed back, I'd felt like a terrible failure—and deeply ashamed—holding my B- in my hand. And as if that wasn't enough—earning a B- and therefore knowing that now I would have to ace all the remaining tests to earn an A in the class—I also felt like I'd let my father down, that I was in some slow motion process of disappointing him with my lukewarm start. For I knew I was expected to do better, not only by my parents, but myself. And not only that. No, I was expected to *excel*, exceeding not just those expectations, but those of the school itself. I was supposed to *shine*.

Instead, I had inexplicably sunk to the middle of the pack and was now up against it. Which probably explains why night after night I had to tell Sudeep that I didn't think I had the time, or that I didn't know if it was for me, or that

I doubted I could successfully manage everything the fraternity might require with everything I demanded of myself academically. Nonetheless, I eventually relented, and why I did wasn't entirely clear to me then nor is it very clear to me now. Perhaps it was because I wanted to follow my father's advice. Perhaps it was because of my friendship with Sudeep, my roommate and closest friend at Irvine. I don't know. All I can remember is that one night I was giving him my list of reasons why I couldn't do it and he was telling me all that the fraternity had to offer us—cultural activities, including, according to him, the best Divali party in California, tutoring with upperclassmen who'd succeeded through the very classes currently fucking me, pretty girls, cricket (potentially), a chance to make lifetime Indian friends *from* India, pretty girls—when finally he said something that befuddled me to the point that I caved.

We were both close to dozing off when Sudeep finally asked, "I mean, dude, why the fuck are you even here?"

Silence.

"Why are you here?" he repeated, his bloodshot eyes on me through the darkness.

"What do you mean?"

"What do you mean what do I mean? Why are you here—in college?"

Because the answer seemed blatantly obvious, I knew it wasn't. These were the kinds of questions being asked more and more around me—by Azada, by my professors, and now by Sudeep, someone so continuously stoned it was hard for me to even take seriously. But I did. I did because I knew that, stoned or not, he was on to something—as usual.

"I don't know," I said, irritated. "For the same reasons you're here—to get a good job."

"A job? Dude, a job is the last thing on my mind. Get with it. Anything you learn here that might get you a job will be worthless in five years. Or you could learn in a fucking library. That's the problem with this country today, too fucking focused on the short term. Never the long term. Just like the stock market—the quarter is what matters and so any investment that might pay off ten, twenty years down the road—and thereby change the fucking world— gets put on the backburner. Too often today I guess it is about getting a job, but I think if you're here simply for that you're shortchanging yourself. College should be about experiences, Rohan. About *life* changing experiences. About trying something new. About," and worked up, Sudeep rose out of bed and sat on the edge and stared at me with his bloodred eyes, "college should be about getting out of your comfort zone and trying to make a difference—a *real* difference."

As to whether joining a fraternity comprised of Indians constituted getting out of my comfort zone I can't quite say, but before I knew it I was in a *kurta pyjama* at the Delta Sigma Eta house, celebrating my induction into the fall rush class with Naresh and Sudeep and nine others who looked as uncertain of themselves as I did. Standing there with my soon-to-be pledge brothers, enveloped in the proud, raucous applause of the current brothers, I couldn't help feeling—despite my deep reservations that I could make any sort of difference given the B- haunting me—that I'd indeed done the right thing—or at least stepped marginally out of a comfort zone that revolved purely around academics and making my parents proud. And even though I'd yet to inform my father about my decision, I convinced myself that he would take pride in knowing that I'd joined a group of men very much like myself. In fact, as I stood there soaking up their rapt applause, I felt as if I was living up to the very advice my father had given me so long ago—for how could I be closer to my own kind than being brothers?

Whatever fears I might have had were temporarily allayed that very night when the girls of Delta Gamma Delta, one of the two Indian sororities on campus, arrived with their new rush class and I saw Padma there before me, looking absolutely luscious in a crimson *sari* that tantalizingly offered the miracle of her flat stomach sumptuously alight with a sparkling silver belly chain. We were equally surprised—and equally relieved— to see each other there amidst the pomp and circumstance, for when we finally embraced, rather than comment on our respective outfits—my *kurta*, her *sari* and glittering belly chain—the first words out of our mouths were identical: "What are *you* doing here?"

"I have no idea," we responded simultaneously, giddy and laughing now at this strange turn of events, and as the night progressed and everyone got increasingly drunk, my prior nervousness, anxiety, and hesitancy shifted to something else, something unclear, a sense of belonging to something larger than myself perhaps, but also a sense that by doing something I had had no intention of doing before I got to college, I was now finally on my way to becoming my own man.

Was *this* what it took? Was this the way? I didn't know. Up until that night I'd never felt anything quite like the confidence or sense of purpose throbbing through my veins as the brothers patted me on the back and the sisters of Delta

Gamma Delta offered me flirtatious congratulations (and two clandestine phone numbers) and, of course, Padma, looking so utterly ripe, steered me to the dance floor and allowed me the pleasure of touching her anywhere I desired. With *bhangra* music pounding we danced the night away, and at one point someone broke out *dandia* sticks and handed them to me and as I clutched them I felt a deep desire to call my father and tell him what I was doing, that I was all right, that I was *with my own kind*—and a *garba* had broken out! A *garba*! *At college of all places!*

Round and round we spun, pairing off in twos to bang our sticks and twirl and bang our sticks again, spinning off away from our partner's joyous laughter to meet someone new, another beautiful girl in a sparkling *sari* smiling proudly and dancing spiritedly, and at a certain point I closed my eyes and lost myself and I felt as if I was back in India at one of the massive *garbas* that always followed a cousin's wedding or *janoi*, *garbas* encompassing over one thousand people, cousins and second cousins and *kakas* and *kakis* and *mamas* and *mamis* from all over Gujarat and the diaspora, and out there under the bright halogen lights with the ivory moon aglow in the sticky black sky the circle would turn and twist and I too would turn and twist and in our collective movement you couldn't help feeling bound to something deeper and more important than yourself, a history that seemed to stretch back before modernity, as if time had folded in on itself, or stopped completely, and there was only the music and the *garba* and the unbroken circle that never stopped, never ended.

Yes, such were the feelings coursing through my body that night as I danced, a profound sense that perhaps the circle never did end, never would stop, that so long as we danced together, it didn't matter where we were or what we majored in or what kind of work we did—the only thing that mattered was that we were there, dancing together, proudly and without shame, writing and revisiting history in the very same breath. And even though I knew that the emotions—and booze—clouding my judgment were transitory, I couldn't stop myself from believing in the dream, of believing that by being here, with my own kind, I would somehow be safe from everything outside—or in.

# 31

The dream turned into a nightmare the very next—or same—morning, when we were awoken in our dorm room at five AM by Darpan, our Pledge Master, the person who, so long ago, had chided me about communists and meth. We'd earlier learned that Darpan was a physics major who already held degrees in biology and philosophy and had gained early admission to Princeton Med. Currently, he rang a bronze cowbell by a weathered *dandia* stick, and by the time Sudeep and I finally stirred from our deep, intoxicated slumber, Darpan was screaming angrily in my face, "Wake the fuck up you lazy fucking pledge! It's time to go to work!"

At the sight of his face inches from mine I fell from my bed, gasping for air. "What?" I slobbered. "How did you get in here?"

"Don't worry about how the fuck I got in here! Pull up your fucking pants asshole—you've got work to do!"

All this as he dementedly beat the bronze cowbell with his *dandia* stick.

We'd been told throughout our induction that pledging was hard, even painful, stuff; we were routinely asked if we were men enough for it; we were also told by the brothers that it was worth the struggle, that from our hardship, pain, and anger we'd emerge stronger men bound together to face the world with courage, conviction, and strength. With the cowbell ringing in my ears and Darpan screaming in my face, however, I thought not of courage, conviction, or strength, but rather sleep, sleep, and, well, more sleep.

Back at the house, Sudeep, Naresh and I, along with our eight other pledge brothers (Pratek, pre-med; Aadav, civil engineering; Nisith, civil engineering, Milan, civil engineering; Tejis, computer science; Ronak, computer science; Kiran, computer science; Vishal, computer science; Vishnu, computer science), stood in full zombie mode staring at the disaster that had become the fraternity house in the wake of last night's festivities. Empty and half-empty beer bottles and cans and red and blue plastic cups were strewn everywhere, some toppled over and staining the rug while those upstanding were typically filled with the pungent stink of cigarette butts; two glass bongs were shattered on the floor, the darkened bong water spilling onto the rug amidst shards of green glass; fast food wrappers were mixed alongside mounds of confetti and glitter and, I quietly noticed, two pairs of pink panties and four used condoms.

By now the sun was slowly rising and birds were gently

chirping and all I could think about beyond my throbbing headache and the sleep I was losing and whose panties those were was my English class starting in about two hours. Darpan's instructions were simple: clean the house so it looked, according to him, "good enough for your fucking mothers to hold a *puja*," and then decide who among us would stay to cook breakfast for the fourteen brothers who lived in the house and would be waking intermittently.

Aadav, our only pledge brother actually *from* India, volunteered for the breakfast shift.

"Are you sure?" one of us asked.

"I don't give a fuck," he said, and then, rummaging through the empty and half-empty bottles of beer littering the living room floor, Aadav picked up a bottle of Bombay Ultra and held it up to the early morning light. He lightly smelled the lip of the bottle. Then drew it to his lips. After he finished he looked at us, said, "Hair of the dog, bitches. Hair of the dog."

When he belched I immediately felt woozy, my stomach burning as a vile substance crept up my throat. I swallowed hard, twice, and then closing my eyes I tried to stay calm by imagining that this wasn't really happening, that this was only a dream—or a nightmare—but when I opened them I was still there, in the fraternity house, my head pulsating, and all I could smell were cigarettes and stale beer and covering my mouth I staggered through the living room, my pledge brothers clamoring behind me, screaming my name, and inside the communal bathroom I kicked open one of the two stalls to discover shit everywhere, smeared along the toilet seat and arcing brown and green across the stall walls, shit everywhere but where it was supposed to be, and recoiling I staggered backwards, my covered mouth unable now to fully prevent what was angrily seeking expression.

When I kicked open the other stall I found someone had beaten me to the punch.

**30**

"You don't look so good," Azada said.

"You have a keen eye for observation."

"Rough night?"

I had just left the fraternity house, was wearing the very same clothes I'd partied in, slept in, and, as of about ten minutes ago, cleaned the bathrooms of shit and puke and anything else born of our bodies known to stain porcelain in, and the sky was clear and blue and we were standing before Roth Hall, home of our English class, surrounded by the few people who still, approaching mid-semester, found it prudent to attend their morning class on time. That I was still one of these pious souls given my situation was perhaps a testament to my filial devotion—or stupidity.

"You could say that," I said.

"You joined a fraternity, didn't you?" she asked, her voice tinged with surprise, disappointment.

"Apparently," I said, peering down at my stained shirt.

"I would've never pegged you for a fraternity guy."

"That makes two of us."

"So what gives?"

I looked down at my clothes, now Azada. "I'm afraid I don't have a good answer for that."

Azada looked into my eyes, and then my filthy, reeking clothes.

"Are you sure you want to go into class like that?"

"I'm afraid I don't have any other choice."

"You look tired."

"You have a keen eye for observation."

She laughed, kindly. "Why don't you go home and get some sleep? I'll take notes and let you in on what went down a little later, when you're feeling better."

"I don't know," I began, even though there was nothing I would've liked more than to go home and go to bed—and have Azada let me in a little later. "I mean, I really don't like to miss class. I've never really missed a class, anywhere, ever, really, so…"

"What does that mean?"

"It means I had perfect attendance from kindergarten through high school."

"Are you serious?"

"Yes."

"So there you go. First a fraternity—now a missed class. You're turning into a typical college kid."

"That's not funny," I said.

"I'm not laughing."

"I don't know," I said hesitantly, glancing at the massive clock adorning Roth Hall about to strike eight-thirty.

"Come on," she said, lightly taking my hand. "You can trust me."

"When will I get the notes?" I asked, my hand still in hers.

"Here," she said, and opening her bag she pulled out a notebook and ripped out a slice of paper and scribbled something. "Here's my number. Call me after you wake up—and shower."

"I'm going to call you," I said, smiling in the grace of my misfortune.

"You better!" she screamed, bounding up the stairs to Roth Hall.

# 29

We met in the library later that night. The purpose, of course, was study, was Conrad, was a serious discussion of everything elliptical and obscure buried within a text whose befuddling contradictions and multitudinous interpretations required diligence and discernment on the part of the reader— these were the reasons, at least on the surface, that we met. But that was only the surface. For I knew, the moment I hung up the phone and felt my heart pounding in my chest as if I'd just broken the most sacred trust, that there was something dangerously exciting about to unfold. And I knew, the moment I saw Azada, seated under the bright lights of the main floor of the library, her long, exquisite black hair down and shining magnificently past her slender, exposed shoulders, that study was only the pretense to a game we both desperately wanted to play—even if the rules we'd been imbibing our whole lives expressly prohibited the other as a possible opponent.

I knew. And, blessedly, so did Azada.

For her lips, once I came fully upon her and our eyes finally met, slipped into the most embarrassed smile I'd ever seen this otherwise confident creature make. She looked at me and then down at the table and the books splayed before her and then back at me and her green eyes flitted with an enchanting cross between innocence and playfulness and wicked guile, a kind of self-awareness that rendered her beauty even more powerful, and it was then that I finally noticed her rose red lipstick, a color that seemed to ignite her luscious lips and enliven her already breathtaking visage. It took everything sensible within me to withhold my compliment, for as I took the seat opposite her at our table and felt—powerless by her allure—the words of flattery dancing on my tongue, I couldn't help glancing nervously around and, noticing the pairs of young men and women dutifully studying around us, found myself sadly aware of the ethnic similarities of their pairing and, thus, remembering my father's words, found myself once more immersed in the pretense, the illusion we were both required to maintain—even as I knew, like she did, that we were desperate to shatter it.

And so, like the good children we were, like the good children we were supposed to be, we sat across from each other under the bright lights of the library's main floor and pretended, at first, to keep our distance, to be eagerly engrossed in scholarship, even as the night grew long and our conversation more hushed and Azada's eyes increasingly held mine with a warmth, tenderness, and yearning that quickly destroyed our dutiful charade. By the time the librarian announced the library's impending closure within the hour, our initial chattiness and flirtation with academics had become a sequence of long pauses where we seemed to speak a silent dialogue, a language outside our time and history, one that knew nothing about what our parents would say or what our respective clans demanded; in our mutual silence, in our sudden shameless staring, I could feel myself coming unglued from something that had held me together my entire life, I could feel myself wrestling with the weight of a thousand expectations, and it was then and only then when I finally acknowledged what I had been lucky enough to admire for the past two hours.

In a whisper so tremulous it resembled a stutter: "Your lipstick. It's pretty."

When she blushed, I knew we were in trouble.

# 28

What had seemed like a stoned pipe dream—and, I mean, let's be honest here, everything coming from Naresh and Sudeep sounded like stoned pipe dreams—had now incredibly become reality as through the credibility of the fraternity's standing as one of the highest ranking GPAs on campus for a Greek organization and, at least in the estimation of the most strident and paranoid brothers, under the auspices of wanting to be politically correct in an increasingly tense national environment where minority persons of a certain ethnic makeup were being treated with increasing hostility and scrutiny, an intramural cricket league had been sanctioned and given the green light by the college. That it took such little time given the bureaucratic red tape typically associated with an institution the size of Irvine College validated—at least according to the ecstatic and proud brothers—the fraternity's growing clout and standing in the community—and India's on the world stage.

For beyond India's increasing participation in globalization and its various trade agreements with the United States that, at that time, were leading to increased business and shared cooperation and, for those in favor of this mutuality, generally lower cost goods for the everyday American consumer, India, immediately following 9/11, had publically and proudly voiced its solidarity with the United States and vowed, as best it could, to assist with the War on Terror. Most obviously, this meant providing a bulwark against any aggression or suspected terrorist assistance provided by Pakistan, a place known for lawlessness and madrassas and whose hostility with India went back all the way to its succession or, depending on your perspective, independence. Of course, what was truly beneath these hostilities, beyond the obvious vying for control of Kashmir and the Himalayas, were ethnic and religious tensions whose history and truth lay far beyond the realm of any outsider's total understanding. Pakistan's mostly Muslim population and India's mostly Hindu population were at odds for something more than simply land; there was something intrinsically nebulous at stake that fueled their discord, something, arguably, cosmic or ethereal that spoke not simply to the material world we live and breathe in, but the spiritual otherworld whose safe entrance mandated strict adherence to intrinsically divisive laws.

As an American-born Indian, I heard countless stories regarding these hostilities, always, of course, from the side of

Hindus who had, throughout their own lives, imbibed their own fear and distrust of Muslims from their own proud, biased clans. Each and every time I heard this distrust—which was every visit to India and now, following 9/11, every time Osama's venomously placid face appeared on the news (which was continuously)—I tried to take it with as much salt as possible, always mindful that I had not been born in India but America and would thus always exist on the margins of her centuries-old history of ethnic strife, colonization, and caste—or so I liked to believe.

For standing on the practice baseball field that day with the rest of my pledge class and over twenty brothers, all of us Indians and, at least nominally, Hindus, I felt as if I—*we*—had leapt from the margins and were creating history, a new American history, a history that echoed the game my father had loved as a child in his village in Gujarat and that he'd taught me to love as a child in Fremont. And so it was for many of us there on that baseball field, a sense of filial devotion mingling with new emotions, purpose, and possibilities, a sense that we were creating something distinctly our own, a game that had made our fathers proud and that we now could be proud of for introducing, promoting, and playing here, on a baseball field of all places. I could hear my father's words in my ear once again— as I'm sure could each of the brothers and pledges alike hear their own fathers—and I could easily imagine the proud smile that would register across his lips as I told him about all we'd accomplished together.

And so perhaps that explains the immense pride I felt standing out there on the baseball diamond and working with my pledge brothers to set up the wickets at second base and the pitcher's mound. The bases had long been removed, as had the rubber on the mound, and thus, after flattening the mound as best we could, after raking down the dirt into as even a surface as we could, we used the chalk we'd brought and drew a large white rectangle stretching from behind second base to just beyond the mound. Together, with the brother's throwing various tennis balls in the outfield (it was decided that tennis balls would be used during practice), the ten of us worked to insert the wickets—three waist-high stumps that protrude from the ground and support what are traditionally called bails, two tiny cylindrical blocks of wood tenuously held between the three stumps and that, if and when knocked off, signal a dismissed batsman, an out—into the hard dirt infield as the crimson sun slid slowly across the clear azure sky. That it was done so easily and with such precision was perhaps not as shocking as the accomplishment momentarily felt—given that over half of us were engineering majors, had the brothers challenged us to put up stands and a *paan* station we probably could've done that too—and well.

Nonetheless, we were sweating by the time we'd completed our task. The brothers told us to stand in a straight line opposite them, and studying our work, they looked upon us with their own kind of impressed, reserved pride. What had begun as a pipe dream born out of weedsmoke had now become a strange new reality: a cricket field had risen from the earth of America's eternal pastime.

Standing beside me, Sudeep cast his eyes on the dirt and said, choking back tears, "It's beautiful. It's fucking beautiful."

"Get this guy a joint," one of the brothers announced. "Stat."

"It's just," Sudeep began, "it's just, you know, think about it.

I mean, really, *really* think about it. This is the future. I mean, look around." He did, only to stop on me. "*This* is the future."

A strange chill ran up my spine.

"Dude," Pratek, pre-med and one of our fellow pledges, said. "You're stoned."

"I don't think that's truly possible," I confessed.

One of the brothers lit a joint. Another lit another.

"Here *batta batta batta*," someone called.


# 27

"So…" Dr. Green began. "What do we know so far? What do we know about the people to whom Marlow is telling his— to use the word of Conrad's unnamed narrator—*yarn*?"

Dr. Green kindly surveyed us in all of our early morning somnolence, perplexity, and—at least for me—feigned attentiveness. Feigned because, well, with Azada in front of me, it was really she who held my attention, even if my eyes gave the pretense of caring about our increasingly circular Conradian discourse. For this was our fourth class since we'd begun *Heart of Darkness* and we'd barely cracked through the first half of the novel; indeed, it seemed that, instead of moving linearly through the text, towards, as it were, Kurtz, it seemed we were instead going backwards, circling towards some silent, implied beginning, fixated not on what takes place deep in the heart of Africa, but rather what drove Marlow there in the first place. And though it should seem rather obvious—novels begin where they begin, right?—our silence confirmed just how lost at sea we were regarding Dr. Green's seemingly straightforward question.

"Anyone? Any takers as to whom Marlow is speaking? Remember, first of all, we are getting Marlow's tale from a narrator who Conrad does not name. That person is there, on the boat, listening to Marlow's tale with a few other people. Is there anything significant we should draw from those other people?"

Everyone turned to the start of the novel, where we assumed the answer must lie. Did it? Our silence indicated skepticism, unpreparedness, perhaps even indifference. Definitely indifference. I thought someone might groan in despair. I thought I might.

Finally, someone spoke up. "Well," a brave soul began, "there is the Director of Companies, some Lawyer, and an Accountant, all of whose names this unnamed narrator—or Conrad—chooses to capitalize." She stopped, then added uncertainly, "I think."

"Good! Absolutely," Dr. Green responded. "So, why do we think he *chooses*—I like that verb here—to capitalize these otherwise generic names?"

A hand rose instantly.

"You don't have to raise your hand. You're no longer in elementary school. And thankfully neither am I. Speak, please." Dr. Green smiled warmly.

"Well, precisely because they are generic, vague terms. By capitalizing them, Conrad makes them what they are—a lawyer, accountant, and a director of companies—but he also makes that *all* they are. And I might be off here—I probably am, this book is driving me crazy, I hate it, I really, really hate it…" This ignited patches of laughter and agreement, including Dr. Green's. "But by capitalizing their names he makes them important, superimportant, perhaps the most important of their kind. Almost like the way we typically capitalize President."

"Very, very good. I think your colleague here is on to something. On the one hand we perhaps have these characters reduced to their function in society—not a person with a name—a name given by a mother or father or God—but a name that explicitly identifies their role in society. Then, we also have the double meaning of having their names capitalized, thus imbuing them with importance. So: what do we make of Conrad choosing these three individuals—or types, as it were, as they cannot truly be called individuals without a proper name—as the audience of Marlow's tale? Why them and not, say, a teacher, a fireman, or, I don't know, a plumber?"

The voice that spoke next I could've recognized in my dreams.

"Because the main subject for Conrad—and therefore Marlow—is imperialism, colonialism, and the horror—to use Kurtz's word—of the very enterprise. Conrad is using Marlow to speak, in his own enigmatic and circular way, truth to power. And the power here resides with this Director of Companies. Remember, it is a company that has sent Marlow into Africa in the first place; we can thus safely infer, I think, that Kurtz was sent to Africa not only sanctioned by the Belgian King to, as we discussed earlier, try and tame the savage under the guise of some noble idea, but really to take the ivory and make as much money for the empire, for the companies involved in the business of empire. For that is what it is, really, isn't it? Isn't imperialism simply a cover for business interests to take what they can from these repressed and war-ravaged people?"

"What about this? What about what your classmate—Azada, right?—has said here?" Dr. Green queried, her eyes sparkling in the morning light.

"I mean," someone began, a guy in soccer shorts and a Metallica T-shirt seated in the back corner, "I think within the context of this novel, perhaps she's right, you know? I mean, of course you need an accountant to keep track of all of the money being made, and of course you need some scumbag lawyer to make it all legal, and so I guess you could make the case that these guys on this boat represent the interests that have driven Kurtz to loot and destroy Africa. Cool. But you're going to have to convince me that imperialism is always about business inter-ests. I mean, some people are calling us imperialists for going into the Middle East, right? That *definitely* ain't about business."

"No?" Azada asked, and I could detect, immediately, a mix-ture of disbelief and disgust. She turned to face him. "What's it about then?"

"Freedom," he replied.

"*Whose* freedom?" she asked.

"Whoa, hey, I'm just saying, you know, that's what *they're* saying. Don't take it so personally, dude."

"I'm not taking it personally, *dude*," Azada replied, trying, as best she could, to restrain herself. "I'm just concerned that we hear this idea of freedom over and over again—from Bush, from the media, from everyone, really, and in theory it sounds great, but rarely do you hear the other side of the coin, rarely do we question the morality of this historic decision."

"And what's the other side of the coin?" This came from a

blond girl, seated near the window, in the first row. Her disgust—or was it simply exasperation—was clearly detectable. "Saddam Hussein is a brutal dictator who once killed his own people with chemical weapons. You're saying we should let him brutalize his people? The guy has weapons of mass destruction. We *know* this."

"He's also insane," someone else chimed in. "We know *this* too."

"That's a false choice," Azada replied. "Saying we have to go to war with someone simply because of the reasons you've given would have us going to war with half the world. Thankfully, we use more discretion than that when dispensing our men and women to risk their lives. Or at least we used to."

"I take exception to that," the blond girl replied, and I could tell it was a struggle for her to repress her emotions. "My brother's in Afghanistan right now, fighting to defend our country. He signed up right after we were attacked. You remember that, right? That *we* were attacked. That *we* were attacked by some crazy Muslim," and here she stopped herself, perhaps aware, as the class drew silent and our collective eyes fell upon her, that there was something loaded in that word—in the way she said it—that hued dangerously close to the line of decorum, tolerance, or political correctness that we, as students, were not supposed to cross.

Or were we?

Where, if not here, could we cross that line, could we test that line, could we cross and cross out and redraw that line to test the boundaries of what could or could not be civil discourse?

Her fair cheeks flushed, the blond girl continued the only way her heart would allow. "I don't know. And I'm sorry if this sounds awful but it's true. We were attacked by some crazy Muslim terrorist or fundamentalist or whatever you want to call it and it needs to be said because it's true. And my brother is there risking his life because we were attacked. And if he winds up in Iraq to prevent another attack then I support him there too. And not simply because I love him with everything I have, but I support him because I know what he's doing is right."

"We've moved a bit off topic here," Dr. Green said swiftly, expertly preventing Azada's response with the cool of someone in command. I don't know what Azada was going to say, but her shoulders were crimson, as was the back of her neck. I wanted to reach out and console her, calm her, but knew better (even though I wished I didn't). "And that's good. That's fine. It shows that even today, in our current time, Conrad still has currency. That's why I chose this text. I'm glad all of you are able to bring so much to it. A central question remains, however, both for Marlow and even our current time: who benefits? Who benefits most from the imperialist act? Or, to put it more broadly, who benefits most from war?"

Her brow raised, she surveyed the class: "Any takers?"

"It just makes me so angry," Azada whispered loudly.

Again in the library, we sat huddled closely together at a table in the corner of the first floor, pretending, as best we could, to study.

"You shouldn't let it bother you so much."

"I know. I'm sorry. I shouldn't. But you don't know what it's like. It's not your people that are going to be killed."

"Are they your people?" It was the question that had been on my mind far too long; strangely, it was also the question I feared asking, for I knew that once floated—albeit harmlessly and somewhat innocently—what had silently and perhaps purposely lay beneath us, submerged like an iceberg, would finally become visible in all of its inherent divisiveness. Of course, it was bound to happen, that we both knew. But did it have to happen so soon? *Before* we'd had the pleasure of, well, each other's pleasure? Damn this war—*damn bin Laden!*

"Of *course* they're my people," Azada responded, recoiling slightly. She studied me in the same astonished way she had the guy in the Metallica shirt in class. "What do you mean?"

"You're from Iraq?"

"You sound surprised?"

"I am." I was.

"Why?"

"Because you told me you were from L.A."

Thankfully, this brought a smile to her face and diffused, momentarily, the anxiety that had furrowed her brow.

"I'm sorry," she said, laughing, shaking her head. "I shouldn't be taking this out on you. You didn't do anything. It's just that I get so angry sometimes and I don't know who to blame because it's so complicated, you know? Every time I think it's safe to blame someone, when I really think about it, I realize they don't even know what they're talking about." Azada closed her eyes for a moment. "It's difficult to talk about because most Americans have no sense of history."

"Like that girl in class."

"I understand where she's coming from. And I admire her brother, in a way. He's braver than anyone in my family. I mean, no one in my family would *dare* sign up to fight these wars. They know better."

"What does that mean?" I asked, thinking, no one in my family would dare sign up for these wars either—and not because they don't agree with the politics behind it. For they did. Our parents easily and passionately agreed with taking revenge against Osama for the crimes committed against America; were you able to secure a candid response, the men, the immigrant men who'd come from India years ago on student or work visas and made their way through the difficult early years and now, with wives that had been arranged and grown children that had been a blessing, with houses and cars and wealth beyond their wildest dreams, they earnestly would confide that the rise of Muslim fundamentalism must be stopped by any means necessary, here and abroad. But never would they suggest—never did I *hear*—one of these immigrant men suggest that their sons or daughters (or themselves) commit to fighting for this cause, however it was sold. For the fathers of our community expected degrees for their children, not guns; even immediately after 9/11, with the horror of that day continuously on television, not once did the thought of literally fighting the War on Terror enter our dinner conversation. It was college and only college. It was college and only college and then the college *after* college.

Azada laughed, and then kindly repeated my question. "'What does that mean?' It means my parents know better. It means my cousins and uncles and aunts know better. Or at least better than that idiot in office, George Bush. These wars, these wars have been going on for centuries, Rohan. They've been going on longer than we've been alive and longer than there's been an America. And yes this is sad and yes this is unfortunate and yes it's totally fucked-up. No one is disputing that. The question, though, or the one that dominates my household, is how long does America think it can stay there? Because this is what you don't really read or hear about in the news, but this is what people from there and who've been there know intuitively—to change that place the way America wants will take years, decades—centuries! And not because these people are crazy or violent or anti-American—like that girl in class probably believes—but because they are proud: proud of their culture, proud of their history, and, yes, especially proud of their religion. And to think that you can just storm in there and blow up the bad guys and somehow change the nature of the entire place—it's like something out of Conrad. It's intuitively ridiculous. I mean, imagine if this was India they were talking about."

"Many have tried."

"And how did it wind up? It winds up the way it always winds up. With a bunch of innocent, poor people dead."

"You're beginning to convince me this war is a bad idea."

"That's why I'm here. To convince my generation, one innocent soul at a time."

"What makes you think I'm so innocent?"

Azada burst out laughing, so much so that I began to blush.

"I'm sorry," she said, reaching out to touch my arm. "It's just…"

"You know I'm joining a fraternity, right?"

"That's right. I forgot. Rohan's a bad boy, aren't you?"

"Whatever."

Azada couldn't stop laughing. Neither could I.

"How's that working out for you by the way?"

"Are you really from Iraq?"

"My father is. My mother's Turkish. Both Shiites."

"Uh-oh. I know what that means."

"I know." Azada smiled wickedly. "I might be a terrorist."

"Azada. Is that a Shiite name or is that the name they gave you when you joined the Taliban?"

Her laugher was a gift. "It's a Turkish boy's name."

"A boy's name? *Nice.*"

"You can see how highly regarded girls are in my family."

"And by family you mean cell."

She gave me a look. A *great* look.

"I'm sorry. Does it mean anything?"

"Azada?"

Her smile signaled a return to a safe place, even if we both knew we were anywhere but.

"Freedom," she replied. "Born free."

"And is that how you feel, Azada? Free?"

"Look at these fucking towelheads," Barun said.

We were sitting on Barun's sofa, Sudeep and me, watching Wolf News' coverage on the War in Afghanistan. Images of the Taliban floated across the screen, young men with beards and rocket launchers and long white robes; bedraggled men wearing white turbans who rode packed into Toyota flatbed trucks with miserable, defeated looks, as if the war they'd been fighting had been going on forever. The screen flashed to our military, black helicopters soaring and then rockets tracing across the clear blue sky and then the footage turned quickly to declassified military film and an explosion of what the gentle, feminine voice narrating the sequence of events described as a madrassa, a school where Taliban fighters were believed to have once been trained, the madrassa decimated with mechanical precision, and immediately following the explosion children were running from the destruction as now a smiling, beautiful blond newswoman filled the screen and mentioned something about freedom, about liberating the Afghans from the terror of the Taliban.

"You know, in their crazy fucking religion, they fucking stone women if they commit adultery. You know that right? I mean, these fucking Taliban, they think that book is meant to be interpreted literally. *Literally*. And you know where they learn that shit? I mean, this is what truly scares me, this is what keeps me up late at night—*this* is why I stay tuned to Wolf News like 24-7. Do you guys watch Wolf News?" Barun looked at us. Seriously. "Dude, you got to watch Wolf News. It's the only reliable news source out there. Fair and Even. That's their motto. Anyway, these fucking Taliban come from Pakistan. Right next to India, bro. That's where they're trained. Pakistan. *Think* about it." Barun raised an eyebrow intensely. "Hey, you guys want a beer? Come, have a beer. Sudeep, grab us some beers from the fridge brother."

Perhaps the most arduous and, arguably, most fun part of the pledge process at DESHI was getting all twenty-five brothers to sign our paddles. What this meant in practical terms was that each of us, the pledges, had an oak paddle two feet long and about eight inches wide that we'd purchased and, with the help of our Pledge Master Darpan, we taped twenty-five pieces of inch-wide white tape down the front and back. Each piece of tape was designated for a brother to "sign" in his own unique way; typically, this meant seeking out each of the twenty-eight brothers in their apartments or dorm rooms and asking them to please "sign" our paddles; once every piece of tape was "signed" the paddle was finished and you, the pledge, were supposedly near becoming a full-fledged brother.

Depending on the brother, you could have vaginas or erections or blowjobs colored in their space, or you could have elaborate drawings of Shiva or Krishna or any other Hindu deity that spoke to that brother's heart. On Darpan's paddle, for example, he had as many as seven Shivas and seven vaginas, each uniquely rendered, each initialed by a brother that had long moved on into the world and who—through the unique bonds of their brotherhood—Darpan remained in contact with, especially the ones working on Wall Street as investment bankers or venture capitalists. Darpan's dream was to start his own pharmaceutical company one day; being part of the fraternity, he would always reiterate to us aspiring, bedraggled pledges, helped build a network of people who could one day help us achieve our professional ambitions. Furthermore, he would expound, as Indians, as minorities in white America, we needed these connections if we ever hoped to rise above the modest successes of our fathers and truly take our rightful position in American society. That a group of ambitious superstrivers like us were so easily hooked by this impassioned rhetoric should go without saying.

Nonetheless, underlying this entire process was our collective fear of what these paddles would *really* be used for beyond just creating a keepsake of our journey. In fact, campus was riddled with lurid stories of fraternities paddling their pledges so hard they drew blood. And that was just the start. There were stories of beatings and brandings, of public humiliations that included making pledges attend class for a week in the same dirty clothes (typically called Hell Week and the final stage of initiation; ours was tentatively scheduled for February), of such severe binge drinking that rumor had it that there had been multiple campus deaths; of course, campus was also simultaneously replete with the very public knowledge that, at least according to the school and, indeed, the law, hazing was illegal and subject to severe penalties. Still, everyone on campus knew hazing went on in some kind of capacity; oddly, in some ways, public knowledge of being hazed—even if only rumor—typically drew interested looks of admiration and surprise, a very real kind of prestige that went with being part of something considered strangely dangerous—if simultaneously juvenile and stupid. Still, for those of us immersed in the pledge process, the question constantly on our minds was: how far was

I willing to go? What was I willing to do, what humiliations were I willing to endure, and what laws were I willing to break to join this fraternity? And, of course, was it worth it?

Mercifully, for the most part, the answers to those questions hovered around cleaning the bathrooms and apartments of our brothers when trying to obtain paddle signatures. Or hitting a six-foot bong (easier said than done). Or even being called at two in the morning when Darpan was drunk and demanding Taco Bell, something that, because of his self-avowed mild-sauce addiction, happened all too frequently. Or, as was the case with Barun, sitting down and having a beer and listening to the news as seen through the eyes of a very, very concerned citizen. Whether or not this was considered hazing I'll leave to the jury.

"And if they're coming from Pakistan," Barun was saying, "then what do you think the Indians are saying?"

He looked at me. I looked at him, then anxiously into the kitchen at Sudeep peering into the fridge. On the television, three very old men were heatedly discussing the need to weed out and destroy militant Islam.

"I'll tell you what the Indians are saying—they're saying the same shit our fathers have been saying for centuries. Fucking Muslims. What are they going to do next? Are they coming here? Of course they are—why *wouldn't* they? India is right fucking next to Pakistan. Fuck, the only reason they don't launch a nuclear bomb is because they know their entire fucking backwards-ass civilization will be destroyed in seconds. You know, they hate India just like they hate America. They hate India for the very same *reasons* they hate America—because of our democracy! Here," Barun said, taking the beer Sudeep had brought him. "Cheers!"

Barun cracked open his Bombay Ultra, as did Sudeep and I, and we brought our cans together awkwardly.

"To India," Barun said.

"To India," Sudeep and I repeated.

We all took a sip of our beer.

"Cheers!" Barun said again, raising his beer, and this time his eyes were alight with something decidedly more palpable, menacing: "To avenging 9/11!"

And like good soldiers, we once more repeated his toast, though this time I felt as if I stood on uncertain ground.

"Oh fuck yeah!" Barun then shouted, patting me on the shoulder. "*The O'Malley Factor* is on!"

# 24

My father's response to pledging the fraternity and our starting an intramural cricket league was centered only on my schoolwork and grades. Was he happy that I'd decided to get involved with campus life? Of course. Was he pleased with the fact that I'd chosen—as he'd somewhat suggested—an Indian fraternity to pledge my time and energies? He was. But his main concern on that Saturday morning I called was perhaps the only concern he'd expressed for me throughout my life, a desire to ensure I earned my college—and eventual graduate—education. And so, on the phone with him for the first time since he'd left me here, perhaps I wasn't *that* surprised that his questions and concerns always circled back to my academic demands. He reminded me that being an engineering major was exceedingly difficult. I responded that I wasn't the only engineering major in my pledge class, let alone my fraternity, and so I felt, actually, that I was in an even better position to be successful than being alone. He reminded me of the need to earn high grades, so as to ensure a strong chance at admittance to the best possible graduate school. I told him that, once the pledge process was over, my involvement in the fraternity would be entirely up to me and that, I assured him, would ultimately revolve around my studies, grades, and personal choice. And while I conceded that perhaps the pledge process might be initially time consuming (an understatement if ever there was one), I tried to win him over by again stressing the cultural aspects of Delta Sigma Eta, focusing not only on their high grade point average (consistently within the top five of all Greek organizations on campus) but also the upcoming Divali celebration, the weekly Hindi lessons, and of course our intramural cricket league.

And what did he do? He listened as I gushed about being considered one of the best bowlers (pitchers) on the team. He listened as I articulated the campus-wide benefits of the league in general and how it fundamentally allowed different student populations to interact with other groups, allowing for Irvine's diversity to truly come together while experiencing and learning about a game rarely played in America. I proudly told him of how fraternities on campus had taken to the game and, while they certainly lacked the skills and history of our group of men, their interest and participation signaled—at least to the administration—another step in increasing racial and ethnic harmony on campus (a harmony, I declined to tell my father, that seemed mostly absent thus far). By the time I got to our demolition of Iota Chi, a white fraternity with no experience playing cricket but, the good sports that they were, had nonetheless decided to join the league out of sheer competitiveness and curiosity, my father was laughing at our hijinks and victories, his mind perhaps returning to his own days as an immigrant student in America, when, as a graduate student at USC in the 1970s, he'd certainly felt out of place, a computer engineer when there weren't many, an Indian when there weren't any, a stranger, as he'd recall at our family dinner table, in a white land longing for home, a wife, and a family of his own.

After I'd told him that, following their destruction, Iota Chi had laughingly told us they'd see us on the intramural football field, soccer field, disk golf field, any other field anywhere, I told my father I wished he could see me out there and I told him how good it felt, after the league in Fremont and the trips to India, to be out there again. By the end of our conversation, our first in too long, I told him I had to go, that we had our second match later against Delta Theta Phi, the Chinese-American fraternity, and everybody was counting on me to repeat my previous performance. He told me he was glad that I'd found something that made me happy, that I had found a place where I felt comfortable.

He also told me to remember why I was there.

The news that Mohammad Jafar al-Sadr, a controversial Muslim cleric, was invited to visit campus in February to denounce American involvement in the Middle East burned across campus like wildfire, igniting the passions of those politically unconscious and further exacerbating the political and racial tensions that seemed, at least to me, to reside in too much of life here at Irvine. He was supposedly a direct descendant of the Grand Ayatollah Mohammad Mohammad Sadeq al-Sadr, a once powerful Shiite cleric whose name had yet to find any currency in American political discourse but whose direct descendent, Muqtada al-Sadr, would soon become, once the war in Iraq reached its apex, one of America's most ruthless enemies. It would be Muqtada al-Sadr—now labeled an insurgent, terrorist, or hero, depending on your political position—who would famously and, in his eyes, righteously send his army, the Mahdi Army, to fight American troops in Basra, Sadr City, and Najaf. Of course, at that time, prior to the war, Muqtada al-Sadr was a name barely uttered by our politicians and leaders; indeed, with America and Americans so focused on capturing Osama bin Laden and with Saddam still in power so as to stifle political opponents such as al-Sadr, his impassioned rhetoric and vitriolic anti-Americanism was then somewhat muted.

Not so much with Mohammad Jafar al-Sadr. To hear the rumors that quickly began circulating around campus, that, indeed, saw campus quickly splinter in ways that were decidedly more complicated than they first appeared, Mohammad Jafar al-Sadr was a cleric in a small mosque in Chicago who had first gained fame (or infamy) decrying America for going into Afghanistan when it was not the people of Afghanistan who had attacked America. Though he agreed that Osama bin Laden had committed the act, he drew further attention for labeling 9/11 not an act of terror but war and vehemently argued that America was incorrect for bombing and destroying the nation of Afghanistan when most of the people in Afghanistan were simply innocent Arabs trying to live their lives and neither agreed with the Taliban nor with the politics of al-Qaeda. Either way, it was not America's job, according to Mohammad Jafar al-Sadr, to go into foreign lands and plant democracy or any other kind of political ideology. Furthermore, Mohammad Jafar al-Sadr went on to claim—outrageously, as rumor would have it—that America deserved the 9/11 attack and that it was America's meddling into the Middle East that had in fact started what he labeled as a holy war. Most importantly, he claimed, America's military bases in Saudi Arabia, the holiest of holy lands and the home to Mecca and Medina, debased Islam and Muslims all over the globe and therefore needed defending. In his eyes, then, 9/11 and, indeed, all the hatred Muslims felt towards American influence—including the Gulf War, which he reportedly mentioned as another instance of America acting not for the ideals of freedom or democracy but rather in its own narrow self-interest, to protect Kuwaiti oil—was clearly justified by the Koran; accordingly—and according to him, in speeches made continuously in his mosque and now infamously throughout America and on the internet—every Muslim had a spiritual duty to defend the Holy Land by any means necessary, be it terror or otherwise. For it was only when America had fully and completely divested itself from the Middle East that the holy war would stop; only then could the idea of peace—and the end of what President Bush called the War on Terror—ever become reality.

And he was coming here. To Irvine College. To virulently denounce the potential invasion of Iraq and to vituperate the War in Afghanistan and to offer his version of what many on campus were calling militant Islam. Indeed, from the very start, as pictures of al-Sadr were published on the front page of our weekly newspaper *New College*, it wasn't uncommon to see students on campus holding the newspaper, their agape mouths staring bewilderedly at Mohammad Jafar al-Sadr's round, heavily bearded face, and then, with confusion, fear, and incredulity, the words "fucking terrorist" falling from their lips. It seemed almost instinctive the way that phrase began circulating around campus in regards to al-Sadr's upcoming visit. Within days of the announcement, campus seemed abuzz with the bewildering fact that a "fucking terrorist" was coming to campus. And to give a speech no less. To discuss, in intellectual terms, his point of view. To rationalize the use of violence against—well, us. Quite suddenly, Irvine seemed fraught with danger and uncertainty, a place where everyone, because of this visit, was becoming more and more politicized and because of that more and more on edge.

He was coming here. Heavyset, green, glowering eyes, bearded and, at least in his picture, wearing a tightfitting *kufi*, a traditional Muslim hat that, on him, sat without decoration or ornamentation but austerely white—he was coming here. Why? And who had arranged it? Who had thought it a good idea to bring someone so divisive to campus, especially now, with the Bush administration threatening Saddam Hussein on an almost weekly basis to allow the IAEA into the country to check his weapons stockpile for chemical, biological, and nuclear weapons—who thought this a good idea? With Osama's crimes still so fresh in all of our minds, with his videotaped denunciations an exact echo of al-Sadr's screed—or al-Sadr's screed an exact echo of bin Laden's—who thought this a *necessary* idea?

According to *New College*, the "discussion," as it had been billed by those who had worked to bring al-Sadr to campus, was put together as a joint production between the Muslim Students of Irvine and, incredibly, the Political Science department. On the late October Tuesday that al-Sadr's picture found the front page of *New College*, an editorial ran alongside the article denouncing the Political Science department's support and involvement in such a "disgraceful, politically incorrect move as this." The *New College* editorial went on to write that it was "shameful that, when the wounds of 9/11 are still bleeding, when the myriad implications of that day on our nation's history have yet to be fully understood, and when men and women of our nation and local community are dying to defend our country from global terror networks such as al-Qaeda and killers such as Osama bin Laden, to invite one of their defenders into our community shows a stupendous lack of timing, tact, and not to mention class." It was, the editors blisteringly wrote, "treasonous."

In editorial fairness, on the opposing page of the paper, the Muslim Students of Irvine, in conjunction with the Poly-Sci department and in anticipation of the obvious backlash, submitted an editorial of their own, claiming, among other things, that the "vigorous need for discussion and understanding between cultures can and will help ensure America's global decisions and war efforts are made within the context of every possible intellectual, cultural, and political framework." Furthermore, the Muslim Students of Irvine (MSI) wrote, at a "time when Muslims all over the world and especially America are being singled out, stereotyped, and persecuted for the crimes of a few disenfranchised bad actors, it was especially necessary that, at a college campus like Irvine, we welcome all points of view and that these points of view, no matter how seemingly disagreeable, be respected, heard, tolerated—and challenged if need be." Only through "hearing these traditionally marginalized voices," the MSI wrote, "can we better understand the needs of our diverse world and the historical consequences of our national actions, both past and present." "Only by supporting these traditionally marginalized voices," they concluded, "can America's core values of freedom of religion and freedom of speech be upheld and seen as the global ideals we believe them to be."

How I felt about al-Sadr's visit—announced on a sunny day late in October, one week before Divali, the Indian New Year and one of the biggest parties thrown by Delta Sigma Eta—was still unclear. Part of me felt that I should be angry that someone who seemingly blamed America for being attacked on 9/11 was coming here to speak. It seemed, on its face, disgusting. Paradoxically, part of me also understood that even the most outlandish voices weren't completely delusional—that there was some truth inside the vitriolic words spewed by al-Sadr. As much of a political neophyte as I was, I wasn't foolish enough to believe that everything our government did was correct, either morally *or* militaristically. *Especially* militaristically. One look at Vietnam was enough to dismantle any argument of governmental purity.

And so, even as I found myself disgusted by al-Sadr's speaking engagement, I also found myself strangely persuaded, as I reread their editorial, by the MSI's position on freedom of speech. Weren't colleges the place where contrasting, even hostile voices could meet to argue and see who held the stronger position? Wasn't dialogue the key to our democracy?

Perhaps. Yet still, like almost everyone else on campus, I found myself staring perplexedly at al-Sadr's glowering picture, at the hate and desire for vengeance in his eyes, and staring at him I couldn't help thinking of the million other images of Muslims I'd seen on the news over the past year, since 9/11: images of Osama bin Laden, images of the Taliban, images of the Ayatollah Khamenei. So many bearded men, so much hate towards America—and therefore me.

I also couldn't help thinking of my father, and the stories I'd hear in India, stories told by *kakas* and cousins, stories replete with deep, historical distrust for the Muslims who lived in their communities, out on the margins. It felt easy, staring at al-Sadr, to hate this man for believing what he believed, for hating America (if, indeed, he truly did) and therefore for hating me.

Of course, what I was really thinking about was Azada—and how this was going to change everything.

**22**

Divali.

Indian New Year.

Back home, fireworks would soar across the Fremont sky as the large Indian diaspora that comprised the deshi community would break free from their everyday dutifulness and publicly celebrate their one true holiday. Mothers would dress in gaudy *saris* of verdant or lavender and young women would dress provocatively in dazzling *ghagra cholis* that left their taut stomachs delightfully exposed to those old and brave enough to stare, and men, drinking with unbridled freedom, drinking as if it were the only night of the year to which alcohol was permitted (excluding, of course, a Niners Super Bowl run), would dance in their *cuffney pyjamas*, drunkenly clanging their *dandia* sticks to whoever passed by as their gold necklaces shimmered and bounced upon their proud brown chests. I always got the sense, during Divali, that my parents and the entire deshi community were celebrating not only the year that had passed or the year to come, but some deeper spiritual connection that wasn't just nationalistic or rooted in filial devotion, but rather a kinship to some idealized history and sense of self to which they were bound and powerless to propagate.

The sense I got from the brothers of Delta Sigma Eta wasn't quite so spiritual or transcendent. Of course, that didn't mean I wasn't impressed by the ambition. More than once I heard one of the brothers proclaim, almost fiendishly, that they "weren't fucking around" when it came to Divali. According to them, Divali was the zenith of their social calendar, an event to which almost twenty thousand dollars were designated and to which, to hear the older brothers explain it, seemed to get bigger every year as more and more Indians came to Irvine in search of something familiar. Because Irvine College mandated that parties of this size and scale have some social utility beyond the admitted binge drinking—or even, in this case, a quasi-religious celebration—DESHI advertised the party as a Thanksgiving food drive; as such, everyone who attended had to bring at least one canned good; typically, most visitors brought at least two and, lately, many of the sorority girls had begun bringing toys, old and new, to the event. So while ostensibly an Indian New Year's celebration, DESHI's Divali Extravaganza became known campus-wide as Irvine's largest food drive, one that not only resulted in copious amounts of food and toys being delivered to various local charities, but also one very large check written by DESHI itself.

The Extravaganza was held at a rented mansion on two acres in Laguna Beach that rested high upon a solitary cliff with private beach access to which they had obtained the requisite permits to use throughout the night. On the beach a bonfire would blaze till morning as a DJ flown in from Mumbai would blast music alongside the crashing tide. Then, the brothers said, around midnight, a *garba* would inevitably break out on the pure white sand; sometimes, in years past, girls would drop their *cholis* and go frolicking into the ocean. It was a sight, they said, even more magical and beautiful than you could imagine. They wished their fathers could see it, so proud would they be.

For transportation, shuttles were arranged to bring girls

from both Indian sororities—and any non-sorority Indian—from Irvine to the mansion beginning at 9; the shuttles would run continuously until noon the next day. Inside the mansion, another DJ from Mumbai would spin on the first floor, perched so as to overlook the pool, the moon, the sea. There, a very dark lounge was set up for dancing and, well, whatever else anyone felt inclined to do. All eight of the bedrooms were stocked with condoms, weed, ecstasy. Food would be catered by Star of India, Laguna's premier Indian restaurant. As for the booze, well, of that there would undoubtedly be an endless supply. And that was just the start, for as I soon found out, we pledges were responsible for decorating the mansion, a task that included more garlands and petals of roses than I'd ever seen—and I'm Indian, I've been to a wedding or two.

The night of Divali, the night before Halloween, a full moon hung in the clear black sky, igniting the shimmering ocean just below the mansion with a magic that infused the night with a dramatic splendor only to be found in California. I felt as if I were no longer coming of age but that I had suddenly stepped into the glamorous movie of my adult life, so beautiful were the surroundings. I could feel it in my bones—especially after the brothers forced us pledges to do two shots of tequila and take a very large bong hit just before the first shuttle loaded with girls passed through the gilded gates. Standing in the mansion with the brothers, eagerly anticipating the start of what undoubtedly seemed the grandest and most ludicrously out-of-scale party I'd ever been to, let alone thrown, we held our shot glasses high in unison, all eleven pledges and all twenty-five brothers, and as we shot them back I felt what I'd been feeling more and more with these young men—and I'm not just talking about the sweet burn of Patron in my stomach. No, what I felt was a real sense of camaraderie, belonging, a feeling that because we all shared a similar history, we also shared a similar future, a future where Divali could and should play a necessary role in the tapestry of our lives.

And judging by the smiles on everyone's lips, I wasn't the only one who felt this way. Perhaps it was the alcohol, perhaps it was the weed, perhaps it was the clothing we wore, all of us, draped in rich, resplendent silk of every conceivable color— white, purple, teal, pink, lavender, crimson, tangerine—our *kurta pyjamas* adorned and ornamented with faux-rubies and emeralds, sequins and stones, our necks—or at least those of the brothers who had anticipated Divali and packed accordingly from home—steeped in gold; or perhaps it was the delicious smell of fried samosas and *badjii*, of decadent chicken tikka masala and vegetable *korma*, of succulent tandoori chicken wafting from the buffet tables set up by the pool, hot and steaming into the cool October night; or perhaps, quite simply, it was Divali itself, the feeling that this indeed was a new year and things would or could be different if we wanted them to be, if we believed them to be—perhaps it was any or all of these things that seemed to band us together like warriors charged with defending our patrimony from being consumed by something we loved deeply but paradoxically understood as antagonistic to our sense of self. Not once but twice did we hold our shot glasses high, and each time one of the brothers shouted "Happy New Year!" we all shouted back not only with pride but also with protective, godly reverence, as if we were on the frontline of some strange battlefield—and perhaps we were.

And so perhaps that was why I inevitably thought of my father and his words. Yes, I could see him looking down on me—as I'm sure my brothers could see their fathers looking down on them—and I could hear his words. I could hear his voice and feel his approval. And pride.

And then the girls came. Sudeep and I were charged with greeting each and every one with a garland of roses and a shot of Ketel One, and every time these fine, delightful creatures stood before us, their dark, voluptuous bodies enchantingly framed in tightly draped *saris* or *cholis*, their brown, almond eyes would flutter and fill with delightful abandon and their lips would slip into the most ecstatic smile and after accepting the garland of roses these beautiful girls would graciously yet naughtily kiss us on the cheek, leaning in close to allow us to touch and smell the comely invitation of their perfumed flesh—*before* shooting their shot. Their ceaseless smiles illuminated a freedom I'd never quite seen before—it was as if now, as adults, as young women in the prime of their lives and liberated from the watchful, protective eyes of home, they could finally play the roles they'd been cast and been dying to perform without having to worry what mommy would say. It was as if they could finally be themselves.

By the time Padma arrived to steal me into the party, I was dizzy from all the flesh I'd been so blessed to taste, my lips and cheeks crimson from the grace of countless girls. Soon Padma and I were out by the pool, lit aquamarine and steaming in the cool night, and people were writhing on the dance floor and sprawled on deck chairs making out and smoking joints and someone offered us ecstasy and I'd never taken it before nor really felt the need but at the possibility Padma's eyes sparkled with lewd desire, ribald relief, and before I knew it we were making out frantically in the bathroom and my hands were on her hips and she wore a thin belly chain of gold that encircled her waist and hooped through a diamond stud glittering upon her bellybutton and overcome I dropped to my knees in the semi-darkness of the bathroom and kissed her there, over and over, running my tongue along the soft, flat surface of her sumptuous flesh and then taking the stud into my mouth I sucked playfully as Padma, sitting atop the sink, spread her legs in tender invitation and when I put my mouth there Padma sighed and when she commanded "Take this!" I heard no admonitions or judgments, only freedom, freedom.

After I swallowed the ecstasy, she kissed me hungrily before dropping to her knees. "I've missed you."

"I've missed *you*," I said, watching her work beneath my silk *kurta*.

"Where've you been?" she asked, her hand tightening around me.

"I've been busy," I said, thinking, or trying not to think, of her. Thinking, she has no place here. She doesn't belong here. She'll *never* belong here. Thinking, isn't that the *worst* kind of thinking? Thinking, good luck with that kind of thinking.

"You haven't been avoiding me, have you? You haven't found someone else to do this for you, have you? Someone else who loves to suck your big, brown, hard…" and revealing me, she licked me from top to bottom before slowly swirling her tongue around my tip—twice. "…as much as I do?"

"I don't think that's possible."

"Good boy," she said. "Because if I hear of anyone else doing this for you," and here she bit me very, very gently on the tip, her teeth coming together for barely a moment—though moment enough for me to clearly get the picture. "It'll be off with your head."

And later, on the beach, the crimson bonfire that roared was framed by a full, marble moon and black sea that urged us all to revel in their combined blessed eternality and as Bollywood hits mixed with nineties West Coast rap we eventually found ourselves pulled closer and closer to the crashing surf, nearly a hundred of us, most of us clothed, some of us not, some of us falling deliriously into it, some of us being pushed, or dared, and somewhere along the way I lost Padma but found my brothers, my pledge brothers, Aadav and Pratek, Sudeep and Kiran, and together we smoked a blunt and watched as the circle of people dancing around the bonfire grew and grew, the colorful *cholis* lit by the bonfire melding into some dizzying kaleidoscope, verdant and lavender, gold and brown, a wellspring of laughter and joy liberated of the need for explanations or justifications, ourselves among ourselves acting only as ourselves, until at one point I turned to them and they too turned to me, all of us stoned and safe, and we confessed our undying love.

# 21

As if our Divali celebration wasn't enough to assure a hangover of debilitating proportions, the following night was Halloween, undoubtedly the biggest party night in Irvine. Now,

Irvine isn't necessarily considered a serious party school by any standard, but on Halloween our modest fraternity row explodes with one playfully haunted affair after the other, a scene that builds (from what I'd been told) from around nine o'clock until the tiny street is teeming with lewd debauchery and the whole thing is shut down by the fuzz around two in the morning. Our house, of course, would be dark, given that we'd already thrown our festivity; our plan, according to the brothers, would be to pre-party there (for those still man enough) and then hop down the line, bouncing from house to house and representing DESHI to the fullest.

Needless to say, I could've packed it in. I could've slept. I *needed* sleep. We all did. That morning, I woke up naked on the beach, alone, with no real recollection of when I took my clothes off or with whom. I presumed it was Padma. But there was a gap in my memory, something missing from around the height of the *garba* and the sun fighting through the early morning marine layer. I did remember naked girls racing into the crashing surf. After that, there was only a blank, and though I was terrified—and ashamed—at having suffered my first real blackout, I was also somewhat relieved in a strange way—for whatever I did, it was done in the presence of people I could trust—or at least thought I could. That I'd let go in the way I did—that *everyone* had—only reinforced the feelings of trust I felt and helped to provide some comfort for my humiliation. Besides, if everyone else was doing it, what was there to be humiliated *about?*

Back at the mansion, cleanup was in progress, and when I emerged from the beach wearing someone's abandoned, black *choli* scarf wrapped around me like a loincloth, there was no embarrassment, only laughter, backslapping, bong hits, and an occasional reference to Gandhi. My pledge brothers looked at me and, with mops and brooms and empty beer bottles in hand, only cheered and jeered, clapping and stomping, whistling and high fiving. All we could do, as our group burgeoned that morning, with members of our pledge class arriving in hilarious forms of disarray from the bedrooms, bathtubs, or bushes where we'd crashed, was congratulate ourselves on having the best time of our lives.

By the time we finally arrived back on campus it was already past three and the instant I saw my bottom bunk I passed out, still dressed in the filthy *kurta pyjama* I'd scrubbed and cleaned the mansion in.

My guilt—such as it was—found life in supercharged dreams haunted by my mother who scolded me for performing so poorly on my report card. My report card was the size of a billboard and posted in our backyard and showed one gigantic F after another and there were helicopters circling our house and people gathered around our backyard to gaze in bewilderment and my mother's wagging finger was three times the size of her head and pointing at me she shook it over and over, blaming me for shaming our family, for shaming India, for disappointing everyone by failing to get into a good graduate school. She told me I would never find a good job, a good wife, a good life. Weeping, I begged her to forgive me as I stood diminished and shrinking beneath her ever-growing finger. I begged her to love me not for my grades but for who I was—her son. I told her I was doing what daddy said, that I was following his advice. I told her I'd learned my lesson. When she asked me what the lesson was I said I didn't know.

I leapt from bed screaming to find Osama bin Laden standing before me. At the sight of the monster I recoiled and smacked my head on the top bunk, gashing my forehead. Blood ran hot and slick across my eyes as I fought to escape the confines of my bunk and elude America's most wanted.

It was only when I heard Osama scream "Dude, what the fuck?" and I noticed the bong in his hand that I realized he was a monster of a different sort.

"Are you all right?" Sudeep said from beneath the massive beard glued to his jaw. He wore a camouflage jacket and a long white tunic. A tiny hijab failed to cover his shaggy black locks. "Here, take this." Surprisingly, it wasn't the bong he passed but a towel. I held it to my forehead to try and stanch the bleeding.

"What the fuck is wrong with you?" I asked. "Why are you dressed like that?"

He ignited the bong and inhaled deeply. *"Dude..."* and flooding the room with smoke he explained: "It's *Halloween.*"

"Of course it is."

"You better get dressed."

"What time is it?"

"Nine." He offered me the bong.

"I'm all right," I said, collapsing into one of our desk chairs. "Where'd you get that costume?"

"Sick, right?"

"That's one way of putting it."

"Allah Akbar," he said, winking at me. "What are you going to wear?"

"I'm afraid I don't have many options," I said, removing the towel, now darkened, to gauge the severity of my injury. I touched my forehead, made a pained face.

"Relax," Osama said. "Take a shower. Get dressed. Have a bong hit. Stay with me, my son, and you'll have all the virgins of heaven."

"That's what I'm afraid of," I said, before foolishly doing what I was told.

Two hours later and absent any judgement, I found myself surveying the tightly packed dance floor in the basement of the Phi Omega Theta fraternity house while trying to drink a lukewarm can of Bombay Ultra from beneath my George Bush mask without spilling the beer (if you could call it that) all over myself. I wish I could say I was the only Bush out that night, but it seemed as if my entire administration—and administrations from years past, for there were quite a few Richard Nixons and George Washingtons about—were out in full to combat what looked like the entirety of al-Qaeda and the Taliban from further wreaking havoc on America. There were Dick Cheneys and Laura Bushes and (these I had to be told) Condoleezza Rices and even a few Paul Wolfowitzes (Deputy Secretary of Defense) meandering around the dance floor, and every time one of us saw the other we waved faux-proudly, sometimes raising a fist in the air, sometimes saluting the other, and there was something disorienting about seeing so many politicians at a Halloween party, something menacing about the hollow likenesses of our masks, about the cheap plasticity of our beatific, horrifically benevolent smiles (especially Dick Cheney, whose long nose hooked over his deviously upturned lips), about seeing so many politicians among so many traditional Halloween costumes—the Freddys and Jasons, the Michael Meyerses and Leatherfaces, all of whom carried a weapon other than a smile.

Nonetheless, there we were—as were the Taliban and too many Osama bin Ladens to count. The last time I'd seen so many turbaned men was on Wolf News. Talk about disorienting. I didn't know whether to call the FBI or buy them a drink. I thought about doing both. The Terror Alert was *high*. Much like the Osamas staggering about. The dance floor was replete with them, white, brown, Black men draped in white tunics and sporting absurdly long fake beards and some of them wore army jackets and held plastic machine guns and at one point a few of them stood in a circle on the dance floor and raised their guns high in the air in mock-celebration, their collective chanting rising above the thumping Tupac in indiscernible melody, a cacophony of voices climbing high into the crimson darkness in search—or ridicule—of some elusive victory, and some of them wore T-shirts with the word TERRORIST or YOU CAN'T CATCH ME or FUCK YOU BUSH written across their chests and twice I bumped into two different bin Ladens and each time he screamed he hated America but loved its porn.

And then he offered me a bong hit.

And then I wondered if this were truly the way forward.

And then there were the girls. As perplexing a sight as the myriad bin Ladens and Cheneys were, equally strange, yet considerably more delightful, were the innumerable girls who'd taken Halloween to a completely different heart. Their goal—such as one could be ascribed—seemed to provoke and titillate, tease and stimulate, to send every young, costumed man's heart aflutter with permissible fantasy. Or perhaps it was more than that—though perhaps it was less. Perhaps I'm being too generous in my description, now removed from the tantalizing superabundance of all that liberated, voluptuous flesh. Or perhaps

I'm not being generous enough—perhaps I'm not giving these beautiful young women the credit they deserved.

For wasn't there—like there was at the Divali celebration—more than a hint of *becoming* in these beguiling, enchanting women? Didn't there *have* to be? Their costumes revealed themselves in ways I'd never imagined a woman would publicly approve; to publicly show themselves wearing such little clothing, to allow strangers to gaze at their most intimate secrets, to command—*demand*—such attention—*and to enjoy it!* To *bask* in it! To allow it to wash over them like some completely deserved, rapturous applause—and then to saunter on in their heels in search of the next pair of helpless eyes to do it all over again. Yes, on Halloween these young girls dismissed any hint of humility, exhibiting instead only supreme confidence—in themselves, in their bodies, in their choice. This truly was an education.

Whether tracing the frilly line of a French maid's garter belt or staring hard at the matching black choker tight around her neck, whether gazing slackjawed at Little Red Riding Hood's crimson skirt as it climbed up her ivory knee or the bevy of Snow Whites salaciously dressed in ruby red lace corsets, whether whistling at the Catholic school girls in their thigh-high checkered skirts and knee-high stockings (and secretly, drunkenly pining for the history that would've allowed me access (without guilt) to the real thing) or just gawking dumbfounded at the girls brave enough to brazenly shed any pretense of playacting and wear instead the skimpiest lingerie they could find—the night seemed to offer every kind of fantasy, every kind of flesh, every opportunity to lose oneself without any hint of penalty or pain.

Until, that is, I saw Azada. Enshrouded by smoke she appeared before me like some heavenly ghost, there for only a moment before vanishing, her fair skin aglow in the sultry darkness like some luminescent idol, a goddess provocatively obscured by emerald veils and shimmering sequins, a belly dancer enticingly shaking her enchanting hips in service to her seductive, magical powers. She was there—and she was gone. Did she see me? Did she know it was I behind the mask? I feared she did and vanished in disappointment. I hoped she did and vanished simply to tease. But how could she? I could barely see from beneath my mask—hard to believe anyone who didn't know I was dressed as Bush could immediately discern my identity.

Still, for that briefest of moments, it was impossible to not sense something, to not feel as if the veiled dancer knew who I was. For there exuded real pleasure in her brief performance: her exposed eyes had locked onto mine in a way that seemed to see beyond our costumes, and her hips—shaking, writhing—hypnotized me with their licentious invitation in a deeply personal way, as if summoning me to reach out of the darkness and seize what we both so desperately wanted.

Panicked yet irritated, strangely embarrassed yet definitely aroused, my heart pounded as I surveyed the crowd, seeking her veiled head and her fair white skin. Was it really her? Or was I projecting some unconscious desire onto the many beautifully clad women on the dance floor? Either way, I stood on edge, seeking her magical beauty once again—even as I knew that were I to find her, I feared what I might do. I feared what I should. And yet still I found myself slithering through the dance floor, giving chase, unable to separate my thoughts from my emotions, the most powerful of which seemed to be—*go get her.*

"Hey, Bush!"

It was yet another Osama bin Laden, though one I knew—Sudeep.

"Look," he said, his arms draped around two girls in negligées. "I found those virgins I promised."

They were unmistakably Indian, their almond eyes and dark skin attested to that. The jury was still out as to whether or not they were virgins. If you stared hard enough, and I was momentarily compelled to, you could see through their sheer, purple teddies and examine the delightful fullness of their breasts, the allure of their thongs. Sudeep, releasing them from his arms, instructed them to twirl.

"This is Oona," he said, gesturing to one. "And this is Oma. This, girls, is Rohan."

"Nice to meet you," Oona said, extending her hand. I shook it, quickly scanning for Azada. Could she see me? Was she watching?

"That's a scary costume," Oma said, coming in close to inspect my mask.

"You like it?" I queried, still scanning, searching.

"Who is it supposed to be?"

I spied Sudeep from beneath my mask, watched his thin lips crease with pleasure.

"What do you mean?" was all I could think to say.

"I've seen this face before," she said, touching me now, her fingers running across the hard plastic nose and lips. "On the news, I think. Is he some serial killer or something?"

I let that sit between us.

"Anyone need a drink?" I asked, and there, on the stairs leading to the first floor, I saw her, paused in invitation, her veils shimmering in the crimson darkness. "Girls, can I grab you all a beer? I was just on my way to grab some beers."

"Hold on, hold on," Sudeep said, barring my advance. "Girls, tell them what you told me."

The girls shared mutually devious looks with Sudeep before turning to me. It was Oona who said, "Well, we're pledges from Delta Gamma Delta, and part of our pledge process, you know," again her eyes found Sudeep's, Oma's, and there was neither fear nor reticence nor even shame there, only confidence and utter control and the exhilarating intoxicant of power, "is to go out tonight and find a pledge and, well, have a three-way with him."

"I told them you'd be perfect," Sudeep confessed.

"You're joking," I said, eyeing him from beneath my mask before noticing the veils had vanished once again.

"If we don't," Oona said, wrapping her arm around my waist and peering up at me with lewd expectation, "we get in a lot of trouble."

"A *lot* of trouble," Oma repeated before wrapping her arm around my waist and running her hand across my chest.

"You think you're up to it?" Oona asked.

"Absolutely," I said, trying, as nicely as I could, to extract myself and race up the stairs. "Let me go get us some drinks and I promise I'll meet you all right back here."

"Promise?" Oma asked.

"Does this look like the face of a liar?"

"You look like the boy next door," Oma said, touching my mask, my face.

"And you two look like trouble," I replied.

"Oh," Oona said. "You have no idea."

Against reason and, perhaps more accurately, instincts, I told them I would be right back. I felt like an idiot saying the words, but I said them nonetheless, said them wanting to believe them, even as I knew that the experience Oma and Oona offered rarely comes along in life—at least without paying for it. So too, I also thought, after the girls had teasingly said "Hurry back" and "We'll be waiting" did the experience—did the raw emotion—I felt upon seeing Azada rarely come along. What about that? Was it any less real?

I was undoubtedly too afraid to give it the proper title, to give it the proper weight, but as I fought through the crowd and up the stairs to the first floor of the Phi Omega house, I purposely yet mistakenly labeled what I felt desire, though undeniably the rawest and most blinding desire I'd ever known. Perhaps I was too drunk to fully understand what had come over me, perhaps I wasn't yet drunk enough, or perhaps I knew full well and was simply too cowardly to accept it, I honestly can't say. All I knew was that I wanted to find her, even if it meant exposing myself in a way I knew would be too painful for too many reasons.

The first floor was in blacklight and decorated like a haunted house, with eerily cut pumpkins glowing in cobwebbed corners and sheeted ghosts hanging from the high ceiling alongside plastic axes and knives and Michael Jackson's "Thriller" was blasting as I took in the throng slamming back booze in blue plastic cups and a wide staircase led up to a balconied second floor where girls leaned provocatively on their backs in lingerie as guys on the first floor leered up at them whistling and begging them to move and shake and often they did, occasionally turning to peer down at the boys and remove their tops, and then I saw her standing at the top of the stairs, alone and sipping a glass of punch and eyeing me in a way that left me breathless, crazed, and on the first step I stopped and stared and knew she knew who I was. I could feel it in my bones. Like she could.

And then she was off, her veils dancing behind her, and I was after her, moving quickly, passing three guys doing a beer bong that hung all the way down from the balconied second story, and everyone was screaming "Go! Go!" as the beer flew down the funnel and through the plastic tube where some brave soul guzzled and guzzled, and quite suddenly something didn't feel right, I could feel someone watching me, and peering down over the second-floor balcony I spotted Padma and Dipika, each enticingly dressed in low-cut nurses uniforms, their skirts high above the knee, and in the blacklight their dark skin contrasted with strange beauty against the white of their uniforms, the white of their eyes, and when our eyes locked Padma held me there from behind my mask for a very long time before smiling drunkenly. Instinctively, I grabbed my crotch, thumbed the bathroom, and then raised a single finger, and fixing her bosom she blew me a kiss and then turned away, whispering something to Dipika, the two of them laughing ecstatically and now pointing to a group of turbaned Osamas, and after a moment they vanished, lost in the darkness, and when I was sure they were gone I turned and saw her at the far end of the dim hallway and frozen Azada stared and I too and together we stood enraptured, afraid, like two people powerless to stop ourselves, like two people lost to reason, duty, history.

When she entered the darkness I followed.

I heard the door lock behind me.

We were in a tiny bathroom, the only light shining through the lone window a full moon's humbling incandescence.

She placed a finger to my lips, my mask's lips.

Held it there and looked into my eyes.

As I hers.

So green, so pure, like something forbidden.

With her finger still upon my lips, she walked me backwards until I was standing against the window, breathless and suffocating and bathed in moonlight.

She teasingly pushed me onto the toilet before laughing mischievously, the tiny bathroom now filled with her provocative melody, her eyes fluttering like butterflies finally freed from their cocoon. It was impossible for me to not take in the fullness of her body, especially her thighs, so white in the moonlight and so close to my touch. A tight, dark-green miniskirt cut diagonally across her waist accompanied by two sheer, lime-green veils that had been tied to dangle enticingly past her knees and in the moonlight the swell of her thighs summoned my touch but when I reached for her there she quickly slapped me away, the echo of her violence ricocheting around the bathroom like some scandalous rumor.

She waved her finger at me, as if scolding a child.

Not yet.

And then she began dancing, very, very slowly, her arms rising up above her head and her hips moving, swaying, shifting slowly from left to right, back and forth, the large silver sequins stitched to her skirt and bra coming together to create a licentious melody, a hypnotizing song rich with temptation and desire, and where she was covered in veils the moonlight seemed to infuse her with a heavenly glow, illuminating her beauty even as it simultaneously obscured her with its spectral illumination, everything hidden and revealed with such sublime ease she seemed both fantasy and reality—of which she was. She was.

With her rapturous dancing, everything seemed in play, unstable, reason and history seemed diminished, games played by fools. One by one she dropped the veils, the first one slipping from her grasp that which had been wrapped loosely around her neck like a scarf and, as she faced me, dangled invitingly upon her enshrouded breasts. She turned away then, her hips still swaying as she teasingly disrobed, veil after veil after veil, her taut, pale body alight in the moonshine. The last veil covered most of her face and with her back still to me she slowly unwrapped it, exposing her long black hair, hair sexily tied up and back and sitting high atop her head like some heavenly crown. I watched as she withdrew the veil and held it out at arm's length for a long, teasing moment before letting it flutter quietly to the floor. There, at her feet, were at least four veils, and I watched as Azada, still shifting, still moving to her own internalized beat, kicked them aside as if finally freed from their egregious purpose. It took everything I had to not touch her, to not reach out and stroke her thigh or kiss her back or wrap my arm around her waist and draw her into my lap. Mercifully, I didn't have to, for soon she was sitting atop me, her hips grinding as she did so. She leaned back slightly past me and caught me with her eyes and together we stared as she gyrated her hips, spellbound by her confidence, her daring, her beauty. Awed by it. Taught by it. Momentarily freed by it. Together we watched as she slowly spread her legs and slowly thrust and then closed her legs only to open them again and reaching for me I wanted to say something, to utter some phrase capable of articulating my desire, but powerless in her spell I could say nothing, only suffocate beneath my mask, beneath George Bush, only watch as she placed my hand on her thigh while her hips conjured a carnal dream and with her as my guide my hand slid further and further up her thigh until finally disappearing beneath her miniskirt.

She immediately stopped grinding her hips and stared at me in the cool silence.

As if offering sanction. As if offering sanctuary.

I could feel her breathing, her breath, and this time when she spread her legs I entered her, her eyes closing and lips parting without sound or shame.

It was at that precise moment that the commotion from outside destroyed our sanctuary. Azada opened her eyes and smiled and tried to ignore it and so did I but the words grew louder and fiercer until we both knew there was no going back and soon we stood peering out the window of the bathroom down into the backyard where two large groups of people, one clearly made up of Osama bin Ladens and faux-Taliban and the other real Muslims, guys dressed in typical Halloween costumes like Jason or Freddy but who now stood with their masks off and at their feet and some of them had real beards and were pointing at the Osama bin Ladens and calling them assholes and even though I was shocked to see Sudeep heading the conflict I wasn't all that surprised.

My shame left me dizzy.

I can only imagine what Azada felt, for before I knew it she had swept up her veils and vanished from the bathroom as I stood shivering in the icy moonlight and soon Azada was standing back behind the Muslims heatedly querying a girl dressed as a toothbrush and the Muslims were calling the Osamas terrorists and the Osamas were calling the Muslims terrorists and Sudeep was clearly wasted and he along with the rest of his posse—some fellow pledges and brothers from DESHI, other guys who'd just decided to dress up like, well, terrorists, and even a few scantily clad girls, Padma and Dipika among them—had begun raising their fake guns and hands in the air and mockingly chanting "Allah Akbar" over and over until finally someone dressed as a murderous surgeon—fake blood smeared across his scrubs, a protective mask tied to his rusted and bloody scalpel—told him to fuck off and when Sudeep told him to go back to his fucking country the murderous surgeon told him to go back to *his* fucking country and this caused Sudeep's group—growing exponentially by the second—to laugh and taunt that this *was* their country and I think it was Padma or maybe Dipika who shouted that they should just ride their magic fucking carpets back to where they came.

I honestly don't know who threw the first punch, but when I looked for Azada she was gone.

# 20

It wasn't until Tuesday night that I saw Azada again. She'd missed our English class earlier in the day, an absence (I assumed) predicated on what had transpired Saturday night. When I finally got the call from her requesting my presence (I had been staring at my phone with her number aglow on it for hours, too terrified to call), I was relieved *and* anxious to hear her voice, given everything we had to discuss.

When we finally met later in the library, this time upstairs by the third-floor stacks in a semi-private cubicle, she was again wearing the rose red lipstick that had come to stir my heart, only tonight it was paired with the necklace from our first day of class, the gold disk inscribed with Arabic lettering. And a headscarf.

I couldn't believe it.

And not only because she looked even more ravishing with her hair obscured than with it voluptuously and visibly falling down her freckled shoulders. Her headscarf was simply emerald green, the very green of her eyes, and inexplicably it brought out their dizzying radiance even more, imbuing them with a mystery, modesty, and exoticism that, combined with the rose red lipstick, left me utterly intoxicated.

And irate.

And because of that deeply ashamed.

"Don't look so surprised."

"Is that how I look?" I asked, taking the seat opposite her. We were surrounded by a handful of empty tables and, beyond our little alcove, books, stacks and stacks of books where we could hear the occasional lost soul drifting in search of some brave mind who'd come long before us and dared to shine light on our ceaselessly absurd folly.

"Among other things."

"I'm just…"

"Exactly."

"No, it's, you know…"

"I can tell you don't approve," she said, as if speaking to her father. And perhaps she was. Perhaps we *always* are. "I can tell you think of me differently now. You see me differently. And you know what? That's fine. Because this is who I am, Rohan. This is who I am and this is who I always will be."

"Where is this coming from?"

"You know where this is coming from. You were *there*."

"About that, about Halloween, look, I want to apologize for that. Things got out of hand, obviously, and I mean, guys, you know, they were *really* drunk and…"

"Rohan, you have nothing to apologize for. And anyway, you can't apologize for the whole campus. And please don't use alcohol as an excuse. You know better than that. Let's, let's try and be honest with each other. Because you know and I know that that's how they feel. It's how the whole campus feels. When they look at us—when they look at *me*—Rohan, I wished you could've seen the looks I got walking across campus. I wish you could've seen the look the librarian gave me when I walked in downstairs. It was as if she wanted to check my hair for a bomb!"

"Azada," I said, trying to laugh it off.

"I'm serious! I could see it in her face. She saw me wearing

this and her mind immediately drew some awful conclusion—
and this is the *librarian* we're talking about! Not some uneducated person on the street! This is the person in charge of *books*!
This is the person in charge of *knowledge*—of *power*! Now think
of what a campus full of dumb college students think?"

"I wouldn't call us dumb college students."

"That makes it even worse!"

"Then why do it?"

"Why should I even have to *weigh* it?" she said. "Why should
it even be a conscious decision? When you see guys walking
with a tiny gold cross around their necks, you think they
thought twice about it? You think they woke up and asked
themselves, 'If I wear this today, what will people think about
me?' No, they simply put it on. And do you know why, Rohan?
Because they can! Because here, in this place, we're supposedly
free to look and say and think how we want. So why should
I even have to think about whether or not to wear this? Can
it not be as simple as deciding what kind of earrings to wear?"

"So it's as simple as that. This weekend happens, *we* happen,"
I said, my heart now caught in my throat—for that's all I really
wanted to talk about anyway. Not what sat atop her head—but
what rested beneath it! Not some piece of clothing—but the
beauty it obscured—enhanced! The beauty I'd touched—and
that had touched me! The beauty that now sat mere inches away
made all the more beautiful by anger!

At the mention of us, Azada blushed and quickly cast her
eyes downward, at what I now noticed was Conrad, open and
highlighted and graffitied with marginalia. Without any hesita-
tion I reached for her then, placing my hand, a finger, delicately
under her chin. Her cheeks flushed even deeper at my touch,

and when I brought her up to meet my eyes, she seemed closer to tears than anything her anger suggested. Where I found the courage to perform such a public act is beyond me, but I did it, I held her there, held her there for all to see, held her until her eyes welled with tears and her lower lip began trembling and it finally seemed as if it was only us and everything else had slipped away.

"*We* happen," I whispered.

"We happen," she repeated solemnly.

"And now this?"

At that she turned away from me and my touch and peered up towards the ceiling.

Tears slid down her face in the silence.

She took a deep breath.

"I don't know what to do," she whispered. "I'm scared."

"So am I."

"You don't know what it's like."

"I have an idea."

"No," she said. "You can't imagine."


# 19

Neither could I have imagined the rhetoric that abounded within the fraternity house later that Halloween night, after the blaring sirens caused the fight to splinter and the brothers to swiftly summon everyone to the house for an emergency meeting. Not in my wildest dreams could I have foreseen what too many of the brothers had to say about the fight and what it meant for the fraternity—and campus—moving forward. Though perhaps I was deluding myself, not only as I sat through the fraternity meeting surprised, but also as I sat in the library with Azada, her hand held in mine and her headscarf loose around her gorgeous black hair. For perhaps that was yet another lesson I was learning, albeit very, very slowly (and reluctantly): that the illusions we live by, the things we tell ourselves—the lies and truths alike—these are things done so chronically and effortlessly that to deny their existence is simply another illusion we use to get us through the day. It was the cost of these illusions—not only on ourselves, but those we love, those we want to—that was finally beginning to trouble me.

For were I to be perfectly honest with myself, I'd have to admit that the things I heard the brothers proclaiming that night weren't entirely surprising—indeed, they weren't surprising at all. What was surprising was how easily I could agree with them! What was surprising was how easily I sat nodding my head in agreement as the brothers began espousing what they identified as the Muslim Problem—even as my heart, at that very moment, was still in the bathroom with Azada on my lap! Though perhaps that wasn't very surprising either! For (again, were I to be perfectly honest) the rhetoric I'd heard that night was merely a variation of what I'd been hearing my entire life, both in America and India, only now stained with the fear brought on by 9/11 and al-Sadr's campus visit. The fear, the resentment, the deep distrust of Muslims, these were things I'd heard from my father and family often throughout my life, and because I loved my father—because we *all* loved our fathers—there was no easier way to make him proud than to agree with his point of view. Indeed, sitting in the fraternity house that night and listening to the brothers' heated rhetoric, it seemed as if my father's point of view was not only entirely reasonable but that, given our current time, mere agreement wasn't enough; now, with 9/11 still so fresh in our minds, with the possibility of invading Iraq and toppling a brutal dictator who (according to the White House) may have weapons of mass destruction, with the knowledge that Osama bin Laden was still on the run and, of course, with Mohammad Jafar al-Sadr, the controversial Muslim cleric, coming to visit our very campus in February—*in only three months*—the time seemed ripe for something *beyond* agreement. It seemed ripe for action.

None of which, I'm sure, would've surprised Azada, had she heard our discussion—which was undoubtedly why I lied when she asked that night in the library where I went following the buzz of the blaring sirens. I'd lied, convincing myself that I was saving her from something else that was certain to exacerbate her already frazzled nerves, even as I knew that the only person I was truly saving was myself—from first having to explain my brotherhood with men who looked like me and whose fathers looked like mine, but more delicately from having to explain my thoughts and feelings about all that was discussed. No, I'd gone straight home, I lied, ran, at the sound of the wailing sirens, as if my life depended on it back to Tarnopol Hall where—and for this I admitted shame and apologized profusely—I helped nurse my roommate, Sudeep, back to some semblance of sanity. When Azada realized who Sudeep was within my narrative, she wasn't at all surprised. Instead, she saw it as yet another awful coincidence in a relationship—and world—that seemed increasingly out of our immediate control.

Of course, confessing to Sudeep being my roommate seemed a minor—if inevitable—offense given the larger truth that unfolded. Back at the fraternity house, around thirty of us were called together, pledges and brothers alike, and as bottles of Johnny Walker and Ketel One circled the basement alongside three tightly rolled blunts, as more than a few brothers and pledges iced their bruised fists and bloody knuckles, I sat and listened as our leadership took to the floor to denounce the newly identified Muslim Problem. It was Darpan, our Pledge Master, who eventually took center stage and articulated what more and more people on campus had undoubtedly begun feeling but, for fear of sounding politically incorrect, kept silent and submerged within the innocence of our idyll. Darpan took to the floor still dressed in his Halloween costume: he, like so many others in the fraternity, had gone as a Muslim terrorist, as some debauched version of Osama bin Laden or Taliban fighter, and he'd painted his beard on with black makeup and because at a certain point he had entered the fray it was smeared and blotchy and there appeared to be a cut stretching from his left ear to his lip. He still wore his white knee-length tunic, stained now in places with blood or jungle juice, and like him there were others—including Sudeep—still dressed as terrorists, as serial killers or rap stars, their costumes darkened with crimson, sweat, and booze, and in the dim, smoky haze we seemed a strange band of brothers indeed, boys acting as men acting as something else entirely, and when Darpan began speaking I found myself listening first as a pledge and potential brother but eventually as something more, an Indian, yes, but an American too, someone who, through no fault or will of my own, was suddenly charged with a cause that *seemed* undoubtedly right and increasingly necessary but paradoxically antagonistic to everything my heart desired.

"What I think we have to start realizing is that they hate our way of life," Darpan exhorted, his dark-brown eyes surveying us through the smoky haze. "They always have. The freedoms we enjoy, the freedoms we cherish, the very things that make up the American dream—a good job and a nice house and a pretty wife—these are things that, at a fundamental level, they detest. And you know why? They hate it because their religion *tells* them to hate it. They hate it because that book they all bow down to five times a day *commands* them to. And we know this. This isn't really news. You don't need some video tape by some towelhead with a beard to understand this. You see this horrible fact throughout the Muslim world. You see it in practice. Iran, Iraq, Pakistan, Saudi Arabia, everywhere. I mean, look at how they live. Democracy? No, never. Not with that book. And so while I agree with Bush that we have to stay in Afghanistan as long as it takes to get Osama bin Laden and destroy the Taliban, I disagree with what some are saying about giving them democracy. Never happen. The cowboy in him probably wants to believe in the ideal—in hope, in democracy. But that's where we disagree, that's where history teaches another lesson. Still, he's right we need to go in there and kill that fucker and the Taliban. And do you know why? Because we need to protect ourselves from those maniacs. And not only there, in the Middle East, but here," Darpan said and then, in the dim silence, he pointed to the ground, "here as well. For believe it or not brothers, here in this very land, in our home, *we* are under attack. *We* are being threatened. I mean, to think that those Muslims are going to bring that al-Sadr fuck to this campus and tell *us* how America is fucked-up. How America is *wrong* for trying to protect itself. I mean, who the fuck do they think they are? At a time of war, when we've already been attacked by them, to think that this asshole wants to come to our campus and speak against *our* country! This is a place for learning—not fucking hate speech! This is a place where freedom and democracy are valued—not dictatorships and the fucked-up belief that girls should be covered from head to fucking toe! I mean, brothers, do you see them? Sure you have. You see them walking across campus, their heads covered, some now even with their entire fucking bodies covered. You know what I think when I see one of them? I think the same things I know you do. I think the bitch has a bomb. I think she wants to blow up the fucking place. I think her husband told her to do it. I think her *father* did. And you know what else I think? I think it has to stop. At this time in our nation's history, something has to be done—yes, my brothers, something has to be done to protect this land, to protect this campus, from al-Sadr and his ilk. And so the question becomes what are we going to do about it? What are we going to do to save this country? What are we going to do save this campus?"

And how could I tell Azada that? How could I tell her she was right?

The following week was, officially, midterms, and so I—like most on campus—found myself drowning in more work than I could handle, not least of which because I'd spent most of the first five weeks of the quarter more engaged in my social life than my academic pursuits. At the start of the school year—and, indeed, during freshman orientation that past summer—councilors and professors alike had warned us that the quarter system utilized by the college could be overwhelming for some incoming students. The pace of learning was fast, they warned, and so it required the kind of personal responsibility many weren't ready for, as the freedom of college compounded by the rapidly passing calendar oftentimes led to a few supposedly smart, ambitious students falling quickly behind—and away. Which was how, oddly, I suddenly felt, especially as I sat looking at my calendar that first week of November and realized, to my dismay and anxious excitement, that we were halfway through the Fall quarter (and only three weeks from Thanksgiving break) and my grades were nowhere near where I (or my father) expected them to be.

Needless to say, I felt overwhelmed. Beyond my feelings for Azada—feelings that both occluded my ability to think clearly while simultaneously forcing me to focus on the only thing that truly seemed to matter—and beyond my responsibilities as a pledge to the fraternity, I had an American History exam on Thursday and a 5-7 page paper due by the end of the following week for Dr. Green; I had a midterm exam on Wednesday in Chemistry for Dr. Xian and the following Monday I had a Calc exam. Given the preceding weekend, I felt rudderless and unable to focus on anything resembling academics. Monday morning somehow faded into Monday night which blinked into Tuesday morning, eventful only because Azada sat in Dr. Green's English 101 class in a crimson headscarf. Her sitting there so conspicuously caused our class's typically conversational mood to descend into a dark, incredulous silence, as if, in her gesture, she had committed some grave offense, and perhaps she had, though perhaps it was us, yes, all of us, perhaps we were all guilty of some strange, terrible crime…

And Tuesday night in the library we two stared in breathless silence, aware of our deepening madness, and rather than Conrad or Chem I fell further and further under the dizzying spell of the most enchanting poison, aware of my folly but also aware of emotions unlike any I'd ever before known. I felt, staring into her emerald eyes, my hand brazenly atop hers amidst the privacy of the third-floor stacks, as if I had finally arrived as a man, as if I'd finally discovered the real reason we're all here. It wasn't school or jobs or the pursuit of money—it was this, this deafening, supercharged silence, a silence whose volume communicated everything perfect and beautiful we're capable of, a silence strangely anathema to everything expected of me.

Wednesday morning I bombed my Chem test. The moment I sat down in class I knew I didn't stand a chance; as someone trained to spend hours studying before an exam, I knew I was unprepared. Midway through the period I looked up from my ignorance and saw my surrounding colleagues diligently completing their tests, the Indians on the left of the room and the

Asians the right, and in the intense silence their cold concentration left me dizzy, their whipsaw brilliance spinning me like a top as they exited by. Seated there, I could actually feel myself falling behind—that it didn't bother me as much as I knew it damn well should spoke to the depths of my quagmire.

Outside the exam I ran into Padma. We'd seen each other only days ago, at the Divali party (good), and briefly at the Halloween party (not so good), yet it seemed like so much had happened since then. A clear blue sky above her, she studied me with a skeptical understanding that intimated she knew more than she let on. I told her it was the fraternity that had kept me away the past few days, that it was those duties that had prevented me from studying, with or without her. In a look of genuine concern, or pity, or perhaps doubt, she told me to start getting it together. She told me I looked like shit. She also told me she was there if I needed her—for anything.

Later that evening, my mother called. I didn't remember the last time we'd spoken. My mother, of course, was quick to remind me—and without any prompting. It had been nearly three weeks, our conversation had been brief, and I was "supposedly" out in the park with some "friends"—don't you remember? I did. I didn't. Everything was a haze, spinning out of control. I realized then how much I missed my mother, the sound of her voice, the calming force of her presence. As a young boy, and even as a teenager, there was nothing more comforting for me than doing my schoolwork at the kitchen table immediately after school while she dutifully prepared our family's dinner. As I grew up, it became equally important for me to let my mother see I was a good and responsible boy by doing my homework in front of her. While she did her job preparing dinner, I felt my own sense of pride doing my job at the kitchen table—I felt my own sense of pride seeing how much pride she took in *me*. Of course, as I grew older and excelled in school, the days quickly passed when she would sit by my side and guide me through my homework; as reading and writing and addition and subtraction became literary analysis and algebra, my mother's limited education—she had only the equivalent of an American junior high school education—was of little real help. Yet it was her presence beside me, in that kitchen, that provided the most help: the sound of her rolling and frying the *puris* and the house slowly filling and warming with the smell of the dough rising in the hot oil, the curried scent of the lentils becoming *dal*, and the potatoes, rich with turmeric, stewing in the *shak*, all as her workmanlike steadfastness was consciously attuned to the clock and five-thirty, when my father would always appear in the driveway, and my mother, anticipating his arrival, would begin brewing his *cha*—that was what I suddenly missed when I heard her voice: I missed her presence, calm and purposed and full of pride. And love.

"How are things going down there?"

"Well," I said, removing Sudeep's bong from my desk, "everything's moving right along."

"It's too easy for you, isn't it?"

"I wouldn't say that," I said. "How are you doing? How is everything?"

"I miss you Rohan."

"So do I."

"What?"

"Sorry, I mean, I miss *you* too."

"Is something wrong?"

"No."

"*Dikra*, don't lie to me. I can hear it in your voice."

"Nothing's wrong, mom. I'm just, you know, I'm really busy. It's been a long week and, well…" I spotted *Heart of Darkness* buried beneath some papers on my desk. "I have a paper to write tonight and…"

"Is it that fraternity? They're not taking up too much of your time are they?"

"Mom…"

"Remember why you're there. You're there to learn, not play cricket."

"I know," I said, and I could see her, see her there in the kitchen amidst her *puris* and *shak* and *dal*, staring at the kitchen table talking to me as if she were talking to me, had always talked to me. "I am."

"Are you?"

"Of course."

What she said next caught me completely off guard: "I heard there was a fight down there."

"Who told you that?"

"I knew it. Were you involved?"

"Mom, what are you talking about?"

"*Dikra*, were you involved? I want to know."

"In a fight? *Me*? Of course not. Why—did someone say I was?"

"I'm hearing a lot of things up here, a lot of things I don't like, and—"

"A lot of things like what?" I said, suddenly fearing the worst. She knew. Of course she knew. How could she *not* know? And how could I be so fucking stupid? To think I could keep it a secret—to think I could keep it a secret in the library. Of all places to meet. There're more Indians in the Irvine College library on a Monday night than at a Dell call center during peak hours. What was I *thinking*? Of course she knew. Mothers always do.

"Well, I heard there was a fight, for one. And that one of the Indian fraternities or some Indians down there got in a fight with some Muslims over Halloween costumes or something. It sounded so stupid I didn't believe it but then Seema's mother, you know Seema, she graduated with you and her mother is from your father's village. Seema's very, very pretty by the way, pre-med, Seema's mother told me the same thing and she also said that someone from the Taliban is coming February to recruit fighters and everyone is scared something terrible is going to happen."

"The *Taliban*? Really, mom? Please, stop listening to Seema's mother. She's crazy. The Taliban is not coming to campus to recruit fighters. That's absurd."

"I'm worried about you. That's all. All of the mothers who have kids down there at Irvine, we're hearing things, things we don't like. And you know I worry about you anyway and you never call and your father says you've joined a fraternity—what am I supposed to think?"

"You think I'm going to join the Taliban?"

"Rohan, listen to me. I love you. I will *always* love you. No matter what. So if you feel any pressures down there, any at all, don't be afraid to take a step back. And if you need to come home for a weekend, don't be afraid to come home."

"Mom, *please...*"

"Rohan, I guess what I'm saying is: I want you to do what's best for you. Do you understand?"

"You want me to do what's best for me?"

"Yes, I want you to do what's best for *you*," she said, before adding: "For you and you alone."

Was such a thing even possible?

# 17

"Going somewhere?"

I was, and while I'd been expecting this moment for quite some time, my rehearsed responses suddenly deserted me, my tongue a brick.

"Study," I said, sweating slightly as I gathered my notebooks, my Conrad, my eyes anywhere but at my interlocutor.

"You've been doing an awful lot of studying lately," Sudeep said, supine on the floor of our room, cigarette in hand, packed bong by his side.

"Well," I said, looking down at him, "this is a college."

"You don't like to study here?"

"Too many distractions," I said, trying to lighten the mood, perhaps change the subject and avoid what I know he must've been sensing for quite some time but what, thus far at least, he'd been unable to firmly identify.

"I can leave," he suggested.

"No," I said. "I'm okay. It's good to get some fresh air every once in a while."

"You're studying outside?" he said, and considering this he glanced backwards from his position on the floor and out of our tiny window. "It's dark."

"Actually," I began nervously, "I'm going to the library but, you know, I like the, I mean, I enjoy walking through the park at night. It's nice."

"The library," he said, perplexed. "Where do you go in the library?"

"Basement," I said curtly, moving quickly towards the door. "Sometimes the first-floor reading room if the basement's full."

"Basement?" he said, and I couldn't tell if his befuddlement was an act or real, suspicious or curious.

"Yeah, I mean, I like it. It's quiet, usually empty. I can concentrate there."

"The library basement," he said, eyes firm on me now. "Wait, which library? I heard we have, like, five or something."

"Kapesh," I said, flushing crimson, feeling as if I'd just fumbled on the goal line.

"Well," he said, his smile all too familiar, "have fun."

"I'll do my best," I said.

Outside of our dorm I stood waiting under the starry black sky and stared nervously up at the half-moon as it sat in the inky blackness white and ominous and heart racing I asked two passing people for a cigarette and a light and after they'd gone I stood smoking, hating the fact that I was keeping her waiting, hating the fact that I had to. The door leading to our third-floor stairwell neither opened or closed as I stood there, and while it seemed highly likely that Sudeep had just rolled over and hit the bong by his side when I left, something about his questions—however completely reasonable—left me on edge. After finishing the cigarette I waited another ten minutes, and then I walked very slowly to the library, cutting through Zuckerman Park but meandering a bit, the cool air doing nothing to cut my anxiety.

Kapesh was gloriously lit up, as it always is, a temple of learning that comprises one of the eight original buildings on campus and that, when I'd first seen it in the brightness of day months ago on our family visit, I'd eagerly imagined as a place where I'd become the man I'd always dreamed of being. Was it still that place? Perhaps, though as I stood at the bottom of the stairs scanning the faces moving about, I struggled to reconcile the man I'd always dreamed of being with the man I was now becoming.

Ten minutes later, on the first floor, I stood staring expectantly at the front door, waiting, waiting, and after an eternity but what was probably only two minutes I was in the elevator and covered by a patina of sweat and after running my hands through my hair and closing my eyes I took a deep breath and then I was meandering haphazardly through the third-floor stacks, zigzagging down aisles, stopping at an occasional shelf to withdraw a book to flip absentmindedly through and then peer over my shoulder to study the empty aisles, and while there was no one, not a single student, I could feel him, all of them, their judgement, their disgust, their rage.

When I finally found her, she sat elegantly headscarfed and dutifully huddled over Conrad, a pink highlighter in hand. I'd kept her waiting for perhaps thirty minutes, and as I stood watching her from about ten feet away it wasn't only her beauty that mesmerized, but her ability to concentrate, to keep moving forward despite everything. I knew she'd heard the elevator, that she'd heard my footsteps, that she'd heard the long, meandering path I'd taken, and that her heart, like mine, pounded out of control. Was she ready to be caught? Was I? And what did it say about us if we weren't?

When she finally looked up, her studious concentration shifted into a smile so beautiful I lost balance.

"Hey," I said, approaching her. "Aren't you in my English class?"

Her smile somehow brighter, she read my drenched shirt and hair and the sweat now pouring down my face for the truth they held, and in her radiant green eyes I saw myself not a young man in the throes of transformation, but a coward too long on the run.

"Dr. Green's, right?" she said.

"Yes," I said, glancing left, then right. "How's your paper going?"

The elevator dinged. Doors opened, closed.

"So far, so good," she said, and here she draped her hand over the cubicle wall.

There were footsteps now, moving very, very slowly across the room.

"I bet you're looking for the Conrad criticism," she said.

Not too far off, you could hear a book removed from a shelf.

"I am. Know where I can find it?"

"Two aisles back," she began, loud enough for anyone on the floor to hear, "make a left, three aisles over."

"Thanks," I whispered, hand extended.

"Good luck," she replied, louder this time, hand in mine.

Two weeks later, our intramural cricket team faced the Muslim Students of Irvine. The matchup had been eagerly anticipated since the advent of the league for numerous reasons, the most relevant being (at the time anyway) each of us knew we'd face our strongest competition in the other. And, indeed, when we finally faced off on that baseball-field-turned-cricket-yard, each of us stood against the other with perfect records, undefeated at 3-0. Of course, our athletic perfection aside, there were now many more reasons why our meeting drew our league's first real crowds, reasons that were whispered throughout campus with the fervent excitement of violent expectation—as I stretched alongside my pledges and soon-to-be brothers on that warm Saturday morning, as the low-cut grass, still wet from the morning dew, stuck to my forearms and back and smelled delightfully of promise, I knew like everyone else that there was something more than just a cricket match going on. I wondered, too, if, during the India/Pakistan test matches, cricket matches that would stretch out over five days, whether they too, on both sides, felt as we did under that rising California sun. For most of India's competition originated from Pakistan and Iran, and so, in some ways, in the ways of our fathers, our battle was very much what we knew it to be when we concocted the league out of thin—or smoky—air: it was a continuation of our family and historical traditions, traditions that gave us tremendous pride to celebrate, recreate. On this day, however, this undeniably true thought pained me, for I couldn't help feeling—as I noticed Azada wearing an azure headscarf filing into the stands alongside a group of about twenty headscarfed girls—that we were trapped in a performance of history that served no one, especially us. No, what I secretly wished for as our team lay on our backs in left field with our knees clutched to our chests, was that the game we were assembled to play on this field was not a game played by our fathers or theirs, but the game we wished for our sons.

"Rupee for your thoughts," Sudeep said.

In a surprise, this was the first morning in a long time that he didn't reach for the bong.

"Just trying to clear my mind," I said, before spotting Padma climbing the stands behind third base, behind our bench. She was with about twenty of her soon-to-be sisters, all of them pretty and cool in their lavender sorority T-shirts.

Sudeep saw where my attention was fixed and said, "Later, *bhai*. You'll hit it later."

Across from us in right field, the Muslim Students of Irvine stood in five rows three deep with their hands extended to the air. Though their cricket team was mostly Pakistani (the association itself, the MSI bragged, was *the* most diverse student association on campus, proudly comprised of Muslims from over twenty countries), they'd decided, long before the announced arrival of al-Sadr and certainly long before our Halloween fiasco, to wear the traditional headwear of Arab Muslims, headwear that, at the time, was most commonly associated with Yasser Arafat, then president of the PLO, or Palestinian Liberation Organization, a group President Bush had labeled as terrorists. Nonetheless, for many Arabs in the Middle East, the PLO and Yasser Arafat represented freedom—or at least the fight for it—and so the keffiyeh, Arafat's headscarf, signaled the same. For too many of us, however, the keffiyeh signaled something else entirely, and the fact the MSI's cricket team had consciously chosen such controversial headwear—and colored it camouflaged crimson to boot—was seen not as a gesture of freedom or unity but a provocation designed to intimidate, distract, and antagonize.

Like we always did before a match, we huddled by our bench, our arms linked tightly together and our heads almost touching. Darpan, his breath reeking of scotch and his dark, furrowed brow dripping with sweat, eyed us menacingly. I didn't know if he was hungover or hammered—or both.

"This is it," he slurred. "It starts here. Now. On this field we let them know who's in charge. On this field," and here Darpan stamped the third-baseline dirt, "we let them know that *we're* in control. Look at them over there, with their fucking hats."

"I believe they're called keffiyehs," said Pratek, our bespectacled pre-med pledge brother.

"Who the fuck are you? The fucking politically correct police? Come here," Darpan said, grabbing Pratek by his polo and bringing his bespectacled nose inches from his face. "I will skull fuck you the moment this match ends if you don't get your shit together. Don't you ever correct a brother. Ever. I don't give a flying fuck what their hats are called. I don't care if they're turbans or sombreros or fucking helmets. Because you know what I see, when I look at them? Do you, wise-ass?"

Pratek shook his head in dumb, terrified silence.

"No? I see a fucking terrorist," Darpan said. "I see someone who hates America. I see someone who hates *India*. I see someone who wouldn't lose a minute of sleep if our entire country were wiped off the face of the earth. And you know what? That's what I want *you* to see," and here he drilled two fingers against Pratek's temple. "That's what I want *all of you* fucks to see. Because if we want to win, that's how we must approach our enemy. With hate in our veins. You hear me?"

Thinking it was a rhetorical question, we just stared at Darpan.

"I said, do you hear me?"

Half-hearted agreement.

"I said, do you hear me?"

This time our agreement was slightly louder and a bit more hostile.

"I said," Darpan screamed, "*do you fucking hear me?*"

Finally our accord erupted with genuine bravado and something dangerously akin to hate and this sent Darpan jumping and stomping the dirt and eventually so did we follow his ludicrous lead and suddenly a chant broke out with someone asking "What time is it?" and everyone responding in unison "Game time!" over and over until more than a few spectators seated behind our bench joined in, their feet thumping hard against the wooden bleachers, and soon the entire stands behind us were banging and kicking and cheering and as our huddle broke and we raced onto the field their cheers felt like warm permission, raucous approval, and I spotted Padma laughing and high fiving one of her sorority sisters and then she was waving at us taking position and noticing me noticing her she offered a slow, playful wave, a slight turn of the wrist, and even though I couldn't see her I could feel Azada's careful gaze from the opposite side of the field. Deeply embarrassed I feigned cool or concentration or both and just grimly nodded my head.

Though traditional cricket rules dictated that someone new bowled—or pitched—to every new batter, given the unsurprising dearth of pitching talent the league decided to mandate only two bowlers per team, per innings. This helped to ensure, at a minimum, that the quality of bowling was somewhat high and our league didn't turn into a home run derby. Furthermore, because a cricket match might last for hours, especially among professional teams, the college limited each game to one innings each. Therefore, each team received only one full run of ten batters to score as much as they could; after they were all out, they had to take the field to bowl and field. Thus far, this somewhat shortened format helped expedite our games, keeping the average time around seventy minutes and the longest—our blowout win over Delta Theta Phi—going just under two hours. And not only did it help speed up the game, it provided the college, and our fathers, with the necessary illusion that we were all, first and foremost, diligent students primarily concerned with academics—and not gallivanting young men with idle time.

I met Darpan between the wickets in the dirt infield. Given the competition, he had decided to bowl alongside me. Outside of practice, this was only his second time bowling to a real opponent and I wondered, reasonably, what his expectations were—and not just for him.

"How you doing?" he asked, his boozy breath rank in the warm sun.

"I'm ready," I said, taking a step back. "You?"

"I'm counting on you today." He slapped my arm. "We're going to need the best you have."

Behind him, cricket balls soared through the air, falling across the clear blue sky like crimson meteors. "No problem."

"Listen," he whispered, "depending on how this goes, we might have to rough them up a little, know what I mean?"

I nodded.

"Good. Depending on how I scratch my balls, you throw inside. Once means somewhat. Twice a little more. Three times, like this," and here he scratched his balls, digging into the side of his crotch before making three obvious and undeniably obscene gestures, "that means I want you to take him out. Got it?"

"Why do I have to do this?"

"First and foremost, because you're a fucking pledge. Got me?"

"Yes sir."

"But more importantly, and you know this, you have more control than I do. I try going inside and I'm liable to send the ball into the fucking stands. I might take out that beauty queen who's been licking your balls all year. What's her name, Padma? No, you're the only one here who can do this—and I'm not saying you have to," he said, while clearly doing so, "but *if* the time comes, it *has* to be *you*."

"Got it."

"Don't look so fucking scared. Besides, if anything *does* go down, you're going to wind up the hero."

"Hero," I repeated, puzzled.

"And you know what happens to heroes, right?"

I glanced quickly behind the MSI's bench and spotted Azada, her eyes intensely focused on the field, on me.

"They get *anything* they want," Darpan said, again slapping me hard on the arm before skipping backwards and calling for a ball.

After he caught one he mouthed the word "anything" before lofting it to me.

I stared at the ball in my hands. Needless to say, the last thing I wanted was to be a hero—at least as Darpan dreamed. I wanted to win the game, I wanted to support my teammates, my brothers, and if striking out some batters or hitting the game winning shot made me a hero—a *real* hero—well, that was great. That was part of the game. But what Darpan suggested was something else entirely. Pitching inside in cricket was, much like baseball, a necessary strategy. There was territory to protect, signals to send. And there was a reason professionals wore heavy padding when they stood at the wickets. Given the size and speed of the ball, people could—and occasionally did—get seriously hurt. Balls have been known to skip unusually high and "accidentally" strike an eye. And so, if need truly be, following that strategy here and now was understandable. Of course, that wasn't really the strategy I was being asked to follow. What I was being asked, what I was being told, was something else entirely, and because of that a feeling of sheer powerlessness washed over me, powerlessness and disappointment and shame, even as I knew I held my fate in my hands.

I vowed, then, to pitch the game of my life. Simple enough. The better I bowled, the less likely any shenanigans would occur, the more likely we win the game like men, like gentlemen. And at the start, things seemed to go that way. Incredibly, the first three batters Darpan and I faced—supposedly their strongest—got out relatively quickly. Eight runs were scored in about fifteen minutes, but within the context of a cricket match, especially one where the teams were closely matched, that was totally acceptable. We knew going in that we would need upwards of thirty runs to win the game, and so as their score was tallied up, I took comfort that, at the very least, we were handling batters who were theoretically considered their strongest and therefore—we assumed—could do the most damage. As per the rules, Darpan and I alternated pitching throughout that early part of the game, one of us fielding while the other pitched, and though we undoubtedly threw some terrible pitches—one of Darpan's was nailed over the left field fence—we were eventually saved by some superb fielding, including a diving outfield grab by Sudeep that sent our side of the stands—now packed with over forty people, some of which were brazenly passing bottles of booze—to scream uproariously.

It was then that we got into a little trouble. Darpan was pitching as their fifth batter came up. Their fourth batter stood at the wicket facing me while the new batter, a stout, overweight kid with long black hair who chewed tobacco and crudely spit its crimson juice in the dirt infield, stood with his back to me and ready to face Darpan. Like most players, he wore heavy gloves and padding that covered his forearms from any stray pitches alongside shin pads, but because he was so stout—he was maybe 5'7"—the shin pads came up past his knees and he more closely resembled a hockey goalie than a cricketer. It was as if one big pad had come to stand before the wicket, and I could tell, even before he did the ludicrously incredible, that Darpan was irritated—and that we were possibly in trouble.

The batsman stood beside the wicket for a very long moment, taking in the high noon sun, so crimson and pure in the clear blue sky. He stared up at it, inviting its warmth, but also inviting something else, purposely so, for after a moment of this some catcalls from our side of the stands began to rain down—sharp whistles, playful taunts, a growing sense of unease. It was then that he did it, a la Babe Ruth. Foolishly and, because of his height, clownishly, he raised his bat and pointed high up towards the outfield, indicating his intentions. At his gesture the MSI side of the stands burst into raucous applause, and there was some laughter in there too, for you got the sense, merely by looking at the pudgy batsman, that he was something of a clown, a joker, someone who had probably been the butt of too many fat jokes throughout his young life and so, in self-defense, had shrewdly decided to turn the joke out from himself and into a kind of armor—or weapon.

Had this been any other game, had this been any other time in history, had he been one of us, perhaps we too might've burst into laughter at his pudgy gesticulation. I almost wanted to. He was so short and fat and the equipment he wore so unwieldy it seemed improbable that he would be able to hit the ball at all, let alone over the outfield fence. Nonetheless, when he raised his bat, I could see Darpan's face darken. The rising temperatures and early game action had already taken a toll on his buzz—or hangover—and he had long ago drenched his polo shirt; his front and back numbers were black with sweat and so too his armpits. All morning he'd been continuously wiping his brow, and at the sight of the pudgy batter pointing towards the heavens Darpan wiped his brow once more and then spit disgustedly onto the ground.

"Whenever you're ready," Darpan called.

"Bring it on, Hadji," the batsman said.

At the word Hadji something altogether menacing washed over Darpan. Hadji. I hadn't heard that term since middle school, when, as one of the few Indian Americans there, the white kids would always tease me for being so smart by calling me not Einstein or genius or smarty-pants but Hadji or Gandhi or towelhead. Among other things. Hadji was a cartoon character, Johnny Quest's trusted sidekick—though a sidekick who talked with an accent and wore a turban and clearly embodied an exotified Indian stereotype. I always felt less than whenever one of my white classmates uttered that dreaded name, as if, by invoking that cartoon's cruel stereotype, I was reduced to something other than what I was—or hoped to be. Well, clearly Darpan was well-versed in the same painful ridicule, for upon hearing Hadji he flashed me a real hard look, one I'd been hoping to avoid.

"I'm going to hit this ball all the way to the Taj Mahal," the batsman said, this time loud enough for some in the stands to hear. Those who heard on the MSI side let loose some guarded laughter or harried him on with taunts of their own; those who heard on our side began whistling loudly, booing vociferously, and calling him fatso.

"I'm going to hit this ball so far you're going to need to call one of your Indian call centers to find out where it landed," he said over the escalating din, before adding, "You hear me Hadji?"

"Let's go fat boy!" Barun screamed from deep in the outfield. "Stop wasting time! The buffet's going to close!"

"Afraid they might run out of curry?" the batsman replied.

"If you get there first, *yes*," Darpan said. "Now shut the fuck up so we can play this game."

"Don't tell him to shut the fuck up," said the batsman's teammate, positioned at the opposite wicket, bat in hand.

"*Shut the fuck up. Shut the fuck up before I call the FBI and tell them I suspect terrorist activity. In fact, I do suspect terrorist activity. Hey, anyone got a cell phone?"

"Fuck you."

"Fuck *you*."

"Towelhead."

"*Towelhead*? You're wearing a fucking towel! Gimme that thing so I can wipe my ass, bitch ass motherfucker."

"Hey," I shouted, spying Azada listening nervously from the stands. "Can we get on with this please?"

"Yeah," the pudgy batsman said, spitting tobacco juice as he dug into his batting stance. "I'm about to put on a hitting clinic."

"More like an eating clinic," Darpan said.

"This one's for you, Hadji."

"Bring it," Darpan said.

He took about ten steps back from where he stood and settled into his pitching stance: feet locked close together, ball cradled in both hands and tucked tightly under his chin, eyes fixed hard at the wicket and the batsman. A hush fell quickly over the stands, the field, and our respective benches. Because I stood directly behind the batter, I could feel the intensity of Darpan's gaze, the hate of his concentration. Was he going to do it? Was he going to do it so I wouldn't have to?

Darpan dropped his hands to his waist and in the day's blinding clarity sunlight glinted off the crimson ball clutched tightly there and after taking a deep breath he strode forward, almost skipping, his arm winding, cocking slowly backward and now whipping, circling forwards, the ball rocketing down into the hard dirt infield where it ricocheted quickly up towards the batsman, close but not nearly close enough, the ball rising from the earth like some delicious offering, a divine gift, and from where I stood I could see Darpan's wide eyes flash and quiet with fear, and then there was only the sound, that clear, sharp, blissfully perfect sound when the ball runs flush against the flat center of a wooden bat, a sweet, melodious crack not unlike a baseball bat crushing a perfect pitch, and in the slow silence that followed we all watched as the crimson ball rose higher and higher, climbing across the pale blue until it looked like there were two suns in the sky.

Because our rules dictated that anything over the fence count as six runs, the batters switched wickets three times, and every time the pudgy batsman touched a wicket he spit crimson tobacco juice at its base like some feral dog marking its territory while clapping his hands sharply in tally, his crimson, camouflaged keffiyeh rising behind him like a flag of war, victory. Rowdy applause filled the air, applause ignited by a real sense of pride and purpose, justification and revenge. For not the first time that day I wondered just how many people gathered together were actually there Halloween night, there when it all started, though I knew it had started long, long before. Still, as the applause fell around us, you'd to have been a fool to believe that the rambunctious cheering was based strictly on performance.

Well, I thought, as the pudgy batsman ended his victory lap and stood facing me at the wicket, as Darpan, standing tall in the high noon sun, eyed me intensely and then brazenly reached for his crotch, it was now my turn to take center stage and perform. I had a duty to do, apparently, a duty I'd signed up for, or perhaps been born into. Either way, with Azada looking on, I foolishly wondered if I could simply drop the ball

I now held in my hands and walk off stage. I also wondered where the stage ended and real life began.

Darpan ran his hand over his crotch before digging in, clawing once, then twice.

I waited anxiously for what I knew was coming next, but it never did.

At least not yet.

The batsman stood at the wicket, eyeing me confidently.

Then, as if his prior excellence had somehow been forgotten, he gestured once more with his bat.

The crowd, still enraptured, reached a rabid, frenzied crescendo.

I looked past him to Darpan, and I'd be lying if a small part of me didn't want him to do it.

Nothing.

I took several steps backwards and held the ball to my chest. I closed my eyes, took a deep breath, and tried to block out the crowd. When I opened them I couldn't help but spy Azada as she stood nervously—silently—amidst the delirium and when her eyes found mine they momentarily softened with hope or relief or simply love before returning to a gracious state of anxiety. I waited for the batsman to take position, and then I was racing forward, my arm winding back before uncoiling rapidly forward, the ball spinning tightly out of my hand and firing down towards the dirt inches from his feet and when it struck it careened upwards, angling not straight at the wicket but hard inside towards his shins and knees.

He'd either been expecting it or had guessed and gotten lucky, for before I knew what was happening the ball had fired behind me like a looping line drive. The backstop was still in place, and because the pudgy batter was a little behind second base when he'd made contact, the ball shot past me and skipped about twenty yards before crashing into the backstop. Pratek was supposed to be fielding that space, but when the ball shot past me it shot past him too, and in his excitement he slipped on the grass, losing his glasses and tumbling to the ground. The ball clanged into the fence, ricocheting before Pratek regained footing, and it was only because the batsman lumbered so that they managed only four runs.

Once again, the batsman stood facing me, his labored breathing now wracked with violent, seizured coughing. He leaned exhausted on the wicket, apoplectic, careful not to crush it under his bulk while simultaneously using his bat for balance as he spit chunks of phlegm and crimson tobacco juice on the dirt. The MSI side of the stands had tauntingly begun to chant "Blowout" in the slow cadence of "Asshole," a chant typically reserved for sports referees who've blown an obvious call, and as the word rose and fell throughout the air my burgeoning irritation sent me peering into the stands. It only took a moment to find her there, bouncing atop her feet and singing playfully along, and for an instant my aggravation burned even hotter, as surrounded by friends in headscarves and joined by keffiyehed players on the field, she resembled not my clandestine desire but rather what too many on this field and across campus and, rightly or wrongly, across America viewed as our enemy.

And for that I wanted to destroy them.

Strangely, or perhaps not, perhaps completely rationally, that thought was suddenly supplanted by something remarkably close to relief, even joy, for I knew what she'd been going through—what they'd *all* been going through—since 9/11;

indeed, what they'd all been enduring and what, to various degrees, anyone born in America of parents from somewhere else inevitably has to deal with, that strange, ugly feeling of not belonging, of not being American, or not American enough, that enigmatic feeling that you will never quite belong, no matter how much money you earn or how perfect your English. And so to see and hear her there lost in the moment afforded me the delight of seeing her suddenly liberated by history, temporarily free of the powers conspiring against her. For the briefest of moments, I could hear her in their chant, could hear her gentle voice screaming "Blowout" as if it was the only thing that mattered, and I thought of that great afternoon in Zuckerman Park when the two of us discussed college, Conrad, our lives. That their joy was at my expense didn't matter. I was happy for her. I was happy for them.

Of course, my sentiments were mine alone, feelings so alien that, were I to share them with anyone, treason would be the charge and banishment not penalty enough. No one had to tell me that. Refocused on the field and the game at hand, I saw Darpan do what I expected him to—what he had to. Once, twice, and finally three times he dug into his crotch, holding himself there with a vulgar obviousness that signaled *fuck you* to anyone remotely paying any attention.

The instant I took my pitching stance, everyone stiffened and quieted around me.

As if they knew what was coming.

As if this was what they'd truly been waiting for.

I wanted to believe that this was just about the game, the context of the game, that this was simply sportsmanship, the logical extension of desire and competition. I wanted to believe these things because I needed to, I needed something pure to find faith. But I knew otherwise. With the ball clutched tightly to my chest and my shirt drenched with sweat, I surveyed the field and studied the players' faces, Darpan's and Pratek's and Sudeep's, and the batsman's too, every face worn and taut and perhaps even afraid. And Padma and Azada, they too, silent and rapt, their beautiful faces belying centuries of hope, ghosts, pain.

I could feel their eyes.

I could feel my father's.

And because of that I did what was asked.

# 15

As only it can, history subsumed the brawl that erupted that day, overshadowing our disgraceful performance with real tragedy and horrific, incomprehensible violence.

Our actions made the front page of *New College* that following Monday, with a sizable headline reading "Intramural Mayhem" and, beneath it, in smaller letters, the contemplative subtitle "Racial Tensions at Irvine?" Mercifully, there were no pictures (I'd had nightmares all weekend long of my face plastered across the front page, a front page that would've been mailed to my mother and driven her to the crematorium) and no actual names other than that of our fraternity and the MSI, as there was no one from the newspaper at our little game and few people on the inside actually talking. It was strictly unnamed sources and secondhand reporting, fake news, arguably, as word spread across campus late Saturday night of all that went down—and speculation exploded of any possible connections to the Halloween brawl and, even more provocatively, to the looming visit of al-Sadr. The article was less than three hundred words (typical for our student newspaper), and though there were quite a bit of inaccuracies and conjecture in the reporting—Did someone really get their jaw wired shut? Did someone really pull a gun?—it still managed to illuminate some level of truth and, more pressingly, what I had anxiously hoped to keep quiet: that a fight between two ethnic groups had occurred on campus—and perhaps not for the first time.

Given that front page news, our editorial page struck a surprisingly nuanced and understanding tone when it decided to comment on the incident on the back page of Monday's edition. In an editorial titled "Patience in an Impatient Time," the page wrote that because "of 9/11, racial tensions across America have generally been on unsteady ground, especially as it pertains to people from the Middle East broadly and India in general. Furthermore, because of the controversy surrounding al-Sadr's imminent arrival and because of the heated rhetoric surrounding President Bush's march to war, it isn't entirely surprising that we see young men and women struggling to understand or come to terms with the political realities of their world, especially the children of immigrants or immigrants themselves who may still have familial or cultural ties to the very places our current administration vilifies or holds guilty of terrorist activity. Though we certainly do not condone violence on campus and expect every student and faculty member to stringently adhere to our code of conduct, and though we would urge all groups involved in last weekend's disappointing enterprise to begin working together with the help of the college to seek resolution to their differences, we do understand that these are confusing times—indeed, historic times—and so to ignore that context would be to misunderstand our current moment. For this is perhaps the first generation in sixty years, since the attack on Pearl Harbor, where young men and women have seen their soil invaded and their brethren murdered—and on television no less. To forget 9/11 and its possible emotional, intellectual, cultural, and even spiritual impact would be to simplify and even ignore reality."

That Monday morning on campus, fueled by the newstory, the editorial, and perhaps most distressingly, rumor, campus felt decidedly different. Charged. Supercharged. Had the fight not occurred, it would've been a short, relaxing week leading up to Thanksgiving break, a week that typically saw campus quickly drain of students as they ditched classes early to head north to the Bay Area or south to San Diego in search of a respite from the crucible of the closing quarter. Campus was closed Thursday and Friday because of the holiday, and I, like everyone I knew, had been eagerly looking forward to going home for some much needed rest and home cooking.

At least before the fight. Now, with our fraternity's name on the front page of the paper for fighting, what I wanted even more than home cooking was to hide myself in the cocoon of Fremont so as to let the drama I'd been central to die down (if such a thing was possible). What I also wanted, and what I desperately realized I needed, was a chance to get some air and a clearer perspective on where my life was going. Academics had taken such a backseat to my campus life—and, more specifically, to Azada—that I could honestly say I felt less and less like myself—the self measured by academic achievement and the parental satisfaction derived therein—and more like someone struggling to hold on to something that had once seemed fundamental but that now, inexplicably, seemed facile and juvenile. Quite suddenly, there were much more pressing concerns, demands rooted not in the falsity of grades or the tenuous illusion of some ideal future but the strange, desperate urgency of the heart and soul, the here and now. That these concerns were so in conflict with my initial academic mission here at Irvine was something I would've never expected or imagined. I knew I was betraying not only my parents but myself, yet still I couldn't—or wouldn't—extract myself from everything I knew my life was becoming—that *I* was becoming.

That Monday morning on campus, on my way to Dr. Xian's Chemistry class—yet another battle I was losing—walking past what felt like the entire campus staring at the front or back page of the student paper, I could feel their eyes and hear their whispers and, oddly, read their excited, proud approval. There were more than a few nods of the head and winks of the eye as people I passed peered up from their paper and, either because they thought they recognized me as one of the culprits from the rumors or simply because my skin color indicated someone antagonistic to the increasingly despised MSI, they signaled their understanding—and support—of some mutual, existential struggle. And not just from Indians, no, this was students of all races. In Chem class, as I tried to sit inconspicuously in the back among the Indians—and as Padma winked conspiratorially across the vast lecture hall from her long held, front-row seat—it felt, as people slowly and then quickly turned to acknowledge my presence, that applause might erupt, so ecstatic were the faces facing me. From *both* sides of the room. American-born, foreign-born, Indian or Asian, winking, nodding, smiling, even pointing or offering high five, their esteemed attention seemed appropriate for a celebrity or hero, not me. But it was. It was. For the first time in my life, I tasted what it was like to be popular. What it was like to be famous. *In*famous. Uncomfortable certainly, yet still, for the briefest of moments, as the restless class struggled to attention while Dr. Xian strode towards the lectern, I understood that, for all of the potentially damaging consequences of my actions, the benefits offered a seductive power of their own. I wanted to flee to Fremont to escape my actions even as I wanted to bask in them for the fame it conferred. It was absurd.

And very short lived.

For midway through Dr. Xian's lecture the entire Indian side of the classroom began collectively checking their cell phones. Intermittent buzzing and humming could be heard throughout the room as the roughly one hundred Indian students began touching their thighs to quell the sporadic buzzing or, after thinking it finished only to hear and feel it restart again, extracting their phones to secretly see who it was. This was long before texting came to supplant practically all voice-to-voice communication, back before the advent of the modern smart phone and its ubiquitous and invasive usage destroyed our capacity to focus on anything for more than seven seconds, and so cell phones had only one purpose: to actually communicate through speech. A task impossible in our current confines. Nonetheless, as people around the room began reading their caller's name or the calls they'd missed, you could feel a palpable sense of confusion and unease scorch the room. Like everyone else's, my phone was furiously abuzz, and when I fished it free I saw my father's name flashing before me. He knew my class schedule, he knew where I was—or, at the very least, where I should be—and so to see his name there (and his two missed calls preceding it) drove my heart to my throat.

En mass the entire Indian section of Dr. Xian's lecture hall rose and, cell phones in hand, quickly fled the room. A polite, dutiful group, we moved as quietly as we could, but our shuffled, hurried footsteps and our unanimous exit caused Dr. Xian to stop his lecture and study us with irritated bemusement. Even Padma, from the front row, quietly but quickly excused herself. He would understand later why we left how we left; indeed, the next time we attended his class we took some time to share with him why we had to do what we did and, understanding, Dr. Xian kindly repeated everything he knew we missed in an English most of us had now gotten used to.

Outside, other Indians had slipped free of their classes and they too were on their phones, their faces shifting from surprise to confusion to horror and back again. There were probably one hundred of us standing outside of Engineering Hall, and had you been an administrator passing by you might've thought we were participating in our own strange fire drill. The words people kept repeating over and over were India, Mumbai, Bombay. Some of us, especially those on student visas from India, broke into sobs, their panicked, powerless faces struck by something incomprehensible.

My father answered on the first ring.

"Where were you?"

"Class. What's up?"

"Are you okay?"

I decided to play that one straight. "Yes. Why?"

"Are you okay? Is everyone there okay?"

"What—yes—why? What's going on?"

"Get to a television as quickly as possible. There's been a terrorist attack."

And then I got it. I knew what had happened.

"Is everyone okay?" I asked. "Have you heard from anyone?"

"We're trying. We're calling."

"How's mom?" I asked, for it was her voice I now desperately longed to hear.

"Just get someplace safe, okay. I'll call you later."

"Okay."

"Rohan," he said, his voice broken by fear. "Be careful."

Back at the fraternity house, our collective silence was deafening as we switched between CNN and Wolf News. There were no bongs being passed, no blunts or bottles, only our stony, sober silence, horrified at the carnage flashing across the screen, at the sight of Mumbai under attack and the distinct possibility that people we knew and loved were possibly dead. As of that moment, there were already over 100 reported dead and 200 wounded. Based on the reporting thus far, there had been three coordinated bombing attacks by roughly ten men from an as-of-yet unnamed terrorist group. Nonetheless, Wolf News speculated that the group had ties to Pakistan and the Taliban and had, as their ultimate goal, the dream of creating a Muslim state throughout Southeast Asia, a state governed by Sharia Law and strict adherence to Islam. Whether there were connections to al-Qaeda was unknown yet, though speculation was rampant.

Whether the attack had anything to do with the heavily contested Kashmir region of India was unknown yet, though there too speculation abounded. What was known and what was being broadcast for the entire world to see was that at least four bombs had gone off in central Mumbai, one at the famous and iconic Royal Crown Hotel and Tower, a five-star hotel, one at Chhatrapati Shivaji Terminus, a central train station, one at the Naik Trident Hotel, closely located to the Crown, and also, disgustingly, one at the Asha Hospital, a women's and children's hospital not far from the two hotels. Smoke rose in black spires throughout the city, and more than once did I think of 9/11, of the bewildering incomprehensibility of that day, a day remade today. It felt as if the entire world were under attack, was at war, and perhaps it was, perhaps it had always been, perhaps it needed to be.

Some of the terrorists were still alive, men with the kinds of beards we'd seen too often on our evening news and even here at Irvine, and in the heart of sweltering Mumbai the remaining few stood defiantly firing machine guns at anyone they could target, their maniacal cries of "Allahu Akbar" echoing above the staccato gunfire like some deranged prayer of the brainwashed, uneducated, principled, pious. Wolf News covered all of this unflinchingly, like some remorseless chronicler of history. Or some supreme creator of it.

I thought then of the Royal Crown Hotel, a place my father loved visiting whenever we were in India. He loved their *cha*, even though, in its Indian five-star quality, it looked and tasted more like some anglicized version of what real Indians would properly consider tea. Nonetheless, he loved bringing all of us there and getting a table and sitting inside the cool, air-conditioned dining room, an Indian who'd made a life for himself in America back now visiting, back now a success. The dining room would always be filled with them, businessmen and locals but mostly tourists, deshis who'd long left the subcontinent and sought the West for their economic dreams and, having earned them, come back with their families to enjoy the best their country had to offer. It was an iconic hotel, nearly 100 years old, a hotel that, as my father told me every time we sat in the chandeliered dining room, had predated Indian independence and been visited by The Beatles and Bill Clinton among others.

And now it was under attack.

Now it was in smoke.

And all we could do was watch.

Like on 9/11.

# 14

Thanksgiving. On that morning, I came downstairs to find my mother in the kitchen and my sister diligently seated at the kitchen table doing homework. A banal, domestic scene, yet strangely I felt a crippling sense of relief, order, as if everything was finally where it should be. Myself included. My mother had been singing alongside a Bollywood song, the house filling with her gentle, high-pitched voice, and like I'd done all my life I followed that voice from my bedroom down the stairs and into the kitchen where, like I had a thousand times before, I found her tending her home. *Our* home. When she asked what

I wanted for breakfast, when her almond eyes shifted from the *shak* she was preparing for tonight's feast to fall upon me, there was no hint of suspicion or doubt, disappointment or anger—only a love I was unsure I still deserved.

Up until that moment I didn't realize how badly I'd missed her—even though I'd missed her, I did. Still, there was something calming in seeing her there in the kitchen, something beautiful about hearing her warm, sonorous voice filling the house, something remarkable in seeing her perform the mundane so assiduously. So dizzy did I suddenly become that I had to grip one of the kitchen chairs to steady myself, my head abuzz with the shame of my actions, the disgrace of my desires.

Behind the kitchen table, tucked into a corner of the kitchen, a makeshift temple sat atop a small side table, a giant teakwood framed picture of Shiva adorned by a garland of fresh white roses and surrounded by smaller pictures of deities, Ganpati, baby Krishna, the voluptuous goddess Laxmi, each of whom had fresh rose petals at their feet. Today, surrounding the pictures, cotton balls dipped in *ghee* burned in tiny silver bowls, and I knew from the surfeit of homemade candles that this was more than the weekly *puja*—something my mother typically did every Saturday before we all breakfasted together. This was a prayer for Mumbai's fallen, for Mumbai itself, her city, the city of her youth. On the car ride from SFO my father had informed me of a second cousin who'd been working inside the Crown when one of the bombs exploded. As of last night, he was still technically considered missing, but we knew, we knew. I inhaled the buttery smell of the candles and studied the deities, Ganpati's elephant trunk, Shiva, blue and menacing, and like a prayer I wished to feel, to be, as I had for most of my life: unquestioning, dutiful, good.

I asked my mother for pancakes.

Later, as the house began filling with cousins, *kakas, kakis,* and friends, we tried watching the football game—Dallas manhandling a Dan Marino-less Miami—anything to help us focus on something normal, meaningless, safe. The males, nine or ten of us including my father and a few older adults, were all in the living room, the men drinking Johnny Walker Black with water or soda or ice, and there were salted cashews and Indian Hot Mix and pistachios and samosas with mint chutney and someone had brought store-made guacamole and chips and salsa, and if you were under thirty you were sitting on the floor beside the adult men as a sign of respect, not because there weren't enough chairs. This was something I'd seen my own father do in India, especially in his tiny village in Gujarat. When a favorite *kaka* of his would come to visit, or when we would go to visit a distant uncle, he and I would always sit on the hardwood floor beside this *kaka*—my actions more childish mimicry than actual respect—and listen as he regaled us with comic, absurd tales of growing up in third-world poverty or colonial India. So it was there and so, on holidays like Thanksgiving or Divali especially, when people from the deshi community were visiting, it was here.

So too with the women. Our kitchen buzzed with the nine or ten *kakis* and cousins who'd arrived, a collective hive of unbridled energy that swarmed from American dish—mashed potatoes, biscuits, turkey, gravy—to Indian dish—*puri, shak,* curry, tandoori chicken, *papad*—querying my mother and kindly accepting her command as if she were the queen bee. Time after time I'd hear a cousin in her thirties ask my mother to let her do it, asking her in Gujarati to kindly sit down, that it was her honor to help, her joy, and my laughing, smiling mother, thanking her kindly, would amuse the women in Gujarati with a story from her youth in Mumbai, of her own mother, of what she would do if someone asked her to sit down in her own house. And with her husband and only son needing to be fed no less. Oh the shame!

I couldn't completely understand the Gujarati, but I'd seen the scene and heard the stories—had, indeed, experienced them firsthand when visiting my grandmother in India—enough over the years to know that this back and forth, much like the back and forth between my father and his favorite uncles or elders, was part of the ritual, the tradition, the order of things. In the kitchen my sister did as she was told in exactly the same way my mother had done as she was told, much like I—seated at the foot of my father and careful not to provide too much detail about college so as to incriminate myself—did as I was told. When one of the men needed a drink, it was my task, first and foremost. When one of my *kakas* needed some food, it was my job to bring the plate closer, to get them a napkin, a fork, some chutney. When they inevitably asked about college— which they did, in their turn—it was never anything serious, never anything about the fraternity or girls. Even though they knew—or believed they did—what was happening down at Irvine. Even though the scandalous rumors had made it all the way here to Fremont. Even though I know they were curious— especially about the girls.

Nonetheless, because decorum dictated otherwise, the topic of girls—let alone sex—was completely off the table, unheard of, as if, by pretending it didn't exist, we wouldn't do it. Or that by ignoring the subject we'd somehow ignore our desires— at least until marriage. Mercifully, or not, marriage was not brought up either. No, the conversation was only polite, only on the surface, primarily concerned with academics, though even there it was so gentle it was almost nonexistent. For what needed to be said? There wasn't an adult male in the room with less than a master's degree and so, if they could do it, certainly their American-born children, children born with advantages incomprehensible to them as children—foremost among them hot, running water—should have no problems at college—let alone life. It was expected, like getting my *kaka* some chutney.

Yes, it was polite—until it wasn't. By halftime the game had failed to provide the necessary distraction and one of my *kakas*, already on his third scotch, told me to put on CNN. With a window into still smoldering Mumbai, my father, cousins, and *kakas* began the commentary, their disgust shifting between English and Gujarati profanity, their analysis vigorously supplementing the reporting and latest from President Bush. The terrorist attack had lasted a total of three days, ending early this morning, and current reporting suggested a total of 164 deaths and over three hundred wounded or critically injured. As was originally suspected, a Pakistani-based Islamic terrorist organization was responsible, and as of that day all but one of the terrorists had been killed in the ensuing gunfight. The man who'd been caught, Aalam Kasab, was very young, my age or perhaps a year or two older, and as CNN repeatedly showed pictures of him firing his rifle I couldn't help hate him, and not only for what he'd done. He was rumored to be Pakistani, though there were some suspicions he'd been trained by al-Qaeda in

Afghanistan. He was caught almost twenty-four hours ago, prompting President Bush, once Kasab's identity had been verified, to issue a statement regarding the horrific attack. President Bush concluded his remarks accordingly: "The leaders of India can know that nations around the world support them in the face of this assault on human dignity. And as the people of the world's largest democracy recover from these attacks, they can count on the people of the world's oldest democracy to stand by their side."

As CNN continued its reporting from Mumbai, as the television journalists and pundits argued and dissected Bush's words and implications—"War with Pakistan? Well, what about their nuclear arsenal? What about President Musharraf?"—the men in my living room applauded his words and felt invigorated by his steadfastness. Finally, one or maybe all of the men in my living room had said, someone is standing up to those people. Finally, went the embittered, heartbroken refrain, those people would get what they deserved.

And as I listened or tried to follow along the only thing I could really think of was Azada. Yes, fearfully I was thinking of *her* household this Thanksgiving and what *her* father and uncles and cousins were saying. Were they furiously engaged in similar discussions? Were they too denouncing the 9/11 terrorist attacks as well as the most recent ones in Mumbai? Were they decrying the slaughter of innocent civilians? Perhaps. For if they were anything like Azada, they too were struggling with things well beyond their control: the workings of madmen halfway across the globe, insane, crazed men who'd hijacked history, their identities, their sense of self and, equally or perhaps more troublingly, the world's ideas of themselves, the way others feared or believed or accepted them—yes, through no fault of their own they'd been hijacked and everything they'd once took enormous pride in—their religion and culture, their language and history—had suddenly and explicably come under attack by forces hostile not only to the new lives they'd struggled—like all immigrants—to embrace in America, but the inevitable march of modernity, that grand, terrifying, utopian future that's promised to every new generation but bitterly withheld by the last.

Of course, I also had to wonder if they were perhaps having a completely different conversation, one in which they somehow rationalized these horrific attacks by articulating—in their own language, much like my father and uncles were conversing in theirs—the deep political, economic, and militaristic engagement the West has long had in the Middle East, ever since colonial superpowers Britain and France arbitrarily mapped what we now consider the Middle East in the hopes of preserving their economic and political influence. Could Azada's family—could she—look upon these current events with anything *close* to surprise? Given everything the average person living in the Middle East has had to endure for the last 50 years—circumstances easily attributable, for the right arguer, to the West—could anyone be surprised at the rage and violence now exploding from the heart—or was it the fringes?—of Islam? And what about the presence—as Osama bin Laden repeatedly denounced, provided we even seriously considered his deranged ramblings—of American military bases in Mecca and Medina, the holiest places in all of Islam? What about *that*?

I couldn't help thinking of Conrad and the heated discussions in Dr. Green's class, of the bravery Azada displayed in the face of what she knew was hostility, even ignorance. Though of the ignorance I was uncertain. For while there certainly may have been some ignorance, there was an overabundance of youth, and because the two generally go hand in hand, to paint my classmates as foolish seemed too easy. No, we were learning, all of us. Yes, "the idea at the back of it," that's what came to mind as CNN broadcast the Mumbai terror attacks and the men in my family vigorously discussed the horror transpiring in their homeland, "the idea at the back of it" and our classroom discussions of how war or colonization or imperialism required something we could all hold on to and "bow down before," some shiny, simple truth that sounds and tastes reasonable but that, according to Conrad, can and ultimately will lead to darkness, moral darkness. According to Conrad, it was inevitable.

Yes, as heartbreaking as 9/11 and the Mumbai terrorist attacks were, and as angered as I was at the groups responsible, and as much as I supported the invasion of Afghanistan I, like practically everyone else in America that Thanksgiving, wanted revenge more than anything. Blood. No matter the cost, no matter the consequences. Osama, the Taliban, those who had aided the Mumbai terrorists—I wanted their blood. Even so, or perhaps incredibly so, what I was learning listening to my father and *kakas* decrying the attacks, what I'd been hearing them say about Muslims my entire life, what I was learning from my social life at Irvine and inside the classroom and from our nightly news, what I was learning from Azada, was that everything that had recently taken place in the world—that had ever taken place in the world—didn't exist in a historical vacuum, that everything, if one is willing to dig deep enough, can be traced back to a starting point. What that precise starting point was—religion, politics, power—was too unclear for me, as it is for most people. Obscured by history. Bound to it. *Inside* it.

Yes, it was all so complicated that to truly understand and take an intelligent position seemed to require a mental and moral balancing act I couldn't seem to sustain for more than two seconds. And so how could Azada? How could *any* of us?

Well, quite easily it seems.

What I was beginning to understand—and what I myself had been doing on campus, what had perhaps gotten me off track academically and, of course, in other ways—was that we too often take the easy way out. We go with our race. We go with our religion. We go with our ethnicity. We go with those who look and sound like us. We go with those who look and sound like us because we know, we hope, that they'll think like us as well. And in that solidarity we seek safety and also acceptance—for our thoughts, our fears, our justifications, and, of course, our actions. For that's what we truly want—acceptance, moral or otherwise. And who could blame us? We're human. And because we're human, we're afraid, terrified of what we don't know. Of being alone. Of being outcast. Of being cast *out*. And so, perhaps because it's easy or perhaps because it's natural, perhaps because that's how we've been raised or perhaps because we're cowards, we seek those who are like us and too often fear those who don't.

And for that I felt ashamed.

When school resumed, campus went on a self-imposed academic lockdown. As if trying to salvage our transcripts from the endless party that had been our lives. Even the fraternity suspended all activities for the last two weeks of school before Christmas break, the brothers summoning us to the house the Monday we returned to inform us that all pledging activities would resume Winter quarter and that now the focus had to be on our grades and doing what we needed to do. Tutoring sessions with brothers who'd taken our classes were available at the house upon request; it was our job, according to Darpan, to take control of our learning and do what we needed to do to be successful. As hard as it was, Darpan instructed, we must focus on our studies and try not to allow what had happened in Mumbai, or had been happening on campus for these past few weeks, to interfere with the task at hand. As difficult as it was to believe, he reminded us, we're here to learn—or at least get good grades. "This fraternity has a cumulative GPA of 3.7," Darpan informed thunderously, before setting us free. "Don't fuck it up."

I'd yet to experience campus like it was those last two weeks. It was as if the chaos of the outside world—indeed, the chaos we ourselves had nurtured—became suspended in time, as if History mercifully vanished. School was the only focus, was finally the only focus. It was a relief. Even Sudeep eschewed the bong for those two weeks and, high on Adderall—something he offered me twice but to which I declined, despite my curiosity—stayed holed up in our dorm room pounding the keys of his laptop and churning out two 12-page papers for his humanities classes. I'd seen him do little more than pledge and smoke weed throughout the quarter, yet now, like some deranged madman, some possessed genius, he read with lightning speed, focus, and excitement, mumbling and occasionally laughing exuberantly to himself as he shuttled between the text clutched in his hand and the text being created on his computer. Was this how it was done? You coast through the entire quarter reading nothing, doing nothing, skipping classes, getting high, getting laid, getting in trouble, and then, at the very end, high on Adderall, you pull all-nighter after all-nighter until you've produced some highly debatable, purposely inscrutable text that purportedly resembled scholarship. Was this college? Was this learning?

Judging by the terrified, paranoid, zombie-like mood that infected campus those last two weeks, the answer seemed unanimous. By Wednesday of the week before finals, the quad was empty, Zuckerman Park almost deserted, our beautiful campus absent of students and the playful commingling and jocular goofing that had come to define Irvine for me up until then. Passing students wore headphones and kept their heads down, their drawn faces and panicked, fidgety eyes lost within themselves; those few brave enough to soak in the spectacular 80-degree sun bestowed upon us those two weeks in December—as the rest of America, particularly on the East Coast, dealt with a blizzard—sat with a book splayed before them and a highlighter clutched in their hands, their focus singular, their minds strangely immune to the sun's intoxicating effects.

Finally, it was strictly business, not business as usual, and we students, facing the firing squad, feverish and terrified and trying to reclaim some sense of the academic goals to which we'd originally arrived, fought diligently—better late than never?—for some sense of salvation.

I spent most of the weekend before final exams studying with Padma, trying to catch up with everything I'd missed in Chem. Exhibiting a stern seriousness I knew she had always possessed but that she'd reserved primarily for her parents and teachers, Padma scolded me for the holes in my knowledge and embarrassed me for the obviousness of my mistakes; she lectured me for my inability to keep up and humiliated me for failing to retain and demonstrate what she deemed simple. In short, she motivated me the way all Indian parents motivate and control their children—and not just for scholastic performance. No, she shamed me, over and over as we checked each other's work and discussed the formulas and concepts on the exam—she called me dumb and lazy and a failure, she called me stupid and, twice, incredulously (and seemingly honestly) asked how she could've fucked someone so fucking dumb. And because I was intimately familiar with this kind of stimulus-response, because Indian children are traditionally conditioned to perform under these exact circumstances, because shame is our burden, it worked. As much as I detested her methods, I respected her aims; I knew she only wanted the best for me, no matter our relationship. That up until then I'd apparently wanted something else wasn't lost on Padma, as it became vaguely clear throughout our weekend cram sessions that any more sexual contact between us would take place only under highly intoxicated circumstances—if at all. And that was fine. There was someone else I wanted.

Dr. Green's English 101 class had student-professor conferences during Week 10 so there were no formal class meetings, only one required conference where we discussed strategies of revision for our final term paper. And during final exams, we had no scheduled class meeting either, our only task (other than revise our final essays) to submit our final term papers to her mailbox in the English department. Finished were the heated discussions about colonialism, imperialism, narrative structure, morality, Kurtz, Osama, Marlow, Bush, or even terrorism. Finished—*finally! After a lifetime!*—were the discussions about thesis statements, transitions, topic sentences, quote integration, and MLA style. Of course, so too was Azada finished: never again would she be seated there before me, headscarfed or not, the early morning light slanting through our classroom window, her fair, freckled, exposed shoulders angelically aglow and stirring me to touch, lust, dream; no longer would I hear her voice crack the dialogue like gunfire and bravely challenge the facile, proscribed way of thinking; no longer would I admire her shoulders as they burned crimson at the irrationality of our classmates—the experience was gone, all of it, never to return!

Such was my melancholy when I found her in Zuckerman Park the Thursday afternoon of final exams. Campus was empty, everyone and anyone who could leave—Sudeep and Padma among others—long gone, but there she was, headscarfed and clutching Conrad in her hand.

When she smiled up at me from where she sat in the fading sunlight, I said the only thing that felt right. "I'm sorry."

"You don't have to apologize," she said. "You did what you had to do."

"Did I?"

"Sure. What choice did you have? You did what was expected."

"And you?" I asked, tapping my head. "Are you doing what's expected?"

She straightened her headscarf. "Yet to be determined."

"Still with the Conrad?"

"I'm so stressed," she said, nodding her head. "My paper was a disaster."

"I'm sure it was fine."

"I don't want it to be *fine*," she replied tersely. "I want it to be *perfect*."

"Like you?"

Her blush, so deep, so true.

"I want to see you—I mean, I *need* to see you," I whispered, surveying the park, paranoid suddenly, and because of that angry, and deeply ashamed. "Away from here. Outside all this."

"There is no outside."

"Do you believe that?"

She pulled her headscarf back, revealing a few wisps of her black hair. "Maybe."

"You don't want to see me?"

"I want to see you," she whispered, crimson, ablaze.

"I miss you."

No longer could she look at me, but only down, at the grass, at the Conrad by her feet.

"Can you come back early?"

She nodded.

"Friday night," I said. "Before class starts?"

Again she nodded.

"Here. Right here," I said, then: "No, at the beach. Meet me at the beach."

When she finally looked at me there were tears in her eyes.

# 12

At first we sat on a bench and watched the stand-up paddleboarders glide across the aquamarine ocean as the setting sun colored the sky crimson and saffron until finally the entire canvas was bled of light and when the full moon rose to ignite the black sky and black ocean it was as if there were two moons, two moons and two universes, silver stars shimmering in the sky and silver stars shimmering by our feet, and we sat close, so close, just us, only us and the moon and the stars and the gently crashing surf, and it was almost enough, or more than I've ever known, and I wanted to ask her so many things but I knew better, for once in my life I knew better.

And then we were walking on the beach, our jeans rolled high up our calves, not a word spoken, only the eternal melody of the black surf crashing on the white sand and the moon, like some fortuitous blessing made twice, illuminating the darkness and the way before us and on we walked until there were only cliffs on our right and moons and stars and surf on our left and when I stole her hand she rested her headscarfed head upon my shoulder as we walked slowly, so slowly now, as if to savor the crime, as if to simply be ourselves.

The cliffs became more and more jagged and cut closer to the ocean and at times cut clear across the sand and out into the surf and eroded through the stone were tunnels illuminated by the moonlight and slowly and together we walked through the cliffs until we could walk no more. When she turned to me in the alcove her eyes sparkled like two emeralds set in alabaster, a goddess of flesh alight by the silver moon. Shame curled her lips. After she laid her head on my chest I held her to me like some stolen treasure, some guilty secret, the two of us criminals, outliers, outcasts. Her emerald eyes peered up at me and no longer was there embarrassment on her red lips but something else entirely, confidence and joy and perhaps even defiance, yes, brave, brave defiance, and then she was undoing her headscarf to reveal the part of her she'd willfully obscured from everyone, including me, especially me. In the ocean breeze her long black hair shimmered and danced behind her and after gently folding up her headscarf she placed it into the back pocket of her jeans and heart pounding I watched her glide to the edge of the crashing surf, her long black mane flowing behind her like some shadowy spirit, carnal black magic, and testing it, Azada watched the black water quickly climb up her feet, her ankles, her calves. When the water receded she disrobed.

There she was. Like some eternal truth lay bare. Or some forbidden dream made real. There she was. So frail, so pale, afraid no longer, out there on the edge of reason, history, America. There she was. Azada stretched her arms out beside her and, head turned up towards the black sky and silver moon and constellations of stars, stood in defiance, as if awaiting some final cosmic judgment, or standing protest to the madness of our time. After a moment, she marched into the crashing black surf. Without turning back. Without need to.

For I followed.

# 11

Three weeks later, on January 23$^{rd}$, 2003, President Bush made his case to the American people for invading and liberating Iraq. At Irvine, it was yet another perfectly warm January day, one of a seemingly endless string of them, the temperature hovering just around seventy-eight degrees and campus, unlike it had been for those two stressful weeks following Thanksgiving break, finally returning to its natural state of play. After the hectic first two weeks of Winter quarter had passed and the stress of having to add or drop classes and purchase books and obtain class permits or pay tuition was thankfully forgotten, campus once again resumed more pressing preoccupations: where the next party was, the next boy or girl was, the next beer or bong was. And though the academic intensity that had consumed campus following Thanksgiving was something I relished and thrived in—I salvaged a B in Chem and a 3.4 GPA overall—I did, over Christmas break, occasionally find myself missing the comradery I shared, not only with the fraternity, but Sudeep as well.

Sudeep returned from Christmas break like someone who'd undergone a religious conversion—and perhaps he had. Even before the Mumbai terrorist attacks he'd planned on visiting India with his father for business but, following the attacks and aware of the travel risks involved, his father felt the trip might be more fruitful if they stayed planted in Mumbai with family. His father, a hardware developer for Hewlett-Packard, had, according to Sudeep, a growing side business that for the past five years required biannual visits to India. There, his father (and occasionally he) would travel to Bangalore and Chennai to visit the heart of India's rapidly expanding—and decidedly cheap, when compared to American wages—business environment, a place where more and more American corporations were moving their customer service operations and, to a lesser degree, manufacturing (China, according to Sudeep, seemed to have the monopoly on that). Though this did have the unfortunate effect of costing jobs for too many of us here, in India, it had the converse effect of providing what were locally considered great jobs, jobs that lifted Indians into a new, burgeoning middle class and infused many of their lives with the kind of disposable income too many Americans used to take for granted. It was this corporate cost-shifting—commonly known as offshoring or outsourcing—that was driving this new Indian economic boom and that intrigued Sudeep's father with the business opportunities newly available in his native country.

And so, prior to this previous trip, having visited India more frequently than certainly myself but many of our pledge and fraternity brothers as well, Sudeep would talk avidly and proudly about the changes taking place in India, reporting with vigor and excitement about not only the physical transformations (the high-rise call centers and dazzling, air-conditioned corporate parks that sprawled fortresslike within Chennai and Bangalore) that signaled India's inevitable rise, but the cultural changes as well, the fact that now, in contrast to our parents' youth, actual dating was something increasingly—if reluctantly—tolerated and though public displays of affection were still culturally off limits (and deep sources of shame), things, at least for historically sexually conservative India, were slackening, modernizing, social mores were shifting, and as more and more educated young women and men entered the urban workforce from their rural villages and tasted real economic freedom for the first time in their lives, you could feel, as Sudeep had tirelessly suggested prior to his most recent return, a real cultural change that left him not just amazed, but proud.

The Sudeep that returned from India following the Mumbai terrorist attacks had nothing to say about India's cultural or economic developments but rather, with his newly shaved head and stony demeanor, offered instead a terrified, intimate assessment of what Islamic fundamentalism looks and feels like to the victimized at ground zero. Gone were the long, curly black locks that gave him an intellectualized, hippie affectation. Missing was the stoned jokester who couldn't resist sarcasm, self-mockery, and academic procrastination. Rooming with me now was someone radically changed by experience, his disgust fraught with fear and sadness and the folly of humankind. "There was still blood on the walls," he recounted to me, the Sunday before classes started. "My father, because of his business contacts, got us into the Crown. It's still open, but under the tightest security you've ever seen. Like trying to get on an airplane, only worse. We were searched, stripped down to our underpants.

Soldiers with machine guns watching us, making sure we didn't have anything, making sure we didn't have a bomb. They confiscated my camera. I couldn't believe it. But when you see it, you realize. You realize you don't need to take a fucking picture because the imagery gets seared into your head. Like the images of the planes crashing on 9/11. How could you ever forget? Even if you wanted to you couldn't forget the smoke and rubble and all of those brave police and firemen running into that carnage—that crumpled steel and dust, as if civilization had reached its inevitable violent end. I'll never forget it. I mean, how could *anyone* forget it? How could anyone forget the sight of people jumping from their floors because of the smoke? Remember that? Remember watching the people as they fell a hundred stories down? Remember the chaos? That awful feeling of *not* knowing. Even Tom fucking Brokaw had no idea what was going on. Who did it? Was it an accident? But when the second plane hit, you knew it wasn't an accident. America stopped that day—America woke up. Well, so has India. But honestly, I think they've always known it, known it in ways you and I could only hear about or see on TV. Known it in ways that, until 9/11, we really couldn't even imagine. Why do they hate us? Why do they hate others? Where does the hatred come from? Well, when you see the blood on the walls, when you see the dust fall from the sky, you realize that what took place was the work of madmen. You realize that what took place in Mumbai and New York, what's taking place in Afghanistan and Pakistan and Iran and Iraq, is the work of men possessed not by the human need to try to love one another but rather that crazy fucking book, that book they bow to ten times a day. *That's* what drives them to give their lives and steal the lives of others. *That's* what drives them to cover their women in black from head to toe and stone their women if they do not comply. No, you don't need a camera to remember because when you see the blood, you'll never forget. Blood pooled in the main lobby. Blood pooled in the dining room. Blood everywhere, the blood of average, working men and women going about their lives and then—boom! In the main lobby, right by where you check in, there was a hole in the wall so fucking big you could drive a rickshaw through it. Never seen anything like it. Never hope to again."

Sudeep's firsthand recollections of Mumbai made him somewhat of a celebrity around the fraternity house, and by the time we all gathered there on the 21st of January to watch the State of the Union, we'd all heard some approximation of his story and felt, much like he did, a visceral disgust and dizzying sense of anger. Even as the pundits on Wolf News analyzed leaked excerpts of the speech prior to President Bush's delivery—excerpts that, it became increasingly clear, were focused on Saddam Hussain and Bush's rationale for preemptive invasion—brothers and pledges alike were questioning Sudeep on what he saw, how it had affected him, and what it meant. His stony, blood-soaked memories mixed with their own knowledge—knowledge that had been influenced over Thanksgiving and Christmas breaks by their parents and the ceaseless media coverage on CNN and Wolf News—solidified the terrifyingly chaotic narrative that had inexplicably come to frame our young lives. First 9/11, then Afghanistan, then the Mumbai terrorist attacks, quite possibly a war in Iraq, and now, here, at Irvine of all places, *in only three weeks*, the arrival of Mohammad Jafar al-Sadr—our world seemed to be spinning further and further out of our control, the orderliness and sense of purpose we'd all once imagined as young boys doing our homework and getting good grades continuously disrupted by forces beyond our grasp, by men halfway around the world, strangers—yes, it was a sense of powerlessness we all felt, a terrifying, mystifying, incomprehensible sense of powerlessness that left us angry in our impotence and shattered any illusions of order we'd once naively imagined. There seemed to be only disorder, only chaos.

And so it was to President Bush that we looked for order, for some sense of direction, for some sense of hope. Needless to say, he didn't disappoint. Had you been walking by the fraternity house that night—indeed, had you been walking anywhere on campus, from fraternity row to the Student Center—you might've mistakenly thought the Super Bowl was being played, so quiet were the streets and so raucous our collective applause. Bongs and blunts and bottles of booze were being bounced around the packed, smoky living room as, on Wolf News, with the Terror Alert High, our President made it clear that the course of America "does not depend on the decisions of others." "Whatever action is required," he bravely informed us, "whenever action is necessary, I will defend the freedom and security of the American people." To these critical lines near the start of the address, the applause was deafening, both on the House floor where President Bush stood before a joint session of Congress and among us as well, for there was suddenly acknowledgement that, independent of other nations and of our allies, our President was determined to do whatever was needed to ensure our safety as a nation. Upon hearing those lines, we all sprang to our feet and began high fiving each other, excited by our President's toughness, his cowboyesque America-defenders-of-freedom-and-democracy-against-the-world attitude, but also relieved, deeply, deeply relieved at the protection his words afforded, for us as Americans first and foremost, obviously, but also for places like India, the poorer nations around the globe who believed in democracy and freedom and had suffered from or been threatened by Muslim fundamentalism but lacked our military or intelligence infrastructure. Our President was speaking for all of us.

He was also, as he began laying out the crimes committed by Saddam Hussain and his Iraqi regime, awakening America—even if we didn't fully realize it then—to a new world order, something later coined The Bush Doctrine, a political policy allowing for preemptive war. In other words, President Bush was suggesting that our country—and his administration specifically—would snuff out any potential threats to our freedom and security *before* being attacked, before another 9/11 could occur. And who could argue with that? Who could argue with the safety he wished to provide? When our President argued that, before "September the 11th, many in the world believed that Saddam Hussein could be contained. But chemical agents, lethal viruses and shadowy terrorist networks are not easily contained," our collective response was agreement, vocalized, loud, raucous agreement, because we knew, we knew that these terrorist networks were not "easily contained," we lived it on 9/11 and we saw it in Mumbai. Even Sudeep, someone so previously hypercritical of Bush and his tactics, even he rose in applause and, screaming at us, the television, and Bush, screamed, "Fuck yeah! Kill that crazy fucking asshole! Get those WMDs! Blow his ass to hell!"

On the television, inside the congressional chamber, our President's words also struck accord, for as the camera panned to the Democrats now standing and clapping on the House floor, there didn't seem to be any disagreement on their faces or fraudulence in their support. Whether they were being respectful or polite or simply playing politics I can't be sure, but when the cameras lingered briefly over Senator Hillary Clinton—someone I remembered because my father was an avid supporter of President Bill Clinton—standing in applause, I had to believe that she supported our President's position and that if she, a Democrat, a Senator, a former First Lady, believed Bush's reasoning, then certainly my father would, then certainly I *should*. Yes, as Bush made the case for preemptively invading Iraq—"If Saddam Hussein does not fully disarm for the safety of our people, and for the peace of the world, we will lead a coalition to disarm him."—the cameras paused over many faces, from members of his cabinet that had constantly been in the news since 9/11—Powell, Cheney, Rice, Rumsfeld—to the few Democrats from California I could recognize—Senators Feinstein and Boxer, Representative Pelosi—and in their stern faces and clapping hands you could see clear understanding, a sense of duty, and, perhaps most importantly, total agreement. Yes, onscreen and in our fraternity house, there was an electric sense that we were all in this fight together and, though we did disagree on many things, on the singular issue of our time— our nation's safety—well, on that there was only unity.

Whether it was intelligent, rational, or morally correct to believe that invading another country alone, before they had actually attacked us, was, at that moment, beside the point—or perhaps it wasn't. Perhaps it was precisely the point Bush was trying to communicate. We will not wait for another 9/11. We will not wait for another Mumbai attack. We will not wait for those fostering hatred against America to spread their deadly ideology. And because we will not wait for our own destruction *it is morally correct, it is wholly rational to do what we need to do.* Perhaps the point was, given the threats facing us at that moment in our history, given the fear, anger, and unshakable paranoia that had gripped America since 9/11, given the fact that Saddam Hussein had, according to the British government, "recently sought significant quantities of uranium from Africa" for building a nuclear bomb, America could no longer wait for action. Look what it got us on 9/11.

Up until that night, I had paid little attention to State of the Union Addresses; up until Irvine I had paid little attention to politics in general. But the world had clearly changed. Or perhaps it hadn't. Perhaps it had always been this way and would always be this way and the only thing that had changed was me—yes, perhaps I was changing and I was finally becoming aware of the powerful forces underpinning and circumscribing my existence. Was that it? I don't know. What was undeniably true was that President Bush was telling us what we—what I—wanted to hear, what we needed to hear. He was giving us a narrative that made sense and that felt right and that, at least on the surface, seemed to offer protection from everything conspiring to disrupt our lives and steal our futures. If we followed him, if we agreed, if we trusted him, there was a future there, the future we'd always wanted, a future free of hijacked, crashing airplanes and exploding car bombs and radical terrorists. There was a future of graduate degrees and good jobs and nice houses and beautiful children playing in the California sunshine. And so whether invading Iraq was moral or reasonable or even effective seemed utterly irrelevant. As did how history would judge him—or us. The only thing that mattered was we had been attacked, we were being threatened, and we were Americans. The only thing that mattered was what we were going to do about it.

# 10

"Please, *please* don't tell me you bought into that bullshit last night," Azada said, standing in the doorway of our private study room on the (thankfully) empty third floor of the library. It was as if she'd been trailed or even chased across campus, so shaken did she look. Her white headscarf was translucent with sweat, and there was a never-before-seen vein throbbing down the center of her damp, pale forehead. Her green eyes flitted anxiously around the room, struggling to find focus, order, me.

"Please sit down."

"Why? Why should I sit down when I know you believe him, when I know you support him?"

"Because I love you."

"Do you?" she asked, moving towards me now, the door closing and locking behind her.

I'd never said it before, never had the chance. Was this love? I didn't know. Up until that point in my life I'd only read about it in books or heard about it in songs or seen it in movies.

Nonetheless, I'd never felt anything akin to what I was feeling now, to what had been supercharging my days since not only that night at the beach, but that morning in Dr. Green's class and that Halloween night at the fraternity party, when the world finally paused and there was only her beauty, her bravery, her incandescent spirit. Lust, desire, those I'd certainly felt and been lucky enough to taste since my father left me here so long ago. But this, this was terrifying—and because it was I knew it had to be that elusive, magical, essential emotion we're born to crave but that, in cultures like mine and cultures like hers, is too often silenced and dismissed in the name of family, foolishness, class or caste.

Terrified, shaking now myself, I said, "I love you Azada."

"Prove it?"

"Is that what you want?"

"Yes! No! I don't know! I don't know *what* I want! No—because I do know what I want. Do you know what I want? I want a *normal* life! I want to go to class and not have people staring at me like I'm going to blow up the fucking school. I want to go to class and learn and talk—*just like everyone else!* I want a President who cares about all of his citizens and not just the richest few! And if I can't have one then I want to be able to protest him every fucking day without people thinking I'm anti-American or some religious nut because I look or pray differently! And you know what else, Rohan, I want to fall in love with who I want to fall in love with and I want to be able to hold their hand in public and not hide out like criminals in some fucking library! Is that asking too much? Is that *crazy?*"

And because we knew, given our circumstances, that it was, and because we knew it shouldn't be, and because we knew that, were we to be truly honest with ourselves, it was not just President Bush to blame but rather our own cowardice and fear and steadfast filial devotion (among other things), Azada crumbled sobbing into the chair beside me. I wrapped my arms tightly around her and pulled her towards me and let her cry. She cried for a long time. For all that was. For all that wasn't.

"What's wrong with us?" she eventually asked.

I wiped the tears from her eyes, her face.

Her headscarf had loosened, become disheveled.

"May I?"

She nodded.

I undid her headscarf, liberating her long black hair.

"You know, the first time I ever saw you," I said, gently folding up her headscarf, "it was your hair I couldn't get enough of."

"Yeah…" she said, still sniffling, but softening now, "That's what they all say."

"I mean, don't get me wrong, when you walked into class, it was like—I don't know, it was unlike anything I'd ever seen before. You were so breathtakingly unlike any girl I'd ever seen before. Your shoulders, your green eyes, your freckles," and here I leaned in and kissed her exposed shoulder and the pink dots speckled across her fair skin, "but your hair, when you walked into class, it shone so brilliantly in the morning sunlight—I mean, I don't know, it was like you were imbued with some magical power or something. I couldn't believe it when you actually took the seat in front of me."

"It was the only one left."

"Was it?"

"I don't know. Maybe. Must've been."

"The world works in mysterious ways, doesn't it?"

At this she blanched. "No it doesn't, Rohan. The world works the way it does because people are afraid. Afraid to do what's right, afraid to do what's right for them, afraid to fail, afraid to share, afraid to disappoint, afraid to trust. To call it anything other than that is to—I don't know—believe in superstitions."

"Like this," I said uncertainly, offering her the headscarf. "What do you call this? *Fashion?*"

"I never said I was immune. No, I'm disappointed to say I'm as guilty as the rest of humanity. What keeps me up at night is wondering whether or not I'll have the power or strength to change that."

"Is *that* what keeps you up at night?" I asked, my hand now on her thigh.

"Did you tell your parents about us?" she asked, resting her hand upon mine.

"I'm ashamed to say I've never told my parents about *any* girl, not just the gorgeous Muslim I'm secretly in love with some four hundred miles away at college. Have you told your parents about *me?*"

"Why do you think that is? Why do you think it's so hard for us to do what every other kid in America does with relative ease? You know, in my high school, I had a lot of girlfriends, most of them, my closest friends, were Middle Eastern, girls I'd known all the way back to the second grade, but some of my newer high school friends were, you know, everything, Black, white, Asian, Hispanic, mixed, whatever. Palisades High has a very good mix of students, very diverse, more diverse than this place, if you can believe it."

"Everybody got along?"

"Does everyone get along here? No, I'm not saying that. It wasn't perfect. I mean, it was still the Pacific Palisades. It was still high school. It just happened to be in one of the richest neighborhoods in America. But it was still a public school, you know, and some of my friends, they came all the way from East L.A. or South Central or Koreatown because their parents knew that Palisades High usually meant getting into a good college. But obviously, yes, there were issues—money issues, I guess what you'd call class issues. Obviously very academically competitive. And of course racial issues, that goes without saying—but even with those racial issues, I don't know, as cliquey as high school was, I still managed to have a nice mix of friends. Anyway, the thing that always got me, that made me crazy, actually, was all throughout high school, whenever one of my friends dated a boy, they had no problems telling their parents about it. Whether or not their parents liked him or approved is really another question, I guess, because it was still high school and what parent wants their kids having sex in tenth grade? But never did my friends express fear of what their parents might say regarding *who* they brought home—at least racially speaking. Actually, that's not entirely true, because Amy—she's Chinese—she was like me. Always told me she had to date an Asian. Told me she was forbidden otherwise. And not just any Asian, but a Mandarin-speaking Chinese. That's what her parents demanded from her—alongside straight As of course. Which she delivered then and I'm sure she's delivering now at Yale. Anyway, I'll never forget our conversations. 'Not just any Asian,' Amy used to lament, 'but a *Mandarin*-speaking Chinese.' 'I don't even speak Mandarin,' she'd say, 'why should I care that he does?' But it was important to her parents, you know? They spoke it, and parental relationships are very strong in their culture. So that's what they wanted—and Amy, so smart, so sweet, she was going to give it to them even if it meant going through high school alone. Which she did. Because—surprise! surprise!—there just weren't that many Mandarin-speaking Chinese walking around Palisades High. My Black and Hispanic friends, however, they had no problem dating anyone—white, Black, Latinos from Cuba and Peru and even Spain—and they didn't think twice about bringing someone home to meet their parents. And this was going on in the tenth grade, mind you. I remember feeling so happy for them that they could not only date—because that was something in and of itself—but that they could date who they wanted, no matter race or religion. Of course, alongside the happiness I felt for them—and I did, I truly did—I also felt jealous and sad because what they weren't even thinking about was the only thing on my mind. Because, like Amy, my parents also had expectations."

"Had? Or have?"

"Exactly. And now, because of everything that's going on, they've gotten *worse*. It's as if things have hardened into something so intractable and my parents, they've made it clear that as American as we like to think we are, we're still considered outsiders and that's why it's even more important we stay together."

"Do you think that will ever change? I mean, I'm not trying to compare my situation to yours because I get what you're saying. I do. I just wonder if there'll ever come a time when you think we'll stop being considered outsiders."

"I don't have answers to that, Rohan. Given everything that's going on, I'm barely able to focus on the answers for my Spanish

101 test. I'm a fucking mess. I can't sleep at night. But I'll say this. Think of the way African Americans are treated in this country—and they've been here since it was founded. Really, *really* think about it. Think of the racism that still occurs all over our country. *And they've been here for over four hundred years.* You think being racially profiled because you have a funny name and dark skin at an airport sucks—trying being a Black man driving in the wrong neighborhood. Try being a Black man with a supposedly 'Black' sounding name sending out resumes. Good luck getting the job. It's disgusting. In a country where equality, justice, and freedom of speech and protest are supposed to be the cornerstones to our democracy, we still have a hostile environment to anyone who *isn't* white. And I know it may sound crazy—and honestly, Rohan, as an English major, I feel crazy saying it. Because I don't want to believe it. It breaks my heart to even think it. Because, I mean, it flies in the face of everything moral and decent this great country is capable of. But at the same time I'd be an idiot if I denied what's going on here—and what's about to happen in Iraq. If something is immoral or wrong I like to believe we have an obligation to say and do something about it. To me, that's the value of a liberal arts education. I know you engineering majors might have other concerns, but to me, I don't know, I hope I have the courage to do what's right—even though I certainly know that's easier said than done. So, to answer your question: Do I think they'll ever come a time when we'll stop being seen as outsiders? I have no idea. But let me say this: invading Iraq won't fucking help."

"You don't think we have a right to protect ourselves?"

"I knew you believed him," she said, incredulous, embittered, green eyes aflame. "I knew you *agreed* with him!"

"He's our *President*, Azada. You think he would lie to his own people?"

"Are you really asking me if a politician would lie?"

"You know what I mean. The facts are the facts, right? Saddam *is* a brutal dictator. He *did* gas his own people. Don't you think he deserves to be removed?"

"Why should we, as Americans, feel we have the right to invade any country we want—for any reason we want? Or, in this case, *no* reason."

"He's putting together a nuclear arsenal. He has chemical weapons. He has weapons of mass destruction! Come on Azada! Certainly you don't support someone like Saddam having this kind of technology? He's a threat to his own people—he's a threat to us!"

"So is North Korea! So is Iran! Where is the speech arguing for invading those countries?"

"Perhaps that time will come," I found myself saying, even though I knew I was well out of my league intellectually, and because of that I felt deeply ashamed, not only for the positions I may have been parroting, but for the possible consequences of my ignorance.

"Are you *crazy*? What are you *saying*? Now you want to invade *those* countries too?"

"That's not what I'm saying, Azada. What I'm saying is—"

Infuriated, Azada cut me off and shot to her feet. "Have you read *1984*?"

"Azada, please, I'm sorry. Please sit down."

"Have you read *1984*? You know, by George Orwell?"

"What? No. I mean, I don't think so. Why?"

"Perpetual war, Rohan. That's what our," and here she angrily made quotation marks in the air with her fingers to accentuate her disgust, " 'President' wants. And do you know why, Rohan, do you?"

"Azada, please, look, I'm sorry."

"You're not sorry. You agree with him. And I guess that's your right, even though it's morally reprehensible—and not to mention intellectually lazy. But let's be honest, I'm in the minority here. Do you know *why* our President wants perpetual war? Do you know *why* he wants to keep his people in fear, in fear of being attacked by Iraq or Iran?"

"Tell me, Azada," I said, and by now I too had become irritated with her pedantic sarcasm, by her strident certitude. "Please, enlighten me O hallowed English major."

"I'm afraid the answer is so mundane and obvious it'll seem ridiculous."

"I'm listening," I said, rising from my seat.

"Money," she said, before bursting into tears. When she repeated herself it was almost inaudible, so bereft of breath was her voice.

"Azada," I said, moving towards her.

"Don't," she said. "Don't." She gently wiped her face with her headscarf and then, unfolding it, began to cover herself. "There's going to be a protest Thursday afternoon. *Against* the war. We're going to start at the Student Center and march down to Chancellor White's office. We want him to take a public position against the war." And then she looked at me in a way no girl ever had. "I expect to see you there."

"Azada…"

But she was already gone.

**9**

Tue to her word, at around one o'clock the following Thursday afternoon an MSI-led anti-war protest convened outside the Student Center. Like most of campus, I was heading to class—Dr. Rock's American History 102—when I encountered them there, a group of about fifty-five and swelling, picket signs rising and falling in their hands, placards of Bush and Cheney and Rumsfeld and Powell with the words "War Criminal," "Liar," or "Show Us the Yellowcake" stenciled in red across their cartoonishly enlarged faces. My curiosity— and heart—compelled me to stop alongside the mass of students watching at the foot of Zuckerman Park, our shared disagreement and uncomfortable distrust mixing with genuine concern as to what might transpire. My primary concern was obviously for Azada, for somewhere among the protestors her strong, beautiful voice was undoubtedly echoing those around her—and her expectations of me. Our rendezvous last night had ended terribly, and in the intervening, sleepless hours I'd tried to puzzle a way through what was obviously a difficult situation. For what Azada asked of me was something with which I vehemently disagreed, and so to join her today simply because she asked seemed to embody the very fear she believed too many of us easily exhibited. Nonetheless, I loved her, loved her in a way I'd never before known, and so as I watched the protest growing under the golden sun, as I unsuccessfully surveyed the headscarfed, chanting women for

Azada, I had to wonder if it was love—and not politics—that dictated I join her.

What also gave me concern as I failed to locate Azada among the protestors was the sight of so many young women wearing full-length burkas, their entire bodies in total blackness, completely obscured, any sign of their individuality or self buried beneath their black shrouds. On a typical day (whatever that meant at Irvine), you might see one or two girls fully covered, oftentimes walking with a group of girls wearing headscarves or even dressed like typical American girls, legs and arms and hair innocently exposed to the yellow sun. Today, however, the entire vortex of the protest churned with women covered in black, at least twenty of them by my count, and in their presence—or absence—I felt strangely uncomfortable, terrified, as if the sight I observed was taking place not in sunny southern California, but Kabul or Medina. A bearded man wearing a keffiyeh stood on a crate in the center of the covered women and, wielding a bullhorn, led the protesters through a litany of slogans: "Make schools, not bombs!" "What do we want? Peace in the Middle East! What do we want? Proof!"

To my surprise, and disgust, I felt angry at all of them, the women especially, repulsed that they would purposely choose to dress in such a way when protesting my government. Even as the thought pierced my mind so did the answer, yet still it hovered silently out there, before me, before all of us watching this strange, disconcerting scene: What gives them the right?

"You know," a familiar voice instructed me, "they wear bombs in there. The men, they recruit women as suicide bombers."

I turned to find Padma and Sudeep.

"I'm serious. It's a strategy that dates all the way back to the

French occupation of Algeria. These days it's mainly Hamas but Wolf News has been reporting the Taliban might try it in Afghanistan, even India. There could be someone out there right now with a gun or even a bomb. And you don't know. You don't know becuase you can't see."

At that, Padma and Sudeep shared a look, one that would've bothered me—*should've* bothered me—were I who I was only months ago. But I was changing, and so what I read in their shared affection did not ignite jealousy, or even sadness, but rather a strange disappointment, an utter lack of surprise. Their parents would be proud.

To that I only replied: "I gotta go."

"Where do you have to go?" Sudeep asked, his cleanly shaved head gleaming in the sunlight.

"Where do you think?" I gestured to the ivied buildings surrounding us. "Class."

"Class? What class?" Padma inquired incredulously.

"American History."

"American History?" Sudeep shook his head. "*This* is American history. Look!" He pointed to the protest. "This is history in the making. Look at this shit—look at them! Fuck class. You're protesting here, with me, with all of us. We're going to teach those fucking Arabs a lesson in American patriotism." In the high, golden sun, his chestnut eyes sparkled with a dangerous mix of purpose and belief. Sadly, so did Padma's.

"Dude," I said, searching for a lie. "We have a test."

"Fuck your test. Tell him you went to the protest. He's a fucking history teacher. He'll understand."

"Maybe he will. Maybe he won't. That's a risk I'm not willing to take," I said. "I'll see you on the backside."

As I was about to make my escape, Sudeep grabbed my arm and pulled me towards him. "What are you willing to sacrifice?" His face was only inches from mine. "Why are you even here?"

"What? Dude, I'm here to learn," I said, struggling for freedom.

"Not here," he said, indicating the ivied campus enveloping us. "Here." He pointed to the ground. "Why are you *here*?"

"Let me go."

"Answer his question," Padma said.

"Let go of my fucking arm."

"The minute your test is over, we'll be expecting you in front of Chancellor White's."

It was his use of "we" that irritated me most as I dipped away from the Student Center and raced towards class. It hit me then that I'd been hearing that word a whole lot lately, that in fact I'd been hearing it my whole life. *We'll be expecting you. Stay with your own kind. We only want the best for you. We only want you to be happy. We will defend America's freedom.* Everywhere I turned, another We. Such a simple, harmless pronoun, a word seemingly rich with love, yet the irritation I suddenly felt at Sudeep's presumptuousness—among other things—gave quickly to anger, claustrophobia, and for the first time in my life I despised the seemingly endless Wes to which my life had been circumscribed. Whether familial or political, fraternal or ethnic, they were everywhere, loving, instructing, prohibiting, pronouncing, expecting, believing, shaming—yes, they were everywhere, promising me something they believed I needed, but something that, at that moment, seemed hostile to any sense of *I*.

Dr. Rock, tall, thin, lanky, white, early thirties with a ruddy complexion and fiery red beard, sat atop his desk loudly rapping his fingers when I entered the room. At the sight of him there I paused uncertainly, his blue eyes fixed upon me, and then I quickly took a seat in the last row. This was not my usual seat, which was in the front, but there was clearly something in Dr. Rock's eyes that made me even more anxious than I already was. Of the thirty students enrolled, only about ten of us were actually there, and in the minutes leading up to the start of class Dr. Rock studied us intensely, fingers drumming on the hardwood, expression sliding from incredulity to disappointment to perhaps even shame.

He waited for the bottom of the hour before he finally spoke.

"Did you all hear about the protest?" he asked, blue eyes narrowed in scrutiny.

A few of us nodded. One person actually replied in the affirmative.

"Then why are you here?"

Uncomfortable silence. Not to mention painful disappointment.

"I'm willing to bet that some of you here today had perfect attendance in high school. I'm also willing to bet that those of you that did actually think it was some kind of accomplishment."

He let this sink in.

"Do you hear that?" Theatrically, he placed a finger to his ear.

Our classroom was on the first floor, the windows, as always, were open to the warm weather and cool ocean breeze, and even though we were over five hundred yards from the Student Center and Chancellor White's office and our room didn't even face Zuckerman Park but rather some trees back of campus where, normally, sparrows chirped alongside Dr. Rock's dry, circular lectures, our room was nonetheless flooded with chaos, with the strident, tinny bullhorn clamoring for support and unity, with the palpable, uneasy feeling that something was broken, breaking.

I closed my eyes and hoped Dr. Rock might ask someone to close the windows.

"Listen. Do you know what that is? That's the sound of freedom. That's the sound of America. Go make it for yourselves."

And then he was gone, off his desk and—incredibly—out the first-floor window, leaving us with our perfect attendance to make America for ourselves.

I was the last one to leave. I sat alone in that empty classroom until two o'clock dreaming of what it would be like to be somewhere else, or live in another time, or be someone else, not the child of Indian immigrants but the child of someone unencumbered by the pressure and shame I felt weighing upon me. Every decision before me held its own disastrous consequences, required its own unique courage. Did I have the strength to do the right thing? What was the right thing? What was the right thing for *me*?

If you support the war—which I did—then perhaps the right thing was to go and voice your opinion. It's your right. It's your obligation, as a citizen and an American, especially in light of 9/11, Mumbai, and the WMDs Saddam possessed. For as much as I dreamt of being somewhere else or living in another time—as much as I knew that was a young person's nostalgic dream in even the best of times—the awesome truth was that I was alive at this time, in the year 2003, young and alive in the shadow of a monstrous attack on American and Indian soil, and to try and ignore or pretend otherwise was not only naïve and irrational, but dangerous to my fellow citizens. Of course, to pretend that I wasn't in love, to pretend that Azada didn't exist, to pretend that what ached in my heart for the first time in my life was something that could easily be cast aside, wasn't that equally naïve and irrational? Well, perhaps no more naïve and irrational than my desperate belief that Azada and I would ultimately make it in the face of our parents, cultures, or history. Yet still I did! I *did* believe! I believed because I believed in love, because I believed in what I was feeling, and, quite suddenly, in ways I'd never before considered, I believed in America. I believed because I *had* to believe.

Yet even buoyed by belief, I'd still, as the clock struck two and I rose to leave the empty classroom, reached no conclusions; I'd shamefully made no decisions. My earlier feelings of anger and claustrophobia mixed with my love for Azada had left me in a kind of intellectual paralysis as, outside, I followed the obstreperous disorder raging some five hundred yards before me. I was tempted to turn around, return to Tarnopol Hall, and take a bong hit, to try, as Sudeep did before his visit to Mumbai, to smoke away the life and history unfurling around me. But I didn't; I couldn't. As intellectually paralyzed as I felt, to simply run away seemed scandalous and cowardly.

No, more than anything, I needed to see Azada, to make sure she was all right, to see her lime-green eyes there in the golden sun and somehow ensure nothing had—or would—happen to her. Earlier, I'd been unable to locate her in the din, and so perhaps she'd yet to arrive. But I knew, as I made my way to where, now, over five hundred students stood stridently screaming their support for President Bush and the war and, clearly in the minority, about two hundred students, led by the MSI, stood vehemently against, I knew Azada had to be there, deep in that sea of clamorous conviction, that raucous, turbulent cacophony of what Dr. Rock labeled the "sound of freedom."

The MSI-led anti-war protesters were attempting to march in a circle directly before Chancellor White's office, but because there were so many of them—and because, more distressingly, they were clearly being pushed forward by the pro-war demonstrators outnumbering them four to one—they resembled an elliptical, slow moving mass of people growing visibly stressed and irritated with every passing moment. As before, there were an inordinate amount of women clad in full-length black burkas, not only in the center of the mass, but now also interspersed throughout the anti-war contingent. If earlier the anti-war group was mostly Muslim students, by now they had clearly attracted a significant mixture of other students, Black, white, Asian and Hispanic, and together they tried—heroically, I thought—to stand tall and strong against the pro-Bush forces pushing against them. The sound of the entire endeavor was unlike anything I'd ever heard before, a din so aggressive and angry and passionate only a fool would earnestly believe that compromise could ever be found in such an undertaking.

It seemed that the pro-Iraqi invasion, pro-Bush group had been initially led or organized by Irvine College's Young Conservatives, a group with what I'd thought had very little clout or presence on an otherwise liberal campus. Nonetheless, I thought, as I watched alongside hundreds of other students positioned just south of the protest by Zuckerman Park, Orange County was known for being somewhat of a Republican enclave in an otherwise liberal, blue state, and so perhaps that was why they'd felt compelled to organize against the MSI, perhaps that was why they were able to garner so much immediate support. Of course, were I to be truly honest, it didn't take much to galvanize support and antagonism against *anything* favored by Muslims at that time, and so perhaps I shouldn't have been so stunned to see such a public outpouring against the MSI's cause, either here at Irvine or anywhere in America. No, this protest, much like the upcoming campus debate by the Muslim cleric Mohammad al-Sadr, was something with which too many here already disagreed, feared. What I was witnessing now, I couldn't help thinking, was only the beginning, only the burgeoning manifestation of the fear that, for most of the students here at Irvine, had been born on 9/11 and become an awful part of their everyday lives. This wasn't about the merits of the war—as it may have been for Azada and the MSI—this was about *fear*.

Of course, I couldn't blame them. I understood their fear. I feared al-Sadr's arrival just like they did. I feared his criticism, I feared his anger, I feared the beard. And I feared Saddam Hussain and Osama bin Laden—and who wouldn't? Our President had clarified Saddam's intentions; 9/11 had crystalized bin Laden's. And so it seemed reasonable that to *not* fear Saddam was the crime, to *not* want to defend America was, as Azada so tersely put it, "intellectually lazy." Yes, I wanted what most of campus wanted, what the Young Conservatives wanted: a good education, a good job, and a country and life uncontaminated by the fear of terrorism.

So why couldn't I join them?

The Young Conservatives—about two hundred young men and women—stood at the center of the pro-war camp, easily identified by their crimson T-shirts, shirts proclaiming, in white block letters, "Irvine's Young Conservatives Remember 9/11." It was a slogan only a fool would disagree with, and so it easily and effectively animated support and, more importantly, antagonism. The hundreds of students swarming around and behind the Young Conservatives waved signs that read "Remember 9/11?" and "Proud to be an American," "Saddam Supports Osama" and "Got Yellowcake? Saddam Does." Countering the MSI's placards of Bush and the others in his administration were enlarged signs featuring Saddam and Osama, the words Terrorist or Anarchist or Dictator scrawled in crimson across their faces. And as if that wasn't enough, as if the T-shirts and signs, chanting and screaming didn't effectively communicate their position, there were flags, American flags, small, large, or medium-sized, it didn't matter—there seemed to be so many flags waving and flying throughout the pro-war contingent it felt as if they were welcoming home heroes from the front and not vigorously arguing its opposite.

Whether it was organic or planned was unclear, but nonetheless the sight of all of those flags waving and fluttering under the clear blue California sky had a powerful, inspiring effect, reminding me, and perhaps not only me, of that Sunday after 9/11, when the NFL kicked off its season amidst legitimate fears of terrorist activity. On that Sunday at Candlestick Park, my father and I stood alongside sixty thousand before kick-off and, after a moment of silence immediately followed by the lightening beauty of twin jetfighters racing overhead, the entire stadium proudly raised the flags given to them upon entrance and sung—or tried to—"God Bless America." And I say tried because, at that moment, even the most hardened and cynical had to shed a tear, as I, like my father and the thousands around us, felt the freedom to grieve, to cry, and, surrounded by those fluttering flags, momentarily cast aside our differences and come together in our shared loss.

Yes, perhaps I was not the only one inspired by the sight of so many American flags, for as I struggled to locate Azada—and avoid Sudeep—amid the raging sea, the Young Conservatives—led by two perfectly tanned, blond-haired, blue-eyed beauties seated atop shoulders and singing through bullhorns—ignited the crowd through their own raucous version of "God Bless America." Like some patriotic religion, the song spread quickly throughout the crowd, unifying the din into one serene melody, and by the time the lyrics "Stand beside her, and guide her" were being sung even I—alongside many of the politically idle yet cautiously curious onlookers—was mouthing the words.

It was then I spotted a vantage point more conducive to locating Azada—and avoiding Sudeep. On the second floor of the Student Center was a large, open balcony overlooking the start of Zuckerman Park, the Chancellor's office, and the rest of the quad. Though there were quite a few students up there watching the protest, I knew that, if I could make it up there, I could easily secure a position and somehow find Azada. It was only when I'd stepped outside onto the second-floor balcony and successfully secured a spot at the railing overlooking Chancellor White's office that I realized I'd made perhaps the biggest mistake of my life. Whether it was inadvertent or not, I still, even to this day, can't say.

The Young Conservatives loudly led their supporters—including some up on the balcony—into a patriotic climax, a flag-waving crescendo culminating with the lyrics "God bless America, my home, sweet home!" Raucous applause

immediately erupted, followed by shouting, antagonistic fin-
ger-pointing, and, for perhaps the first time all day, an empty
water bottle soaring from back of the Young Conservatives' side
and landing atop one of the anti-war protestors. Who precisely
fired it was unclear—a protestor, simply an onlooker—but the
sight of that bottle flying through the clear blue sky seemed
to change something, sanction something, and before even a
minute had passed another had been lobbed from the Young
Conservatives' side, and then another. Rather than invite calm
or pause, these (at first) empty water bottles evoked laughter
from the pro-Bush side, as you could see and hear students
turning to each other and, strengthened by their numbers,
proud of their country and, perhaps most uniformly, enraged
by their enemy, a growing consensus of continuation blossomed.

It was then I saw Azada—and everyone else. All of them.
Padma, Dipika, Sudeep, Pratek, so many people I knew, all
of them deep in the action, the muck, the sound of America,
while I, shamefully, watched like some cowardly bystander. I
felt, then, the pain of my paralysis, the shame of my ambiva-
lence, the embarrassment of my inaction. I also felt fear. Dis-
similar from my, and our, collective fears of terrorism, this fear
was not in response to some future, distant threat—no, this
was the fear of knowing that someone you love was about to get
seriously hurt—and there was nothing you could do to stop it!

Azada stood courageously on the edge of the ideological bat-
tlefront, at precisely where the Young Conservatives had drawn
their line and were making their charge, the two sides brush-
ing against each other and, in places, commingling, colliding,
people who were once colleagues or friends screaming bitterly
at each other, over each other, and she was there, wearing a

crimson headscarf and bravely holding her ground against all those who opposed, and when I located her she immediately peered up through the chaos as if sensing me, and for what felt like an eternity our eyes locked, her green eyes shifting from surprise to disappointment to a clear sense of betrayal.

And like the shameful coward I was, I could only watch.

It was then the Young Conservatives-led group truly began pushing against the anti-war protestors and, where meeting resistance, shoving people. It was not a conscious move towards violence, but rather, at least from my vantage point, a sad and inevitable shift in mentality given the circumstances, something that too often occurs when groups of young men and women collide to espouse deeply held views—or even share them. Still, to be clear, the shoving originated from the pro-Bush side, a group outnumbering—indeed, crushing now—the other by at least five to one. I'd been hoping, prior to locating Azada, that our campus police would step in to break up the entire thing and send everyone safely home before this unsurprising development. Oddly, there were only six mounted campus police officers overseeing the entire protest, and for the most part they'd been on the margins, outside the center, watching and letting things unfold as if there was possibly nothing that could go wrong. And yet, as the water bottles increased in number, eventually to be joined by epithets and physical confrontations, the police, clearly noticing these developments, didn't raise a hand or blow a whistle, failing to intervene, or perhaps not wanting to.

I wanted to tell Azada to run, to leave this place and save herself, but I didn't. I knew she was committed to her cause. I knew she believed what she believed. I also knew she—like

I, like all of us—had nowhere else to go. Yet still, as our eyes remained locked within the swirling pandemonium, as fights erupted now all around her, I longed for the power of my love to truly express myself to her, to myself, to everyone—I longed for the courage to become the man I'd always thought I was, or felt I should be: a brave man capable of doing what was truly right. Just like her.

I felt this longing no more acutely than when Sudeep emerged from the chaos to stand directly opposite Azada, his forehead agleam with sweat, his visage aglow with rage.

Instinctively, Azada returned her focus to the disorder swirling around her and, discovering Sudeep directly before her, expressed surprise, recognition, and finally fear.

He spit in her face.

And like the shameful coward I was, I could only watch.

# 8

The following day, the entire front page of *New College* was dedicated to reporting of the protest, as was the entire back editorial page. The picture featured most prominently on the front was of two young women trying to escape the madness, fully covered in black burkas save their blue, terrified eyes. Behind them, plastic water bottles and rocks were caught midflight, the blurred faces and bodies composing the background a riotous canvas of mostly red and black. The headline read "War Zone:

Protest Turns Violent as Passions Flare" and was followed by an article that mostly explained the escalating situation and peaceful conclusion. Eventually, the mounted police officers stepped in (obviously too late for my own liking) and, with the help of some Young Conservatives and members of the MSI, quelled the escalating tension before peacefully breaking up the protest. According to the paper, and like I thought at the time, those who had initially instigated violence had had no real political intentions but, rather, were there because, as the paper reported through interviews from anonymous witnesses, "they were looking for trouble. It had nothing to do with the war. They were simply troublemakers looking to start something." Nonetheless, the paper reported, there were members of both factions who, perhaps enflamed by the moment, fell victim to the provocations and "lost control of their stated goals and crossed the line into violence and hate speech, actions that have no place in any fair and respectable civil society, let alone a campus as esteemed as Irvine."

As to whether or not our student paper was being honest in attributing part of the violence to both factions I cannot say. Perhaps they had witnesses who saw the violent provocations from both sides. I'm sure it would've been easy to find someone willing to offer such testimony. But I saw what I saw. I felt what I felt. And for anyone to suggest that the anti-war protestors had instigated or responded to the rising tension with violence seemed to me grossly unfair and, indeed, sloppy journalism. For not only were they clearly the minority, but given the context, it seemed ludicrous that they would respond to any provocation in a way that might damage their political cause and strain their already fractious relationship with the campus at large. Yet still it was there, printed in our paper for everyone to read and interpret, implying—what? That the MSI may have *deserved* it? That they brought it upon *themselves*? It was only one little detail, one little detail perhaps easily overlooked, and yet I found it grossly inaccurate, implying some perverse kind of mutual responsibility I knew too many on campus were too eager to believe.

In a surprising turnaround given their earlier denunciation of the MSI's desire to bring Mohammad Jafar al-Sadr to campus—a visit, incredibly, that was only days away—the editorial board seemed to ignore my fear of implied mutual responsibility, writing that the protest had "tragically cut open for the entire community to confront—and here we feel compelled to explicitly name Chancellor White and our campus police—the anger, fear, passion, support, discord, and perhaps even ignorance surrounding the rhetoric and foreign policy of the Bush administration." Furthermore, the paper suggested, "it would be foolish to pretend that there was not a distinct racial, ethnic, and religious dimension to both sides of the protest and that what took place here on campus was not, in some respects, emblematic of the rising cultural concerns, questions, and tensions in America today. Therefore, it is imperative that all student, academic, and administrative leaders come together to immediately begin a much needed dialogue regarding next week's visit of Mohammad Jafar al-Sadr. While this page initially lambasted the MSI and the Political Science department for arranging this visit, we've shifted positions given recent events, most notably President Bush's desire to lead us into Iraq and the combustibility of yesterday's protest. For what seems tragically clear to this board is that, especially in times of war, open and unfettered dialogue is needed to ensure fair hearing—not only needed, but expected. As such, no matter how potentially reprehensible we may find Mohammad Jafar al-Sadr's political positions, his voice must be given free, peaceful space to be confronted and challenged. Indeed, this board feels it is the duty of this campus to uphold the value of free speech and protest, values that, based on what took place yesterday on campus and what is taking place in Washington, seem to be under siege. For without those core values, without the ability for all voices to be fairly and respectfully heard, free thought in this country will forever be threatened, as will the America we all love. As such, this board reverses its earlier position and calls for leaders of our college community to ensure that Mohammad Jafar al-Sadr's visit next week occurs under safe, respectful circumstances, mindful that this campus, the state of California, and the United States of America are places where freedom of speech and peaceful assembly are enshrined not just in our Constitution, but our hearts and minds as well."

Needless to say, the change in the editorial board's position regarding al-Sadr came as a shock to me, as it did many of the brothers I encountered at the fraternity house when summoned there late Friday night to bring our Pledge Master Darpan Taco Bell. The final stage of initiation, a process known as Hell Week, was about to begin the following midnight, and, as the name suggested, it was billed as the harshest period of hazing we would ever endure. We would be pushed, we'd repeatedly been told, to our limits. Beyond it. And while rumors abounded campus wide of an attrition rate of twenty percent, of pledges being hazed to death or drinking to death or quitting under duress—or even, scandalously, being excluded by the brothers at the very last minute—I still assumed (naively perhaps) that, whatever the week would entail, however stressful this last step, it was something that, however crazy and juvenile, would still exist within the bounds of reasonableness and otherwise typical collegiate hijinks. We were Indians after all.

Sadly, in spite or because of the climate on campus and beyond, we were now living in a time where what was or was not reasonable seemed to change by the minute, no longer fixed by some essential truth or moral center but rather (or so it seemed to me) wholly infected by political expediency, national pride, race or religion. We had once been stirred to life by the simplest and noblest of ambitions: academics and making our parents proud. As I stood in the brightly lit basement of the fraternity house and saw the absurdity to which I'd been tasked, I felt swiftly and painfully cast away from those lofty goals. Worse, I felt shame and anger at my father for his seemingly innocuous advice proffered not so long ago (yet so long ago indeed). Incredibly, I felt shame and anger for so childishly following it.

Six of my pledge brothers, led by Sudeep, stood working on it in the center of the room. Within the brightly lit basement, their eyes flitted with mischievous purpose and sinister pleasure as, between pasting swatches of paper and pausing to meticulously study their work, they brought beer, blunt, or cigarette to their lips. What—or who—it was was both readily apparent and simultaneously unclear, yet in its purposeful crudity you could feel the secret of its dark implications, the carelessness of its makers. Currently, he hung from a hook on the ceiling, and even dangling from above the paper-mache figure was at least six feet tall, his long, scraggly black beard—the only thing currently colored on him—his only identifier.

"Where the fuck have you been?" Sudeep inquired when finally noticing me at the margin. A half-empty liter of Absolut Vodka stood by his feet.

"Yes, young pledge," began our Pledge Master Darpan. "Where have you been? And where are my chalupas?"

"Here," I said, handing him the bag.

"Extra mild sauce?" he asked, digging through it.

"Of course."

"Excuse me?"

"Yes, sir. Sorry."

"I don't know what they put in this sauce, but the shit has me hooked."

"Yes sir."

"I could shoot this shit straight into my arm."

"What the fuck happened to you yesterday?" Sudeep asked.

"Yes, young man," Darpan said. "Where were you during the protest? You were expected to be there."

"I had class, sir," I said.

"My ass," Sudeep said, running his hand over his shaved head. "I saw you."

I was tempted to ask where he'd been last night, why he hadn't slept in our room, but I knew the answer. Out celebrating. I also knew the dangers of pressing him, the conversations they probably shared in bed, their disappointments about me. For the moment, I decided to play it safe: "On my way to class."

"I saw you after. Standing on the balcony."

"I saw you too," I replied, aware that, by admitting being there, I was further opening myself up to scrutiny—or worse.

"So you were there?" Darpan said, drizzling mild sauce onto a chalupa. "Were you lying earlier?"

"By the time I got out of class I couldn't get to where everyone was. So I decided to see what I could from the second floor of the Student Center. Sir."

"And what, exactly, did you see?" Sudeep asked.

"Nothing I'm proud of."

His eyes, posture, hardened, a gesture I immediately mirrored.

"Yes, I'm sure from up in the stands everything appears easy to judge. For those too afraid to fight for what they believe in, for what is right, the actions of the brave and willing may seem irrational, troubling, or even radical. But on the ground, things aren't quite so simple—things aren't quite so black or white."

"Spitting in someone's face," I said, "that's pretty fucking black and white."

Sudeep drew a cigarette to his lips and pulled hard on it. "The bitch got what she deserved."

"For protesting war she deserved to get spit on? An American? In America?"

"What makes you think she's an American?"

"The same thing that makes me think you are," I replied.

"You sound like the editorial board," Pratek, our bespectacled pre-med student, replied. He was wrapping wet paper around the giant figure's leg. "What good is freedom of speech if you're dead? What good is freedom of protest if you're dead in the ground?"

"Yes," someone else chimed in, "tell that to the people who died on 9/11. Tell that to the people who died having *cha* at the Crown Hotel."

"Exactly," Sudeep said, and here he reached for the bottle of vodka by his feet and drew it to his lips. He held it there for three seconds before continuing, "Freedom of speech, freedom of assembly, watery abstractions that have their place, certainly, but only when we are secure. Security always comes first."

"Well, spitting in that girl's face certainly makes me feel more secure."

"What's wrong with you? I know you get it. I know you remember 9/11. India. *We were attacked*! By Muslims! Where is this coming from? I mean, don't you support the war?"

"Of course I support the war. I just feel like maybe things are getting a little bit out of control," I said.

"My son, I'm sad to report they've *been* out of control," Darpan said, wiping his mild-sauce-stained hands on his shirt. He belched before continuing: "Ever since that day two years ago, our worlds have changed. We are now the generation of perpetual war, the sons and daughters who will forever know war so long as we are alive. There will be no end. And there will be no outside of war, or history. As such, as men, we are offered two choices: action or inaction."

"Excuse me, Pledge Master, but they are not even choices," Sudeep interjected, his drunken eyes twinkling with conviction. "Our actions are predetermined—from even before our birth, from before our fathers'."

"Here, here!" Pratek cheered, rising to his feet, beer in hand.

Someone shoved a beer in my hand and swept me into the group's celebratory toast.

"And this," I said, before guzzling my entire beer. "*This* is action."

Our attention turned to the paper-mache figure dangling from the ceiling.

"This, this is only *part* of our action."

"*Non*violent action," Pratek added, winking at me.

"Yes, Gandhi would be proud," Darpan said wryly.

"Do I even need to ask?" I said, dizzy suddenly, suffocating.

"This," Pratek announced, "is Mohammad Jafar al-Sadr."

"Or Osama bin Laden," said Sudeep. "Or any Muslim man you'd like it to be."

I wanted to rip free from my brown skin. "And why, exactly, is he—*that*—here?"

"We're going to send them a message," Pratek said. "We're going to let them know that their radical ideology is not welcome here."

"Please tell me you're not serious? Please tell me you're not going to do what I think you're going to do?"

"I think you mean," Darpan said, his hand on my shoulder, "what *you're* going to do. Together. As a group. This is a pledge activity. Spoiler Alert: A Hell Week activity."

"What if someone did this to—I don't know—an image of Gandhi? Or—fuck—Abraham Lincoln? What if someone did this to George Bush?" I implored Sudeep, searching him for that stoned, skeptical humanities student I'd met so long ago. "How would you feel? How would your mother?"

"Apples and oranges. Not all ideologies are created equal. Not all ideologies ask of their followers to kill or fly fucking planes into buildings. Or kill innocent civilians in hotels in India. No, what occurs in the name of Islam, Rohan, is not even on the same level as what occurs in the name of Hinduism—or Americanism for that matter. Hindus can't even kill a cow for fuck's sake—how are they going to kill innocent civilians? No, there are ideologies—religions—*countries*—that practice and preach peace and tolerance and there are others that preach war—and

Hinduism is the former and Islam, as we've sadly seen in our lives, is the latter."

"Amen," several pledges shouted, their half-drunken beers clanging together.

"Does this preach tolerance? Does this preach peace? I think there's a bit of a contradiction here."

"This is simply the ultimate manifestation of what our editorial board calls freedom of speech," Sudeep said. "If that terrorist can come here and espouse his violent ideology—an ideology that many here on campus undoubtedly support and believe or they wouldn't have invited that clown here in the first place—then certainly the student body of this esteemed college can offer a response."

"Do you have any idea how insulting this is?" I asked.

"Do you think we're stupid?" Pratek said. "We understand what we are doing."

"I don't think you do. I don't think you truly know how offensive this is," I said, and then: "You're going to get us expelled—maybe even killed."

"It's meant to be satirical."

"In what way?"

"It's not finished yet. Just wait. You'll see."

"I don't know if I can be a part of this," I said.

"Hey," Pratek said, "the editorial board wants freedom of speech, right? Well, we're going to give it to them. Aren't you for freedom of speech Rohan?"

"This isn't freedom of speech, Pratek. This is *hate* speech."

"That's what they want you to believe, Rohan," Darpan said. "If we offend their sensibilities we engage in hate speech, as if criticism of their faith or their dress is somehow off limits.

They like to apply a double standard—denouncing America and American military involvement is perfectly fine, calling America the devil and an international nuisance is acceptable, arguing that America deserved what took place on 9/11—or that the Indians who died at the Crown were somehow enemy combatants—that is all perfectly fine and reasonable—and protected under the First Amendment. Encouraged, celebrated, even. Look, look world, look at how tolerant we are! But this, this is somehow construed as hate speech? No, what we're going to show them—and what we're going to get the campus *really* talking about—is the cultural hypocrisy at stake, the double standard that certain groups clamor for when they feel offended. Is this offensive? Certainly. In its crudity and final role it will undoubtedly incense and enflame passions. But is it hate speech? Or is it instead speech that should be just as protected as the shit that cleric is going to say later this week?"

"You're telling me that this is simply about the First Amendment?"

"Of course not," Sudeep responded. He drew another long pull off the bottle of vodka by his feet. "But we can tell your conscience needs something loftier to believe in other than our simple desire to show these people that their version of Islam does not belong here in America. We want to provoke them, to teach them to get along like the rest of us—or to go back where they came from."

"You're the son of immigrants! You all are! And so are they! Do you have any idea how fucking stupid this sounds?"

"What are you saying?" Sudeep said, and stiffening he staggered slowly towards me. "You know, if I didn't know any better, I'd think you liked these fucking Muslims. What? Are you dating one? Is that where you go late at night when you're supposedly studying?"

"I don't know what you're talking about."

"You don't know what I'm talking about?" he asked, his eyes and nose all I could see.

"Look, listen," I said, taking a step back. "I support the war. I support Bush. I hope we go in there and blow Iraq to shit. I hope we kill Osama bin Laden and Saddam Hussein. But to suggest that students who happen to be Muslim are somehow part of the problem, or do not belong, or are terrorists—"

"Do you know that girl?" Sudeep asked, stepping closer.

"What girl?"

"You know what girl," he slurred. "That bitch who got what she deserved."

"And what if I do?"

"I knew it. You're fucking her aren't you? *That's* where you've been. You're fucking a terrorist."

"She was in my English class."

"And?"

"And I don't like your fucking tone—or your questions."

"The fuck you say?" Sudeep barked, his shaved head agleam with sweat.

"Guys," Pratek chimed in, "we're all on the same side. Chill out."

"Are we?" Sudeep asked. "I don't think we are."

"You need to chill the fuck out," I said.

"You need to fall in line."

"If this shit," I said, pointing to the paper-mache figure, "means falling in line, I think I might be better off somewhere else."

His face immediately darkened, his bloodshot eyes flooding with rage. "How did you get so lost?"

"I'm not lost, Sudeep, I'm just trying to be reasonable, *please*."

"You're a *disgrace*," he slurred, before shoving me hard in the chest. "Sleeping with the enemy. Sleeping with that *trash*."

I knocked him out cold.

# 7

"I don't know what I'm doing here," she said, contemptuously studying me seated on a bench.

"Please," was all I could muster. "Please." I tapped the open space beside me, peering up at her in all of my powerlessness, my cowardice. "You've come all this way."

We were back at the beach, under the high noon sun, the surfers, taut in black wetsuits, gliding across the ocean like magicians mastering the same spectacular trick.

With irritated reluctance she took the seat beside me and, mercifully, we sat there in silence for a while. Watching the surfers escaping the crashing waves. Watching the children racing heedlessly towards the shore. Watching their parents calling cautiously after them, their anxious laughter rising and falling like the tide.

Finally, Azada said, "It's so unfair."

I let that sit between us before saying what I'd called her to do. "I'm sorry."

"Is this how you want to go through life, Rohan? Continuously apologizing for your inactions?"

"Someone has to."

To that she had no reply.

"If it's any consolation, I punched him in the face," I said, knowing it wasn't, knowing it only made it worse.

"That's what they want, you know? To provoke a response," she said, finally turning to me. The warm ocean breeze suddenly picked up and sent her black headscarf aflutter. A lock of black hair sprang free to momentarily dance between her green eyes. I watched mesmerized, like I was that first day of English class, like I was that night she defiantly marched into the very ocean before us.

"You're beautiful," I said, finally.

Her eyes immediately welled, the dying breeze liberating a solitary tear to escape across her now flushed cheek. I reached for it before the wind could steal it away, and touching her with only a finger I gently wiped away her tear and then, slowly, secured her lock of hair beneath her black headscarf.

"I've never said that to anyone before," I said.

"First 'I love you,' then 'You're beautiful,'" she remarked. "What's next?"

"Will you marry me?"

At that we both laughed uneasily, embarrassedly.

"Do you think," she said, her eyes again filling with tears, "that you'll marry an Indian girl?"

"Indian, Hindu, Muslim, American, Republican, Democrat—is that all there is anymore? Is that all we are? I'm sick of hearing about and thinking about and worrying about who I am or who I'm supposed to be," I said. "I'm suffocating."

"This coming from the man who's about to become a full-fledged member of Delta Sigma Eta."

"Right now I'm not their biggest fan. Nor am I theirs."

"You could always quit," she said, her voice betraying her excitement.

"You'd like that, wouldn't you?"

"It would certainly make things easier."

"Would it?"

"No," she said, and in her sharp certainty I could sense she'd already thought this through. Unlike me. "Rohan, I'm sorry to say there's nothing that could make this any easier."

"This isn't how I envisioned my freshman year of college."

Azada exploded into an unrestrained laughter so innocent and pure she sounded like one of those children frolicking in the surf. I couldn't remember the last time I'd heard her laugh. I couldn't remember the last time I'd heard anyone.

"That makes two of us," she said ecstatically, laughing so hard she nearly fell from our bench.

I couldn't help but join her. For wasn't it funny? *Life*? Or, rather, what our lives—what *we*—had become? Once upon a time we were those children in the surf, mesmerized not by politics or war, race or religion, love or lust, but rather focused only on the hilariously essential task of trying to keep our balance and stand up straight against the rolling tide. And now? Well, now it seemed as if we were constantly engaged in a desperate struggle to find some kind of balance between the myriad identities fighting for our souls, the seemingly irreconcilable selves at battle with our hopes and dreams, pasts and futures. Would it ever end?

"Did you really knock him out?" Azada said, and this time the tears streaming down her face were born of joy, relief.

"Cold."

"Cold," she repeated mockingly, inching closer to me on the bench, our thighs and shoulders touching now.

I wrapped my arm around her then and together we watched the children free in the surf.

# 6

An inscrutable fog enveloped the full yellow moon as the clock struck midnight and we stood anxiously awaiting the start of Hell Week by the backdoor of the house in swimming trunks and plain white T-shirts with the fraternity's Greek letters on our backs. Upon arrival, we were forced to reluctantly acknowledge that every window of the house had been blacked out, obscured by cardboard, bookshelves and, in at least two instances, mattresses. That this portended nothing good sent our steaming breath commingling with chainsmoked cigarettes as mumbled, halfhearted assurances were passed around with a bottle of Jack Daniels, neither of which did anything to assuage our collective fear or alleviate the rising tension. Sudeep, his nose broken and left eye blackened, eyed me from the edge of our group with tempered rage until I openly apologized. A surprised mixture of embarrassment and understanding washed over him then in the hazy darkness as vocalized relief rippled through our tiny band of brothers, a relief that eventually became a desperate feeling of unity and comradery that bound us before the mystery held in that blackened house. Sudeep, reaffirming his leadership position, huddled us closely together, our arms linked and shoulders tight, our collective breath steaming into the cold, murky darkness.

"Whatever is asked of us," Sudeep began, his voice firm and taut, "we must do. Whatever is tasked of us, we must do. And I know that may mean doing or saying things we don't want to do or may not think smart or right. During those moments, we must try and remember that there is always a higher purpose, always a higher aim for our actions, always a reason that those who came before us deem worthy. For Destiny is inscrutable, and so what the brothers ask of us, we must comply. We must comply and we must trust that they have our best interests in mind. More importantly, we must also remember that there is a world beyond ourselves and sometimes we are called to make sacrifices for it. We may not want to, but we must try and remember what others have done before us—we must try and think of the sacrifices *they* have made. And while I know there is fear here, I want us all to remember that while fear is a healthy, normal response, it is also the easy response. It is also the selfish response. It is the response that divides and fractures; it is the response that leads to defeat. And so, whenever you feel fear and feel like quitting—and I know we will, we *all* will—I want you to remember that if we're all here for each other, then together we can find the courage to face the challenges that await us. For we are only as strong as our weakest link. Which is why, when you feel that fear rising up and you feel like quitting, I want you to turn to your pledge brothers and ask for their help. I want you to look into their eyes and reach for their hand and find the courage to push through. For if we are together, as one, I know we can stand tall and get through this thing."

"Are you *banchods* ready?" It was Darpan, holding open the door, a door leading to darkness.

And then we were filing cautiously into the house, shuffling blindly through the darkness of a long hallway where distant, deranged screams echoed alongside maniacal laughter and somewhere in the bowls of the house someone was repeatedly screaming my name and punctuating it by shattering bottles, the crashing, splintering sound of breaking glass following my name, sung out like some sick taunt, over and over again, and perhaps it was Sudeep who whispered not to worry about it, to block it out, or perhaps it was Pratek, I don't know, but when I reached for him there in the darkness there was no one, nothing, only my heart pounding in my chest. Panicked, I froze, desperately awaiting those who had entered behind me to come crashing through, but it didn't take long before I realized they, too, were gone.

Alone in the darkness, I shivered, foolishly wondering if perhaps I'd been spared.

Wishing I had.

And then I was tackled onto the floor and, pinned down onto my chest by at least two people, an eyeless, mouthless hood was forced over my head. Instinctively, I gasped for air, suffocating beneath my shroud while fruitlessly screaming: "I can't breathe! I can't breathe!" I could hear neither laughter nor menace from my captors as my hands were handcuffed behind my back; there was only the sound of my own terrified screams filling my ears, polluting my hood and mind like some toxic gas. I was dragged kicking and screaming into an adjacent room, thrown upon a wooden chair, and left for so long I eventually passed out.

I was awakened by a bucket of freezing water thrown in my face.

"Wake up motherfucker!" someone screamed, his voice unrecognizable.

Another bucket of freezing water was thrown in my face, sending me heaving and hyperventilating awake. I wanted to grab my chest and wipe the water from my eyes but my hands were still handcuffed and so, instinctively, I struggled in my chair, impotently wrestling with it in the hopes of breaking free from the darkness.

"Hey, hey, hey," he said, punctuating each "hey" by slapping me hard in the face. "Where the fuck do you think you're going?"

I could only gasp for air, freedom.

"We've been hearing some terrible things about you Rohan, things we hope aren't true."

My cold, damp shroud clung to my face, chilling the air I fought to breathe.

"Things like, I don't know, you have a hard time following directions. Things like you no longer want to be here. Are these things true?"

Terrified, confused, I shook my head.

It was then my chair was quickly tipped backwards and inverted, with my head angled downward and my feet above me. In this position, my head slammed into the ground, resting there before someone grabbed my legs and yanked me slightly upwards. I could see nothing but darkness, could only feel the numbing anxiety of being locked in such a vulnerable position, a feeling not unlike being a child at the dentist and having your mouth forced open and tongue pushed aside while he digs, drills, and scrapes inside you. I felt equally powerless and even more anxious than a child at the dentist, and while a little voice somewhere inside me reminded me that this was for my own good (much like the dentist) and, if anything, just a game, a more resounding voice argued desperately for liberation—not only from my anxiety and powerlessness, but also, oddly, from the identity I believed I needed, an identity as increasingly suffocating as the mask stuck to my face.

"I know what you're thinking right now," the voice said. "You're scared aren't you? Of course you are. You know, one of your guys, he shit his pants when we did this to him. He shit his pants and he started crying and then he quit. Just now, Rohan. I'm not kidding. He was crying so hard we had to let him go. He broke, Rohan, like a twig. Pratek. You remember Pratek, right? But you know what we told him, as he walked out the door crying in his shitstained pants? We told him the same thing we're telling you now: if you quit, it's over for you here. Irvine is done. We will fucking ostracize you from every social or academic activity on campus. We will make your life a living hell. You think this is hell, Rohan, this is nothing. In fact, any California college where a chapter of our fraternity exists—UCLA, Cal, UCSB, wherever—you're finished on that campus. You don't have a chance. Ostracized, Rohan. Graduate school, law school, med school for our good little Pratek? I told him to fucking forget it. I told him, 'Pratek, there's no safe place for you now. You cannot escape us.' That's what I told him as he cried like a little bitch walking out the door. That's the price for going at it alone. You'll be worse than a *Dalit*, Rohan. Lower than an untouchable."

He was close, so close I could taste his breath—a punishing mixture of weedsmoke and vodka—through my shroud.

"Now, the way this works is, we're going to ask you a sequence of questions, Rohan. And if you tell the truth, you're going to be fine. If you tell the truth, Rohan, believe me, this will go so quickly it'll be over before you know it. And when it's over, at least for tonight, you'll have drinks and maybe even some food and maybe you'll even see some of your fellow pledges, depending on who's, you know, left. But we need the truth from you Rohan. If we don't get the truth, we'll know it. And if we don't get the truth from you Rohan, well," and here he paused, slapping my chest twice before adding, "we have ways of getting it. Of—how do you say?—*extracting* it."

The water rained upon me out of the darkness in one long, icy torrent, filling my mouth and throat and lungs with frigid menace.

"Do you get it?" he asked.

I struggled to regain my breath, my senses. I violently spit and coughed out what had caught in my throat.

"There you go," he said. "Good boy. Spit it out. Here, let me help you." And incredibly, he cut a tiny slit at the mouth of my hood.

I desperately drank down the fresh air in long, frantic inhalations.

"Calm down, buddy. There you go. Now, I'm going to ask you a question, okay? And I want the truth. Because if I don't get the truth, well, the next time the water won't last quite so short. In fact, I can't even predict if the water would stop, okay?"

"Yeah," I said, still breathless, still locked in a downward angle, my head nearly touching the floor. "Sure. Whatever."

"Good. Do you support the war?"

"What? What war?"

"Don't get cute," he said, kneeling near me now, his boozy breath once again upon me. "The War on Terror."

"Of course," I said, still gasping for air, for some sense of calm.

"Do you support the War in Afghanistan?"

"Yes."

"Do you support the invasion of Iraq?" he asked.

"Yes," I said.

"I don't know if I believe you. Guys," and here he was addressing the unknown and still unnamed others in the room, perhaps the person holding my feet and whoever else was watching. I wondered, then, how many of my future brothers were engaged in this absurdity. How many of them were sanctioning this? Sadly, I realized that all of them were, even if they weren't actively engaged in this embarrassing process. For even if they disagreed, even if they weren't in one of the many rooms of this house playing along, their silence sanctioned it, their absence excused it.

"Guys…" he said. "What do you think?"

Again, a freezing torrent fell upon me, stealing my breath and senses and shocking me nearly to tears.

"Please," I screamed, shaking my head to avoid the onslaught. "Stop! *Please!*"

"Stop guys," he said. "It's okay Rohan. Come on, you're fine. You're fine. We're almost done, okay? You're almost done here."

A moment passed where the only audible sound was my frozen lungs wheezing for air.

"Now, do you support the invasion of Iraq?"

"Yes, of course!"

"Good. See guys, I told you he was on our side. They didn't believe me, Rohan. They doubt you, you know? And when I heard it was you they doubted most, well, I was stunned. I was stunned because you are our cricket hero! You performed so admirably on the field—so heroically! I still can't believe it, Rohan. I'm one of your biggest fans, you know. You're like our Roger Clemens. The way you throw the ball, the way you did what you were asked, the way you fucking nailed that guy—I mean, you were fucking great Rohan. I really mean it. And so, between you and me, I don't know what the fuck these guys are talking about when they say they don't trust you or can't count on you."

"You can count on me," I wheezed.

"I know, Rohan," he said, patting my chest. "We're going to convince them tonight. So, you support the war."

"Of course!"

"Even though you weren't at the protest two days ago…"

"I was at the protest!" I screamed, terrified of another drenching.

"That's right. Up on the balcony of the Student Center, right?"

"Yeah," I said, still breathing heavily.

"Why were you up there and not in the mix with the rest of your patriotic brothers?"

With my wet shroud frozen to my face, all I could see was darkness. My eyes blinked rapidly, searching for some semblance of shadow or light, but there was only black.

"I had a class, a test. He canceled it, but by the time I got back it was impossible to reach everyone."

"You had a test."

"Yes."

This time, the water had ice in it, and while I instantly locked my mouth, shards of ice nonetheless made it through, forcing me to cough and expel what I'd accidentally inhaled. This allowed more icy water into my lungs and I could only close my eyes and hope for it to pass, for it all to pass.

"You had a test?"

Breathless, I could only nod.

"But if you hadn't had a test, you would've been with your fellow patriots, correct?"

"Yes."

"We need to know that we can count on you, Rohan. Can we count on you?"

"Of course."

"Because if you support the War on Terror and the wars in Afghanistan and Iraq, then I hope you, like us, are willing to do whatever it takes to win, right?"

The descending silence was filled with my struggle to breathe.

"Are you willing to do whatever it takes to win?"

"Of course."

"Let me ask you something, Rohan, what do you think when you see a Muslim wearing a headscarf?"

"What?"

"You know, on campus, when you see a Muslim wearing the full burka or a headscarf, what do you see? What do you think?"

"I don't think anything."

It was then someone shoved a wet rag into my mouth, locking it open. The water that cascaded upon me was again freezing, and with the rag in my mouth I had no escape from the suffocating sensation of drowning.

"Ro, Ro, Ro, you're too smart not to think anything," he said, removing the rag from my mouth. "We want to know what you think when you see one of them walking across our campus."

"I think," I said, gasping, coughing, "I think…"

"Yes?"

"I think…"

"You think…"

"I think there goes the enemy," I said.

"That's my boy! Ro, Ro! Fuck! And you all doubted him! This motherfucker ain't no joke! You ain't no joke! Fuck! The enemy!" He exploded in delirious laughter, stomping in the puddles on the wet tiled floor. "Rohan, should they be allowed to wear those disgusting things here, on our campus?"

"Of course not."

"Of course not," he repeated, before erupting again in raucous laughter. "And why not? I mean, shouldn't they be free to practice their religion as they see fit?"

"This is a state-funded institution; therefore, there should be no outward displays of religion."

"This motherfucker!" he screamed. "And you all doubted him? Rohan, I think you are our most devoted disciple. Truly I do. Aren't they hideous when they wear those things?"

"Disgusting," I replied.

"You know, we have something planned for you all. You know what I'm talking about, right?"

"I do."

"Can we trust you Rohan? Can we trust you to do what's right?"

"You can."

The rag was again forced into my mouth, followed once more by a downpour colder and more sustained than any before.

"That wasn't very convincing. You need to convince us that we can trust you."

"You can!" I screamed, after I'd recovered from the shock. "You can! You can!"

"Do you remember what I told you about Pratek? About what happens to people we cannot trust?"

"Yes," I said, a sickening dizziness rising from within me.

"Say it," he commanded.

"Outcast," I finally said, before vomiting everywhere.

Cast out.

**5**

The next 24 hours transpired in a fog of binge drinking and marijuana smoke. While we'd all been led to believe that Pratek had quit in fear, we were all relieved to find him with us the following morning, hungover and terrified, his nerves, like all of ours, frazzled and desperate not to again undergo what had just occurred. As much as we could, we all tried to keep each other up; we told each other it was just a game; we told each other we were here for each other; and we also told each other we had no choice but to stick it out, all things we believed or had to believe or perhaps simply wanted to, so terrifying was the alternative we'd been given. When dawn struck we were dismissed for class, given seven hours to complete our campus duties; we were not allowed to change clothes or shower, and so while some of us—Sudeep and myself included—managed to sneak back to our dorm rooms for a few hours of much needed sleep and toothbrushing, we all crossed campus—like every other fraternity pledge immersed in the joys of Hell Week—reeking of sweat, fear, and booze and still dressed in last night's clothes, the Greek letters emblazoned on our backs a warning to all who stopped to notice the bedraggled souls seated before them in class.

And then we were back at the house and playing a game called Pledge Jeopardy. With a keg of Bombay Ultra, Darpan and two other brothers played host as the eleven of us, broken up into teams of five and six, competed to answer questions about the history of the fraternity and our chapter in particular. Every time the other team answered correctly the other team had to drink; every time *your* team answered a question wrong *you* had to drink—each team pounding full pitcher after full pitcher until the entire keg of beer was killed. We each wore a trash bag around our neck to prevent the need to run to the bathroom to vomit. Pratek puked first, then Aadav, and eventually we all did over the course of that dizzying four hours, our drunken laughter and pats on the back driving us closer to each other in ways we'd never known with others, or would ever know again.

After the keg was finished we were taken outside and, brazenly, publicly, told to play a game called Dizzy Izzy. Two massive Slip 'N Slides—children's backyard games from the 80s—were soaked and set up side by side; on each end were cricket bats. Still in teams, we stood—or tried to, given how drunk we were—before our respective Slip 'N Slide and, with the brothers watching and cheering, with some of them placing bets as to who would eat it the worst, we were told to stand the cricket bats on the ground and twirl around them for sixty seconds, our foreheads locked as squarely as possible onto the handle. And then we were told to run to the other end—if we could.

One by one, back and forth, we all twirled around the bats and attempted to run towards the other end, where brothers, many now drunk themselves, waved us home. It was a futile endeavor. I took only a step before staggering over and then crashing down the drenched Slip 'N Slide towards the other end. Pratek walked sidelong into the fraternity house wall after spinning around the bat, unable even to take a step onto the Slip 'N Slide, crashing with a hollow thud that sent him staggering backwards two steps before finally falling flat on his back. We surrounded him with concern, his smile, dumb, content and perhaps amazed at where his life had taken him, a look that drove us to laugh and cry and wonder who would fall next.

We all did.

# 4

After being released from the house at five o'clock that morning, we were told we needed to be back by four sharp. We were allowed to shower and sleep and, if we even wanted to, attend class. In those blissful eleven hours of escape, I somehow managed to do all three, saved by a schedule that saw only two classes meet for fifty minutes each. First I slept, then showered, and then ate to try and sober up. It was a long time coming. I don't think I'd eaten that much at our dorm room dining hall all year. Chicken fingers never tasted so good, coffee so refreshing, and the anonymity of sitting completely alone at the back of the dining hall was a pleasure I'd never before known. It was a pleasure to be alone with my thoughts and myself, a joy so rich I seriously considered keeping it forever, for I knew the date, I knew what was coming—we all did, even as we pretended not to by innocently eating our breakfasts and pretending to ignore the freshly delivered stacks of *New College* with his face upon it.

Eventually, like the good boy I still thought I could be, I was off to class, Advanced Calc at 12:45 followed by Humanities 101. Given what I'd endured, and given my seriously mixed emotions, I felt oddly rejuvenated, like someone who knows they're almost through a horrible ordeal and if they can just push through everything will turn out all right. As to whether or not I was capable of pushing through—or even truly wanted to—was something still unclear. For he was here. *Finally.* Mohammad Jafar al-Sadr was here.

The time had come.

Back at the house, a surprising—and terrifying—amount of fraternity brothers were seated in the living room where the bigscreen television was on, a muted Wolf News anchor silently conversing with, according to the name on the screen, the White House Press Secretary. The energy in the room was nervous; brothers tagore talking with each other animatedly, asking pledges to run downstairs to the kitchen and bring them food and drink and even ice for their bong. Cigarette and weed-smoke occasionally filled the room alongside their anxious, excited conversation. Like most of my fellow pledges, I studied the room with fear and surprise, uncertain as to what was going to follow. Was all of this in anticipation of al-Sadr? Was this the final meeting where our actions—and my humiliation—was to be set in stone? I thought then of the awful paper-mache figure hanging still unfinished in the basement. Since Hell Week had formally begun some fifty hours ago, little had been said of it, and whatever had been mentioned was done jokingly, in passing by someone seemingly unconnected with its design and planning, its horrible implications and possible ramifications undiscussed and kept in some future yet restless abeyance. But it was there. We knew it was there, and try as we might—try as *I* might—to pretend it didn't exist, the truth, like the future, was something from which I could not escape.

Nor, it seemed, could America. For the primary reason so many brothers had convened at the fraternity house was not—as I'd feared—to discuss the arrival of al-Sadr and what to do about it. At least not exactly, and certainly not at first. No, they, along with the rest of the world, were tuned in to see and hear Secretary of State Colin Powell address the United Nations Security Council and sell to the world the truth about Iraq's weapons of mass destruction. It was—I was informed by several brothers—critical that America build a coalition of nations before invading Iraq. While we were certainly the ones leading the charge, and as we were the ones who'd discovered the link between al-Qaeda and Saddam Hussein, it was our job, the brothers passionately informed me, to garner international support and not go it alone. And this was a critical, necessary step that had to begin today, February 5th 2003. All to prevent another 9/11, they said. All to prevent another Mumbai.

And so, like President Bush's State of the Union address almost two weeks ago, our fraternity house sat mesmerized—and in occasional applause—as Colin Powell made America's argument not with "assertions" but, as he continuously reiterated, with "facts" "corroborated by many sources." In a style measured and gravely serious, Colin Powell logically presented America's argument for invasion by highlighting how "the Iraqis have never accounted for all of the biological weapons they admitted they had and we know they had," his long chain of evidence painting a horrific picture of the danger of a chemically weaponized Iraq, a country, according to Colin Powell *and* our President, hiding a surfeit of WMDs, blatantly engaged in a prolonged agenda of clear obfuscation, and with clear links to various terrorist groups. The living room was mostly silent, with rarely the sound of a beer can being exhausted to distract us, and more than once I glanced at Sudeep, his shaved head agleam with sweat, his furrowed brow shifting from anger, to disgust, to fear. When Colin Powell described Saddam Hussain's past use of chemical weapons against his own people, when he discussed the destructive power of anthrax, Sudeep blanched, as did many of us in the room, myself included. It was all too much.

When it was finally over, the anger against Saddam Hussain and his regime was real, as was the fear of any WMDs getting into a terrorist group like al-Qaeda. Even I felt that *something* must be done, that we, as the most powerful nation in the world and, obviously, victims of one of the most heinous terrorist attacks in recent history, had a moral obligation to prevent this man from possessing these dangerous chemical weapons, and while all of the brothers passionately discussed the need for immediate invasion—and, indeed, for going in alone without the aid or approval of the rest of the world—I had another voice in my head, one who's soft cadence countered the zeitgeist, and challenged its ultimate vision.

But I couldn't say any of that.

Not here, not now, not to these young, terrified men. Indeed, in the news coverage following Colin Powell's speech, the pundits on Wolf News seemed to reiterate the very same discourse permeating our fraternity house, and perhaps most of the houses across America. There was no time to lose. There was no time like the present.

It wasn't long before I was corralled by Darpan and Sudeep, Pratek and Aadav. I knew what was coming, and because of that I bummed a cigarette and stood there, surrounded by my own kind, smoking in the tense silence. Finally, he was here, bringing with him the future I could no longer avoid.

"The war begins tonight," Darpan eventually said, smiling at us, at me.

"The war begins tonight," Sudeep repeated, his hand now upon Pratek's shoulder.

"The war begins tonight," Pratek repeated, his exhausted eyes alight with the need for action, revenge, for something heartbreakingly akin to acceptance.

When it was my turn I did what was expected.

It took some time, but Azada finally noticed me standing in the twisted shadows of the distant palm trees. Her emerald eyes met mine and without pause or shame she smiled and perhaps she blushed because she peered down at the steps of the Wilcox Theater where she'd stood and I'd watched her for over twenty minutes handing out leaflets to those curious, brave, or stupid enough to enter al-Sadr's speech and after a moment of studying the brightly lit pavement beneath her she called over a headscarfed friend and whispered in her ear before handing her the leaflets and then, without hint of fear or shame, Azada strode to where I waited in the shadows some hundred yards away.

A cold, whistling wind sent the palm trees dancing high in the starry darkness.

Incredibly, Azada let me hold her headscarf in place.

"I was hoping not to find you here," I said, after the wind had died.

"Is that why you've been standing here for twenty minutes?"

"You noticed?"

"I felt you," she said, briefly, bravely taking my hand in the shadows. "How'd you manage to sneak away?"

"Well, I'm actually on a mission," I said, unable to stop smiling. "Recon."

"I bet you are," she replied.

"I'm serious. Recon and Taco Bell. Our Pledge Master has a mild-sauce addiction."

"Are you going to tell me what you guys have planned tonight?"

"Only if you do the same."

"We're planning the free exchange of ideas. Freedom of speech. How about you guys? Anything similar?"

"Whatever happened to having the courage to do what's right?"

"I am." As if to convince herself she said it again: "I am."

"You truly believe in what that man is going to say?"

"I believe in freedom of speech, Rohan. I believe that that man has the right to say whatever he wants."

"That's such a cop out," I said, irritated. "I'm disappointed in you."

"The feeling's mutual. Rohan, tell me, what do they say up there at your fraternity house about me, about Muslims? What do they say about Muslims and what do you do about it? Tell me, I'm interested to hear it."

"First of all, I punched the guy in the fucking face. And you know that. Secondly, you're attempting to justify your actions based on a principle. Fine. Okay. But that's not the question I'm asking you. You can believe in free speech and allow that man to talk—but that doesn't mean you have to be a part of it and it certainly doesn't mean you have to support it. It doesn't mean you have to stand outside passing out his propaganda!"

In response to my escalating voice, Azada quickly raised her hand and then, amazingly, drew closer to me. Quite suddenly, the wind picked up, driving the palm trees to bend and shake in the starry black sky and sending our protective shadows forward and back. Overcome, I held her then, held her despite the fear of discovery, scandal, exile. In my arms she wilted, exhausted, like I was, of everything that was beyond the scope of our lives, of everything and everyone that conspired to impose their narratives upon us.

There, within the shadows, I kissed her for the first time on campus.

"I love you," I whispered. "I'm sorry."

"No," she said, her body trembling in my arms. "*I'm* sorry. I'm sorry because you're right. All I do is talk. I talk about doing the right thing, about being brave and not being afraid, and yet here I am."

"You could always leave," I said, an echo of an echo.

"No," she said, as the wind picked up again. "I'm ashamed to say I can't."

"Can't or won't?"

"Does it matter? Rohan, I'm afraid to say I have no choice. As much as I'd like to believe I don't, I'm afraid to say I *need* them," she said, and when she peered up at me her emerald eyes welled with tears, shame and sadness, and holding her I could only stare, powerless like that first morning of class, or all of our clandestine nights in the library, remembering, as I held her, the bravery she'd shown that night she marched defiantly into the surf, the bravery she'd shone all along, the bravery she showed even now.

"I understand," I said, before wiping her eyes.

"Do you?"

"I do. Yes."

"Are you still disappointed?"

"Of course not," I replied, and then, holding her to me, I watched as, nearly one hundred yards away, two police cars parked on the grass before Wilcox Theater, their twirling blue and red lights cutting through the darkness in ominous, protective silence.

Eventually, I summoned the courage to ask what we'd both known since the beginning, "You know what this means, don't you?"

She drew a long breath and then the clouds suddenly broke to reveal the high pale moon and in the blinding moonshine her face was awash with tears and only then did I see the rose red lipstick that had captured my heart our first night together in the library. Her lower lip aquiver, she whispered, "Yes."

"Are you okay with that?"

"I'm not okay with any of this. Any of it," she said, spying the police lights twirling where she'd once stood. "This is all so awful."

"I have to go," I said. "They're expecting me."

"They're expecting me too," she replied, before finally succumbing to the weight.

# 2

Mercifully, my prolonged absence didn't much register back at the fraternity house, as everyone was so locked in to the task at hand—and drunk—that my fifty minute disappearance resulted in little suspicion and even less concern. Darpan simply snatched the Taco Bell bag and then, as reward and punishment, handed me a can of beer and barked

"Drink it bitch." The Bombay Ultra was warm in my hand, and simply holding it was an act of war against my stomach. Bile caught in my throat, and the brief moment of sobriety my excursion had allowed now seemed lost, like so much else. For now, back in the caldron, watching my pledge brothers excitedly admire their paper-mache figure while greedily passing bottles of Crown Royal and Absolut Vodka, watching as they chased each shot with a congratulatory pat on the back and a warm beer, I could only see Azada walking away with tears in her eyes, and the rupture was unlike anything I'd ever known before, or want to know again, and all I wanted to do was tell someone—*anyone*—about it, to share my pain with any of these so-called brothers, and because I needed to believe it I had to think that perhaps someday I would, someday I could, *just not at this time*, and because of that I felt even worse, estranged, like my life had become someone else's and I was afraid to do what I knew was right, and perhaps I was, perhaps I always had been.

Quite suddenly, everything became painfully clear and I knew what I had to do. There was no other option. To reclaim some semblance of self—and to help preserve the little dignity our fraternity had left—I had to prevent this disgrace from ever seeing the light of day. If it wasn't already too late.

"There were police," I said, cracking open my beer and feigning a long pull.

"Where?" Sudeep asked, standing before the paper-mache figure, crudely slathering pink paint where lips should be. "What do you think of this color?"

"Looks about right," Darpan replied, before biting into a mild-sauce-drenched chalupa.

"At the event," I said, "outside Wilcox Theatre. There were two of them. I mean, at least two. There were definitely more coming."

"You know what I want," Sudeep said to no one, everyone. "A cell phone that can take video."

"Get the fuck out of here," Naresh slurred drunkenly. "A cell phone that takes video? You know how big that phone would have to be? Dude…"

"I'm serious. Think about it. I mean, imagine a cell phone that could take video, take pictures. I mean, how awesome would it be to have something like that here, now. We could be making a video of this thing—"

"And post it on the internet," someone interjected, before belching, loudly.

"And post it on the internet, *exactly*," Sudeep said very, very slowly, totally blown away by the concept. "I like that. And then, if it's on the internet, everyone can see it, and people who are down with what we're doing here, I mean, they can reach out to us—and us to them. I mean, think of the power of the imagery," he said, taking a step back from his painting to admire his work. "Think of its ability to inspire."

The lips were bright pink, crude, perhaps even menacing, like some distorted visage of Batman's Joker. They'd—or was it we'd?—purposely left the face the white of the paper-mache, while the hands, oddly, were painted dark brown. He wore real clothes, an off-white traditional Arab tunic that hung near his knees alongside matching pants. Where the clothes had come from I had no idea. A tiny matching hat had been stapled to his head, positioned just above the black, crooked eyebrows set upon his brown, vacant eyes. I had to turn away.

"Someone already has," Aadav offered. "It's called YouTube."

"YouTube?" Sudeep asked, amazed and confused.

"It's a website," Aadav offered, "and you can post videos there. But I think it's still in beta stage."

"What the fuck is beta stage?" Darpan asked, perplexed. "The world is moving too fast my friends. I need a joint to slow it down."

"It's actually pretty cool," Aadav said. "I think it was developed by college kids."

"Those damn college kids. Always up to no good."

"And anyone can post?" Sudeep asked.

"Anyone. And it's free," Aadav said. "Totally fucking free."

"Get the fuck out of here," Sudeep said. "No way."

"I'm serious," Aadav said. "Go get your laptop and I'll show you."

"Laptops are so fucking expensive," someone said.

"What about this?" Sudeep asked, his dark-brown eyes huge in his head. "What about a phone that can take videos, pictures, and access the internet?"

"You're stoned," someone replied.

"What's your point?" Sudeep asked. "Think about it. It could happen. It *will* happen."

"Not in our lifetimes," I advised seriously, now standing beside Sudeep. "Did you hear what I said?"

"When?" Sudeep replied.

I looked at him, hard, and then Darpan, chomping away on his second chalupa.

"There are police. Everywhere."

"What's your point?" he asked.

"Do I have to spell it out for you? Do you want to get arrested?"

At the magic word, a contemplative silence descended upon the room. Aadav and Pratek shot me concerned, terrified looks. Naresh and Nisith immediately lit cigarettes before picking up the bottle of vodka.

"No one is getting arrested. Calm down. Do another shot," Darpan said. "All of you."

The bottle of vodka passed nervously around the room. It found me last.

"You too, Rohan," Darpan said.

"My stomach hurts," I said.

"Good. Do two," he said, patting me on the back.

"What are you so nervous about? Why are you so *afraid*?" Sudeep asked, before gesturing to the monstrosity dangling from the ceiling. "This is your destiny. This is *our* destiny."

"It seems to me you're willing to risk an awful lot—"

"No one is risking anything," Darpan interjected calmly. "You're—*we're*—a bunch of college kids about to play a prank, that's all. These are simply college hijinks, pure and simple. And if you do get caught—which you fucking shouldn't—but if you do, you're going to say you didn't know any better and if we have to apologize we will apologize. That's all. No one will say anything—heck, no one will probably even *care*."

"No one will care?"

"We will be seen as heroes," Sudeep said, looking squarely at Aadav and Pratek.

"Do you really believe that?" I asked them.

"You know, right now, there are young men and women going into that theater because they want to hear what that monster has to say. They want to hear what that monster has to say because, somewhere in their hearts, they *believe* what he has to say—or they want to. Oddly, they think that *we* are to blame for what's happened to us, as if the people in the World Trade Center somehow deserved to die, or the people in Mumbai having *cha* at the Crown were guilty of their punishment. I reject that notion completely."

"So do I," I said, peering into Sudeep's bloodshot eyes. "So does everyone here."

"Good," he said, his shaved head agleam with sweat. "*Chalo.*"

"Wait, wait, guys, listen, we should still go down there. We should still protest. I'm all for it. Let's do that instead. Let's go down there," and here I was looking at Aadav and Pratek, perhaps the two most vulnerable, reasonable, perhaps the only two really listening, "and cause a scene inside. We go in there, sit for a while, and then begin heckling him or something."

"That actually sounds like a good idea," Pratek said.

"That's what I'm saying," I said, rushing over to him. "We go over there, and we, I don't know, we figure out a way to disrupt the discussion. We boo him, we heckle him, we shout him down, we teach that sonofabitch a lesson about freedom of speech."

"But won't that lead to arrest too?" Aadav asked. "I mean, they'd definitely know who we are then, right?"

"They wouldn't arrest us,'" I said, feigning certainty. "We're kids. They'll throw us out, we'll get mentioned in the paper, maybe, and that's that. On to the next thing," and on, I hoped, to brotherhood, where, as a full member, I could perhaps change this entire thing from the inside, or perhaps just disappear.

"Enough!" Darpan barked. "Guys, come here." It took a moment for us to huddle together, but after we had it was obvious to whom the following was addressed, "I want you to think back a couple of days ago. Some of you were asked a few questions. Do you remember that?" Uncertain nods. "Now, I want you to ask yourselves if you're truly willing to pay the price for disobedience. Remember, we want you all here with us. *We* are your brothers. *We* are your own kind." He let this sink in. "Am I clear?"

Again, uncertain nods.

"Am I *clear*?"

"Yes sir!" Sudeep, and a few others, shouted.

"Am I clear?" Darpan's eyes were locked on Pratek and Aadav, standing arm in arm.

The response grew now to include them.

"Am I clear?"

We responded in unison, my voice lost within the crowd.

1

We were mere feet from where Azada and I had been when Sudeep finally stopped us and silently pointed to one of the towering redwoods rising between the line of palm trees curling in the starfilled sky and in the distance there were now four police cars scattered around the entrance to Wilcox Theater and in their spinning red and blue you could see a surprisingly long line of people waiting to enter under the curious eyes of several policemen and you could also see her there too, if you looked carefully enough, like I did. The shame that overcame me left me dizzy, and I was tempted, then, to snatch the vodka we'd brought along, to succumb to and finally become what now felt unavoidable, but instead I secretly drew Pratek's attention to the police cars and together we stared in the cool, black silence.

"Say something," I whispered.

"There's nothing to say," he replied.

"Do you see that?"

"Keep it down," he rasped.

They'd—*we'd*—wrapped the paper-mache figure in white bedlinens like some gargantuan mummy and now, laid flat on the ground, several pledges were working to deshroud him. Sudeep loomed over Naresh and Nisith in the shadows as they delicately set about the task.

"We can't do this," I said. "This is wrong."

"You heard Darpan," he said. "We have no choice."

"Pratek," I pleaded, guiding him slowly back from Sudeep and the paper-mache figure. "Do you really think people are just going to think we're some dumb college kids engaged in a prank? You know how offensive this is."

"I also know what they did to us," he said.

"What do you think the admissions board of Harvard Medical School is going to say when they see this on your application?"

The look he shot me conveyed his quandary, and mine, and Azada's. There was anger, fear, and shame, but more than anything there was confusion, a hopeless, helpless sense of bafflement at everything life had suddenly become.

"What do you want me to do?" he finally asked, his hands to his face.

"What's right," I said.

"You're crazy," he said. "I can't."

"If this happens, what you can't be—what you'll *never* be—is a doctor. I can promise you that."

"You're wrong."

"Tell that to your parents," I said, playing the only card I had left. "Tell that to your *dad*."

"Fuck you," he said, his voice far beyond a whisper.

"What the fuck are you guys doing?" Sudeep asked.

A quick burst of cold, dry wind drove away our protective shadows, and in the clear moonlight we were all momentarily visible, the deshrouded paper-mache figure in his white tunic alight like some medieval idol, and together we turned and stared agape down the hundred yards to Wilcox Theater and the twirling red and blue lights there, breathlessly aware of our sudden nakedness.

Clouds assisted the dying wind to offer us an even deeper level of protection, and under that cover Sudeep strode defiantly to where I'd cornered Pratek.

"Are you two fucking crazy? What the fuck is wrong with you?" he rasped.

"He doesn't want to do it!" Pratek said.

"Do you?" I asked him. He was shaking so hard I thought he might cry.

"No," he replied, his voice cracking. "Yes. I don't know. I don't know anymore."

"Let me be crystal clear," Sudeep said, his shaved head drenched with sweat, "you're both going to do this. Do you hear me? In fact," he said, poking me in the chest, hard, "you're going to light him up."

"What?"

"Oh, yeah, you didn't know, did you? We're going to noose him up, and then we're going to light this motherfucker up. And you're the one who's going to do it."

Sudeep revealed a silver-plated Zippo lighter and flung it at me. I caught it instinctively, its weight a burden in my hand. Om was inscribed in Sanskrit on the lighter.

"Dude," I said, "you can't be fucking serious."

"Do I look serious? Does this look like a fucking joke?"

"You really want to be a part of this?" I asked Pratek, my extended hand offering the lighter.

"What choice do I have?" he responded, and now there *were* tears in his eyes.

"*Exactly*," Sudeep responded. "What choice do you have?"

"What happened to you?" I asked Sudeep.

"I opened my eyes. Open yours."

I peered at Sudeep, and now Pratek, his brown cheeks awash with tears, and we were surrounded now by all of our pledge brothers, Naresh and Nisith, Aadav and Tejis, Kiran and Milan, Vishal and Vishnu, and behind them lay the paper-mache figure and far beyond that stood Azada, doing what she thought she had to, doing what she believed she *needed* to—as did we all, we who'd come to this place so long ago with no clear idea of what to expect, or who we were, or who we wanted to be, and now, our eyes opened by history and heartbreak, kinship and kindness, duty and ultimately doubt, stood on the edge of a place from where there could be no return.

"You're right," I said to Sudeep, to all of them. "My eyes have finally opened."

"Good," Sudeep replied, his hands opened welcomingly before him.

"I'm out," I said.

It was Pratek who spoke first, his reply soaked through with tears, "What?"

"I'm out. I can't be a part of this. And neither should any of you."

"Do you know what you're doing?" Pratek asked.

"I do," I replied, tossing Sudeep his lighter back. "Do you? Do any of you?"

"Let him go," Sudeep said. "Fuck him. Fuck you. You want to go, go. No one is holding you here. No one will stop you. You want to go, fine, go bitch. You fucking coward. You fucking *banchod* motherfucker. Go. But you'd better watch your back, you'd better watch your fucking back because…"

I didn't stay to hear the rest. Nor did I stay to convert the rest of them. I just walked away.

I didn't have to walk long before I could smell the burning.

Or hear the screams.

0

The burning of a paper-mache figure bearing crude resemblance to the controversial Muslim cleric Mohammad Jafar al-Sadr at Irvine College made national news, igniting a countrywide debate about freedom of speech, fraternity hazing, the treatment by and depiction of Muslims and Islam in our national media, and, perhaps most critically, the complex sensitivities surrounding portrayals of Islam in the West. The story was on the front page of the *Los Angeles Times* and *San Francisco Chronicle* for one week straight. It made the *New York Times* for three consecutive days. It even led the *O'Malley Factor* three times, with host Ryan O'Malley, the controversial Wolf News personality, opining that "while the act itself was clearly stupid and insensitive, the young men who participated in this act were engaging in their First Amendment right of free speech, and as such, no matter how much I disagree with their means, they should be spared all penalties and their lives should not be ruined." Echoing Darpan, he continued: "Were they stupid, yes. But at their core they were simply young college kids engaged in a fraternity prank. In my opinion, what they did was much less harmful to America than what the college administration did by allowing that anti-American cleric al-Sadr to come onto campus and spew his vitriol."

The administration didn't hold quite the same view. All activities at Delta Sigma Eta were immediately suspended. The pledge class to which I'd given my freshman year was, once names were discovered and interviews made, put on immediate behavioral probation with the possibility of suspension or perhaps even expulsion, given further investigation. The national charter of Delta Sigma Eta publicly denied their possible membership alongside any future affiliation with or any past knowledge of my pledge brothers. Darpan and a handful of other brothers met the same fate, only they saw their memberships revoked and were now unable to wear the letters they'd once donned so proudly across campus. And all of it was done in the public eye, for everyone to see, for everyone to judge.

As for me, I'd learned my lesson. I'd moved on. I knew that Irvine was no longer a place for me on that night and that I would have to transfer elsewhere to begin again, alone; I also knew that these young men to whom I'd pledged myself were enslaved to a history I could no longer blindly follow, or idly ignore, and that my future would hold struggle and fear and shame. Perhaps I knew it even earlier. Nonetheless, while I was able to remain mostly out of the public eye during the ensuing scandal, and while I luckily managed to avoid any penalties, what I couldn't avoid—what *no one* at Irvine could avoid—was the shame of having been even remotely associated with such an act. It was everywhere, hanging over our collective souls and, at least for what remained of our school year, a burden that darkened our endlessly sunny days. For what I learned was that we were all guilty, every one of us, no matter how far removed from the actual events. And perhaps I'm wrong, but I believe this. I believe that the climate was something we *all* had a part in creating. And while the climate may have existed all along, perhaps long before 9/11, that horrible day only gave sanction to everything alien and terrible roiling deep within us, within all of us. We didn't know it then, but it would only get worse.

I only saw Azada once more. She was walking hand in hand through Zuckerman Park, and I was shading myself under some trees we were both very familiar with. The man whose hand she held daintily in hers was a stranger to me. He was growing a beard, wore a Los Angeles Lakers jersey, and was laughing raucously at something she'd just said. She was laughing too, her white headscarf aflutter as her head fell back and her eyes locked, briefly and pleasantly, onto his. It was then I caught her eye, and as they walked by laughing she looked at me splayed under those trees, and she waved, and I waved back, her smiling lips a pink I'd never before seen.

Two months later we invaded Iraq. One day we'll leave.